# *Summer's*

## Ella Cook

*Where heroes are like chocolate – irresistible!*

EPUB: 978-1-78189-500-9
PRINT: 978-1-78189-504-7

*As always, to my husband: still the voice of my heroes*
*And to the real world "Nick": fixer of ... almost everything*
*And for everyone who didn't get to celebrate last Christmas the way they would have liked to.*

# *Acknowledgements*

They say it takes a village to raise a child – in Summer's case, that was definitely true. And it takes about as many people to nurture a book into being too – and you wouldn't be reading this without the support, encouragement, faith and hard work of a *lot* of people.

So, as ever, a massive thank you to the Choc Lit family and all my "sister-authors" who have been there, offering support, words of wisdom, and friendship every step of the way.

And a massive thank you to the Tasting Panel Readers (Celia Bourgi, Kirsty White, Lisa Vasil, Liana Vera Saez, Lynda Adcock, Carol Botting, Fran Stevens, Elisabeth Hall, Honor Gilbert, Joy Bleach, Rosie Farrell, Jo Osborne, Jenny Mitchell, Sharon Walsh, Gill Leivers, Carol Elizabeth Dutton) and ARC team – I'm glad you enjoyed Summer and her story as much as I loved writing it.

And a special thanks to my editor for the edits (in spite everything going on), and to the Choc Lit team for keeping me organised and helping bring another story of mine into the world.

To the real-world "Nick" who knows exactly who he is, thank you for the late night calls, years of friendship and constantly asking "any good books coming out soon?" I hope you like the fictionalised version of yourself!

And thanks to Ann and the Wordsmiths – who couldn't be better cheerleaders – I really wouldn't been writing this without you.

And thanks to Alex and Dad for putting up with my absentmindedness while I mentally wander around my own little world.

# Chapter One
## *Evelyn*

Evelyn pulled a face as she took a sip of the now cold coffee, then downed it anyway – disgusting or not, she needed every drop of the syrupy caffeinated dregs. It had already been a long drive, and she wasn't used to such long distances, especially lately. It hadn't just been the physical effort of packing everything up that was exhausting. The emotional toll was even heavier, and far harder to bear.

She yawned and adjusted the second rear view mirror to check on her precious cargo in the back. She smiled at the sight of Summer curled up in her starry blanket with Tilly, who had stretched her seat-belt leash as far as possible, so she could rest her ginger and white head in her best girl's lap. Summer's hand rested gently on the Shiba Inu's head and, not for the first time, Evelyn was struck by how unworldly Summer appeared with her pale blonde hair, and the fox-like dog who was always by her side. She was tiny, delicate, and almost ethereal when she was asleep – and a bouncing bubble of energy when she was awake, despite everything. She was smaller, and more delicate looking, than most eight-year-olds, but after the last few years it was hardly surprising.

Since Summer had fallen ill, the little Shiba had become her shadow, following her everywhere as if her very presence could protect the smallest member of her pack from coming to harm. If only it were true.

Evelyn forced herself to focus on the road, and tried to push the negative thoughts away. Every mile closer she got to Broclington took her another mile further from Northumberland, and all the sadness and negativity that

1

had happened there. Though she'd grown up in Broclington, a little Midlands' village, it had been a long time since she'd called it home, and it was somewhere Summer only really knew as a place to visit her nan – not that there'd been too many visits lately. Evelyn shook her head to clear her mind of those negative thoughts. As the cat's eyes and white lane markers raced by, she pictured a tiny shoot pushing its way through the dark earth, coaxed to the surface by the promise of light and warmth. With each mile marker that passed, she envisaged the shoot growing taller and stronger, delving out roots to pull in more strength, until the petals of a sunshine yellow rose started to unfold. With any luck, she and Summer could regrow as easily.

She snorted in amusement at the idea of Summer sprouting petals as she indicated and pulled off at the A46, taking care to leave extra space for the trailer she'd been towing for hours. Roses apparently grew well in horse crap, and she'd definitely had enough crap to last a lifetime. She glanced back at Summer again. Make that two lifetimes – they'd had more than enough crap for two lifetimes, though she'd have gladly taken it all to reduce the load on Summer's young shoulders.

But she had to stop thinking like that, she chided herself silently. The last round of treatment hadn't gone the way they'd all hoped – but it had worked, and Summer was fast regaining her strength. Everything was going to be fine – Evelyn had to believe that. And if she believed it hard enough, it might just come true.

She yawned so widely that her jaw clicked, and she had to give herself a shake. It was just a few more miles, and they'd be there, ready to start their new lives in her old home.

Evelyn winced as she bumped up the kerb and pulled onto the gravel driveway, the crunching stones sounding loud in the quiet car. She finally turned the engine off and stretched the cricks out of her neck before squinting to peer through the darkness into the back seat. Tilly whined softly, and gave Evelyn a reproachful look from her spot half-in Summer's lap. Clearly she was telling her that it was far too late for her girl to be out, and she was less than impressed with all the changes and moving about.

'I know. I'm sorry, Tilly.' She whispered an apology. 'But we didn't really have any choice, and we're here now. Wait with our girl, and I'll get the door open. We don't want her getting cold.'

She paused at the porch and ran her hand over the honeyed stone. It hadn't been home to her for years, but it still felt safe and familiar. She'd been so happy in this old cottage. She stared at the blurred head in the back of the car, and prayed that Summer could be happy here too. Happy *and* healthy. She brushed her fingers against the cold, worn metal of the door knocker when the faded green door swung open, and she was wrapped in a huge hug that smelled of roses, cinnamon and safety.

'Hi, Mum.'

'Oh, Evie. I hate what it is that's brought you back home to me, but I'm so glad you're here. I know it's a few weeks late, but Happy New Year, love.' Evelyn was pushed away and her mum squinted at her in the light streaming from the hallway. 'You look exhausted. Let's get you in, settled, and I'll put the kettle on. Now where is my gorgeous, brave granddaughter?'

'Still zonked out in the car. With Tilly in her lap, as usual.'

3

'You go get her. I've borrowed a junior bed from a friend and cleared out my crafting room for her.'

'I said she could share with me,' Evelyn argued.

'I know what you said, love. But I really don't mind. I'll give you a hand, and hopefully we can get her snuggled into bed before she even realises we've woken her up.'

'Sounds good.' Evelyn yawned, suddenly overwhelmed by tiredness as all the sadness and struggles of the last few months hit her in a tsunami of emotion. She opened the car door, and unclipped Tilly who bounced out of the car and bounded around, yipping excitedly as she greeted her old friend.

'Yes, yes. I'm glad to see you too. Now go water one of my trees before you come in.' Evelyn's mum shooed Tilly towards the garden as Evelyn unclipped Summer's seat belt and pulled the little girl tightly against her.

'Are we there yet?' Summer's sleepy voice was muffled against Evelyn's shoulder.

'Yes, sweetheart. We're here now.' She handed a bag to her mother, and held Summer's head firmly against her shoulder as she struggled to lift her from the booster seat. She was getting a bit big to lift around easily, but Evelyn was still going to keep doing it for as long as she could, even if she did get a few twinges in her back every now and then.

'Good.' Summer snuggled against her neck as Evelyn struggled to stand, her daughter's fuzzy regrowing hair tickling her cheek. 'I'm tired, Mum.'

'I know. Come give Nanny a quick hug, and we'll snuggle you into your bed.'

'With Tilly?'

Evelyn chuckled as she carried Summer through the porch and into the hallway that she'd walked through thousands of times: sometimes sneaking in later than she'd promised, sometimes storming in as an angry teenager, but usually she'd been happy, racing to meet her family or friends. She heard Tilly's skidding claws hit the stone floor. 'Of course Tilly's coming to bed with you. I've never been able to stop her yet, have I?'

'Good.' Summer snuggled tighter.

'Hello, darling.' Evelyn heard her mother's footsteps and voice behind her.

'Hello, Nanny Linda.' Summer stretched her hand out behind Evelyn to her grandmother, who kissed her fingers, making the little girl giggle.

Evelyn opened the door to her mother's former craft room, and gasped. 'This is beautiful.' She set Summer down on the bed. 'Look, sweetheart, your very own princess bedroom.' She fingered the shimmering canopy that pooled over the small bed, all in delicate shades of pink that matched the pale walls and striped rug.

'It's so pretty, Nanny. Is it really for me?'

'Well, you and Tilly. Look.' The older woman pointed to a basket in the corner lined with a pink fluffy blanket.

'Thank you so much.' Summer wrapped her arms around her nan's neck and placed a kiss on her cheek. 'I love it.'

'And I love you.' Grandmother and granddaughter pressed their noses together in an Eskimo-style kiss, and Evelyn felt a pang of guilt that it had been so long since they'd been together. It couldn't be helped, but Evelyn still felt guilty.

Her guilt only intensified when Summer yawned and slumped against her grandmother. 'I'm really sleepy, Nanny. Can I please go to bed?'

'Of course you can darling.' Her easy tone and calm words belied the look that she shot Evelyn. 'You can do whatever you want. Do you want me to tuck you in?'

Summer nodded tiredly as Evelyn pulled her pyjamas out of the small bag she'd handed Linda moments earlier. 'Do you need help getting ready for bed?'

'No.' She grabbed the clothes and washbag and trudged tiredly down the corridor to the small bathroom.

As soon as she was out of sight, Evelyn collapsed on the small bed. 'This really is a beautiful room, Mum. I hadn't expected anything like this. I can't thank you enough.'

'Hmm. You're welcome, darling. You know I like spoiling you both. And I've told you before – you don't have to thank family.' She was still staring down the corridor, clearly distracted. 'I know it's late, but is it usual for her to be so tired?'

'Unfortunately, yes.' Evelyn scrubbed her hands across her face, feeling a lot older than her thirty-six years.

'But it's worked?'

'Yes. That's what the doctors have said. She's in medical remission.'

Linda clasped her hands to her mouth and murmured a prayer of thanks. 'I know you told me over the phone, but seeing you and having her here … it makes it feel more real. But she still looks so poorly.'

'I was actually thinking she was looking much better.' Evelyn shot her mum a sad smile. 'She's been a little champ, but chemo can be really hard on kids, and neuroblastoma is harder the older you get.'

'I know, darling.'

'I feel so guilty. You look at her and think she looks terrible …'

'I said poorly.'

'Fine.' Evelyn shrugged. 'You think she looks poorly, but I think she actually looks better than she has for weeks. And it's all my fault.'

'Cancer like this isn't anyone's fault, Evie.'

'It's neuroblastoma, Mum.' Evelyn was careful to keep her voice down. The walls in the old cottage were thick, but she wasn't taking any chances. 'This has come from cells from my womb. From when I was pregnant. I feel like I've done this to her.'

'But you haven't.'

'Haven't what?' Summer's voice from the door startled them both.

'Haven't … unpacked the car yet.'

'Oh.' Summer yawned again. 'Do I have to help?'

'Absolutely not.' Evelyn pulled the covers back from the bed. 'All you need to do right now is snuggle down in bed, and rest your sleepy head …'

'… And close your tired eyes, and chase dreams across the skies,' Linda finished.

'You know my night night rhyme, Nanny?' Summer climbed into bed and lay down.

'Who do you think taught it to your mum?'

'You?'

'Me.' She nodded and placed a kiss on Summer's forehead. 'Sleep well and dream sweet, my brave girl.'

'Night night, Nanny. Thank you for my bedroom.'

Linda smiled as she headed out of the room.

Evelyn smoothed the covers around Summer's shoulders. 'I'm just downstairs if you need me.' She kissed her daughter on both cheeks, and then her nose. 'You've done so well today. Love you.'

'Love you too.' Summer's eyes drifted shut.

Evelyn watched her for a few moments as she drifted off to dreamland, and fiddled with the edge of the duvet to make it a little smoother. She studied Summer as she slept, taking in the fuzzy, regrowing hair, and dark smudges under her eyes. Her mum was right. Summer looked "poorly". But she wasn't, that was what Evelyn had to keep reminding herself. Her daughter was in remission and starting to recover. And the remission would last. It had to.

Evelyn stood and wiped imaginary fluff off her jeans, took one last look at her daughter, and turned off the light. She hesitated at the door and smiled to herself at the soft scrabble of claws and thump. As nice as Tilly's new basket was, she was clearly happier in her usual position, guarding her best friend from nightmares.

Evelyn trudged slowly down the stairs feeling tiredness add weight to her limbs, but as much as she wanted to curl up and sleep she still had to unpack a car and trailer that was stuffed with what was left of their combined northern lives. And she still had to properly explain everything to her mum. She hadn't been able to face telling the whole sordid tale over the phone or video chat, so had only told her the bare minimum – that she and Charlie were no longer together, and there was little to keep her and Summer in Northumberland. True, the doctors at the Great North Children's Hospital had been brilliant with Summer, but it had been a long drive, and they were happy to jointly consult with doctors all over the world – they already did.

Summer's friendship circles had shrunken and vanished while she'd been ill, and since the GP's practice Evelyn worked out of had merged with another, enabling her to take voluntary redundancy to spend more time caring for her daughter, there seemed little point staying somewhere that they both associated with so much suffering and sadness. Besides, she'd walked away with a glowing recommendation, and she'd find another nursing role easily enough when she was ready to work again. And the hospital nearer her mum would be just as good as the Great North, and it would only be for check-ups anyway, because this time the remission *was going to last.*

Naturally, Linda immediately insisted she had more than enough space for them, and begged Evelyn to move back to Broclington, and in with her – at least for long enough to have a rest, be looked after for a bit, and figure out what she wanted to do. The sad truth was, since Evelyn's dad had lost his own battle with cancer a few years earlier, the house had been a bit big for her mum, and she was probably looking forward to having the company and being able to dote on her only child and granddaughter again.

Summer had been thrilled, and while Evelyn had initially been reluctant to run home, the thought of someone looking after her for a little while was incredibly enticing, and she eventually gave in to Summer's pleading. After all, who was she to really turn down any request when Summer had been so brave and put up with so much, for so long.

Evelyn took a moment to smooth down her jumper and check her honey-coloured hair in the hall mirror, before pasting on a bright smile and heading into the living room, ready to convince her mum that everything was all right. But Linda was having none of it. She was already sat on the sofa, with two wine glasses and an ice bucket on the coffee table in front of her.

Evelyn raised an eyebrow in amusement. 'I thought you were putting the kettle on.'

'I thought this is what might be needed. You do still drink sauvignon blanc?' She poured the glass and pushed it into Evelyn's hand without waiting for an answer.

'Haven't you got work tomorrow?' Evelyn tried to complain.

'Nope, I've asked one of the girls to cover my shifts for a few days, so don't you worry about that. Now sit down, put your feet up, and tell me everything.'

'I don't even know where to start.'

'With the most important part of your story – Summer.'

Evelyn took a large gulp of the wine, enjoying its cool sweetness as it slipped down her throat with far too much ease. 'I won't lie. It's been hard. Really hard at times.'

'I can't believe it's been so long since I've seen her.'

'I know. And I'm sorry for that.' Evelyn wiped away a guilty tear.

'Oh love, I know you couldn't help it. You explained that the chemo damaged Summer's immune system, and that she was too ill to travel. I understand that, and I didn't mean to make you feel bad.' She wrapped a comforting arm around Evelyn's shoulders. 'It's not like I could easily have come to you – not once the winter colds started running through work.'

'It's been awful. Really, really awful at times. The chemo hurt her.' She took a deep breath before confessing the next bit. 'It worked, but only just.'

'I don't understand.' Worry deepened the lines around Linda's eyes – the same bright green as both Summer's and Evelyn's. 'You said it worked.'

'The chemo worked, but the last treatment had to be stopped early. Summer had a bad reaction to it. Her consultant wanted to do another round, maybe two, to make sure they got every single cell, but they couldn't. It's not uncommon for a patient to develop an intolerance to treatment after a few rounds. And she's had more than a few.'

'So what does this mean?'

'I don't honestly know. It's so unfair – this was the treatment that's worked the best, and now she can't have it again.'

'Never?'

'No. Once you've reacted badly once, it's more likely to happen again, and the reaction can be even more severe.' Evelyn rested her head on her mum's shoulder, and they sat there in silence for a few moments.

Eventually, Linda placed a kiss on her daughter's forehead. 'But it doesn't really matter, does it? Because you said she's in remission.'

'Yeah. She's in remission.' She took another gulp of her wine before whispering the words that had been plaguing her, half-hoping that she could limit their damage or likelihood of coming true by not speaking them aloud. 'But what if it doesn't last?'

'It will. She's a fighter, our Summer,' her mum reassured her. 'It will take a lot more than this to stop her. She will be all right, I promise you that.'

'I wish I had your confidence,' Evelyn admitted in a small voice.

'I've got enough for both of us right now. Have as much as you need.' Linda gave her a reassuring smile. 'Now, tell me what happened between you and Charlie.'

'Everything and nothing, Mum. He changed, maybe I did too.'

'Of course you have. How could you go through what you have with Summer and not be changed by it? But that's over now. Isn't there any chance of reconciliation?'

'No. He's hurt us too badly. He just isn't the man I married any more. If he'd been there for Summer, been a good dad, maybe there would be some hope, but he hasn't even managed to get that right lately. He hasn't even *tried.*'

'It's got to have been hard on him,' Linda argued.

'Yeah, but it's been hard on me too. And it's been hardest of all on Summer. Neither of us got to run away.' She sighed sadly and shook her head.

'No, you didn't.' She reached for the wine bottle.

'I really shouldn't.' Evelyn held her hand over the top of the glass. 'I've still got to unpack the car and trailer, and I've got to get up early tomorrow. There's so much to do.'

'Just grab what you need from the car for tonight. Everything else will be fine until the morning, and I'll help then. And what, pray tell, do you have to do tomorrow?'

'Well, once I'm unpacked …'

'Which I've said I'll help with.'

'Yes, and thank you for that. When I've got everything in, I need to make an appointment to get Summer registered with a doctor here, and hand over all her case history, then make enquiries at the school to get her registered so she can start after February half-term, and that's just to start with. I know it's several weeks away, but these things take time. And she's still got healing to do.'

'Well, I can help there. You've already got an appointment with the doctor – nothing too formal in case you or Summer are too tired – but you're pencilled in for three o'clock. You remember Dr Tom?'

'Of course. Is he still practising?'

'Absolutely. His wife Julie is still the surgery manager – and she just happens to be part of my crafting circle and a WI member. They both know all about Summer. If you can't make it tomorrow, one of them will drop round one evening to complete the registration forms. And speaking of registration forms'—she leaned forward and produced a sheaf of papers from the coffee table drawer—'Mrs Snowden, the school administrator dropped these by.'

Evelyn snorted in amusement. 'Another of your crafting circle?'

'Painting class, actually.' Linda's eyes twinkled with amusement. 'So, more wine?'

'Please.' Evelyn held out her glass gratefully. 'You really have thought of everything. Thank you for all you're doing for us.'

'You don't need to thank family, remember? And it's really not a big deal. Just a few favours from friends who want to help.'

'Well, I still appreciate it.'

'You're welcome. Now, do you want to tell me what "everything and nothing" means when it comes to explaining Charlie's disappearance?'

Evelyn took another fortifying gulp of wine, before launching into the sordid, gruesome tale.

# Chapter Two

*Jake*

Jake sauntered out of the café, The Brockle's Paws, and had to do a double take as he sipped his coffee. He snorted in amusement; for a moment, he'd thought there was a fox tied up outside the general store, sunbathing in the winter sunshine. It was too early in the year for most of the tourists who visited, and he knew almost all the animals locally, so the creature must be new.

'Well, hello there.' It jumped up as he approached, clearly recognising him as a dog lover, and danced prettily, stretching towards him on the end of a sparkly leash. Though she seemed friendly, Jake took his time and let her sniff at his fingers before rubbing her ears. She yipped happily and butted his hand playfully.

'Aren't you just the prettiest thing?' He twisted her collar slightly to peer at her tag. 'Tilly. What a pretty name for a lovely little fox.'

'You know, she's not actually a fox.'

Jake found himself looking into the brightest green eyes he'd ever seen on a human, peering out at him from between an equally green bobble hat and scarf. He had to bite back a grin at the perturbed face and folded arms: the little girl was right.

'I know.' He moved back to let her untie the leash, but Tilly continued to nuzzle at his fingers, fawning for more attention. 'She's a Shiba Inu, isn't she? Maybe about nine or ten years old?'

The green eyes widened in amazement. 'How did you know that?'

'She told me,' Jake teased gently.

'Who are you talking to, Summer?'

15

'It's not me, Mum. Tilly's making friends.' The little girl grinned up at a woman and Jake did his second double take of the morning. She was absolutely stunning – the same green eyes as her daughter were surrounded by a mop of curly, honey-blonde hair, against creamy, freckled skin and glossy pink lips that curved into an easy smile. There was no suspicion or concern in those striking green eyes – just curiosity.

'Is she, indeed?'

'I … umm …' Jake cursed inwardly. Why was he such an idiot? The moment a pretty girl smiled at him, it was like his brain suddenly lost the ability to communicate with his mouth and all his words suddenly became stuck. And this woman wasn't just a pretty girl. She was beautiful.

'So, who is your new friend, Tilly?' She paused for a moment, before giving him another warm smile. 'Well, looks like she's feeling shy, so I'll have to manage the introductions myself. I'm Evelyn Jon— *Matthams*. And this is my daughter, Summer. It seems you already know Tilly.' She held out her hand.

Jake stood, and shook it, wondering briefly why she'd stumbled over her own name, but he was too polite to mention it. 'Jake Macpearson. You must be new to Broclington. I'd remember this foxy little lady.'

Summer tugged at her mum's hand. 'He's teasing. He knows she's really a Shiba.'

'You like dogs then.'

'It's in the job description. I'm the local vet. I wouldn't be a very good one if I didn't like animals!'

Summer laughed, and Jake smiled with her.

'Do you have a card? You're right, we're new here – well, I'm returning, these two are new. But I'll need to set up an appointment soon for Tilly.'

'I don't, but I'm heading back to the surgery now. If you're not busy, you can walk with me and we can get her registered. It's only a few minutes away. Though most things in Broclington are.' He laughed.

'That would be good, thanks.' Evelyn glanced down at Summer. 'Feel up to exploring a bit more?'

'Yeah.'

'OK then. Where are we going?'

'Just across the village centre. I'm based in The Burrow's.' He set an easy pace, and wondered why he'd just put himself in this situation while he wracked his brains for something vaguely intelligent or interesting to say.

Evelyn saved him the worry. 'It's been a while since I've lived here, but I don't remember a vet. Last time I lived here, it was a drive into town or call-out. Have you been here long?'

'I set it up about six years ago. Wanted to come home after I'd finished my studies and placements, and like you said, there wasn't a surgery here, so it was pretty welcome.'

'Makes sense.' Evelyn fell quiet as they walked, while Summer chattered happily to Tilly, telling her that she didn't need to worry because this vet was a nice one. Jake flexed his fingers inside his pockets, watching his breath puff into the cold, fresh air, while he tried to work out how to fill the silence before it became awkward.

He started slightly when Evelyn clapped her hands together and pointed to him triumphantly. 'I've just realised who you are. Macpearson – you're related to the doctor, right?'

'Yeah. He's my dad.'

'We must have been at school together,' Evelyn mused aloud. 'Who was your form tutor?'

'Allan Cooper. Yours?'

'You were a few years ahead of me, then. I had Jo Smith.'

'Probably why I don't remember you then. Sorry about that.'

'Well, if you're apologising, I should too,' Evelyn replied easily. 'Or we could just gloss over that, and pretend this is the first we've met.'

'Sounds good. So what's Tilly's appointment for? Boosters and flea treatment?'

'How did you know that?' Summer looked at him in surprise. 'Did she tell you?'

'Sort of,' Jake admitted. 'She looks like she's really well looked after, and doesn't seem unwell. She's friendly, and clearly well-loved. Am I right?'

'Yes. She's my best friend, aren't you Tilly? I haven't got any brothers or sisters, but I've got you instead. And you're much better, aren't you?' Tilly answered with a happy yip. 'See?'

They stopped outside a converted stone house where the front garden had been replaced with gravel for parking and a swinging sign painted with different animals hung from the gate post.

'Here we are.' Jake unlocked the door and held it open proudly. He'd worked really hard to set up the surgery, and was incredibly pleased with everything he'd achieved.

'Badger Hospital?' Summer ran her gloved fingers over the wording on the door. 'But Tilly's a dog, not a badger.'

'I look after dogs every day,' he reassured her. 'Most of my customers aren't badgers. It's just the name I liked.'

'How come?'

'Summer, don't be rude,' Evelyn chastised gently.

'It's OK.' Jake could happily talk for hours about his work without getting tongue-tied once. 'One of the first animals I looked after was a baby badger.'

'That's so cool!' Summer was transfixed. 'What happened?'

'Well, it was when I was young – probably only about your age – and we had a really mild winter, which meant a lot of animals woke up from hibernation, and had their babies early. But spring was really, really cold and we had more than ten inches of snow that lasted for weeks.'

'Oh no!' Summer cried. 'What happened to all the early babies?'

'Well, I told you my dad's a doctor, and the village didn't used to have a vet. So when people found poor little cold babies, they brought them to us. One of them was a badger.'

'And you looked after him?'

He nodded, suddenly feeling a bit nostalgic for those old, simpler days. 'He was really little – his eyes were barely open – and he needed to be kept warm, and be fed every couple of hours. I made myself a bed in the living room by the fireplace, and slept by him for three nights, feeding him every time he woke up and mewled for food. Dad said I saved his life.'

'Was he OK?' He was surprised to see Evelyn was watching him as intently as her daughter. He hadn't expected his story to be that interesting to her.

'Yeah, he was. When the snow thawed, we were able to get him to a specialist wildlife rehabilitation centre. When he was big enough, he was released into a nature reserve along with other young badgers who had been rescued that year.'

'You saved his life! That's so cool.' Summer's comment filled his heart with warmth.

'Yeah, I guess I did. That was when I decided I wanted to be a vet. If not for that little guy, I could have ended up doing a really awful job. Or something really boring. I don't think I'd do very well in a boring office job.' He remembered belatedly that a lot of people had "boring office jobs" and flashed an apologetic look at Evelyn. 'Sorry.'

She laughed. 'Don't worry about it. I couldn't be an office worker either. So, you named your surgery after the animal who inspired you.'

He nodded. 'That, and it seemed appropriate to have another badger-themed business here.'

'Did you know they sell badger cakes in the café?' Summer asked, wide-eyed. 'Mum said we can have one later, but not before lunch. There's badgers everywhere here.'

Evelyn chuckled, filling the surgery with the light happy sound, and Jake felt a twinge of something akin to longing. For some reason he couldn't understand, he felt protective of her – of them both – and wanted to make them smile, and laugh, like that again. He shook his head, trying to clear the feeling. He'd only just met them, and they weren't his family. He was probably just feeling a bit overtired after staying up late with a foaling mare at a local farm.

'Do you know why there's badgers everywhere?'

'Coz people like badgers,' Summer replied, like it was the most logical thing in the world.

Jake laughed, touched by the innocent answer. 'They should do, shouldn't they? Badgers are cool. But it's not just that. Brockle is an old, old word for badger. So Broclington means "Badger's Town". And there are lots of badgers in the woods round here.'

'Awesome!' Summer's eyes lit her up and she looked up at her mum. 'Can we go find some badgers? Please Mum!'

Evelyn pulled a face. 'I think badgers are quite shy, and it's very cold. Most of them are probably still snug in their setts.'

Summer's face fell and Jake instantly berated himself for creating this situation. 'Your mum's right, but when it's warmer, we run badger walks sometimes to help raise money for the local wildlife rescue centre. If you're really lucky, some of the badgers who have been released can still be spotted. I could let you know when the next one is.'

'Yes please!'

'That would be good, thank you.' Evelyn smiled. 'Shall we sort out Tilly's appointment? I'm worried we've already taken up too much of your time.'

Jake wanted to argue with her, to explain that he'd enjoyed chatting with them but instead he reminded himself that she was probably just being polite and wanted to get going. He pulled out the large diary from behind reception, and ran his finger down the entries. He was expecting his next patient in a few minutes, but had

21

space in a couple of days. He agreed the time with Evelyn and gave her a copy of the registration form.

'Thanks so much.' Evelyn smiled.

'You won't forget about the badger walk, will you?' Summer begged.

'No. I'll let you know,' Jake promised, wondering how early would be too early to organise the next event, even while mentally berating himself for the thought. He held the door open, reluctantly.

'Thanks Jake, we'll see you in a few days, won't we Tilly?'

'See you then.' He waved as they left, then closed the door against the cold, and went to put the kettle on for another coffee. Clearly the first one hadn't done its job in waking him up properly, because he still felt very odd. He returned to the window and watched the trio as they headed back towards the village centre. Even as they approached the corner, he could see Summer waving her hands around animatedly as she said something that was clearly exciting. For the briefest of moments, just before they crossed the road and turned the corner, he could have sworn Evelyn glanced back towards him. But then he shook his head against the foolish thought.

He definitely needed that coffee.

Summer skipped cheerfully by Evelyn's side, chattering happily about her "new friend" the vet who was so nice even Tilly liked him, and how cool it would be to meet badgers. Evelyn didn't have the heart to remind her that badgers were shy, wild creatures – in all her time in Broclington, she'd only seen a badger a handful of times, and always from a distance. She didn't want to tell Summer she'd be lucky to even see one – and would probably never get to pet one like she'd planned. And she didn't tell her that Jake was probably just being polite to a new client. Summer had always been such a friendly, happy, outgoing child, and she'd spent so long in isolation only meeting doctors and nurses, that Evelyn didn't want to discourage it.

She unlocked the front door, and knelt to wipe Tilly's paws while Summer raced ahead to talk to Nanny.

'Summer, shoes!' She shook her head, trying not to laugh at the healthy exuberance of her beautiful daughter. She thanked God every day that she got to see Summer smile like this. It was funny, she'd never really been particularly religious – until Summer had gotten ill, and now, despite not going to church regularly, she still prayed all the time. Just a quick, few words here and there, but a prayer nonetheless.

'Sorry, Mum!' Summer skidded back into the hall, and sat on the stairs to tug her boots off before racing back towards the kitchen. Tilly bounded after her, barking cheerfully, and Evelyn followed at a more sedate pace.

'We've got a couple of hours before we need to go meet your new doctor, what do you want to do?'

'Not see another doctor!'

'Summer Marie …' She hesitated over the last name. 'Summer'—she knelt down—'I know you've seen more than enough doctors to last a lifetime, but you do need to be registered with one here.'

'I know.' Summer rubbed at an invisible spot on the floor with her toe, her bottom lip starting to stick out. 'But I was having such a nice day. Do we really have to?'

'Yes, we really have to.'

'And the doctor is a friend of mine,' Linda reassured Summer. 'He's really nice.'

'OK. I s'pose. If I have to.'

'I'm afraid you do.'

'But I'm still not happy about it.'

'I know, sweetheart.' Linda rested a hand on her granddaughter's fuzzy head. 'But I think I might have something to cheer you up. How would you like to try a Brockle cake?'

Summer's eyes went wide. 'Is that like the badger cakes we saw today?'

'Exactly like. Chocolate, vanilla and cherry in a stripy, delicious cake. Would you like one?' she teased gently, as she got the plates from the cupboard.

'Yes, yes, yes, yes, YES!'


'How do you know he's going to be nice?' Summer dragged her feet as they approached the surgery.

'Because Nanny said he is. And he was nice when I lived here.' Evelyn gave her a brief hug. 'And you met his son Jake this morning, remember? You liked him, so you'll like his dad.'

'I don't like my dad.' Summer stuck out her bottom lip.

'Oh, sweetheart. Just because me and your dad are having some problems at the moment, it doesn't mean he doesn't love you.'

'He didn't come to the hospital with me.'

'He had to work.'

'So did you. If he loved me, he would have come.'

Evelyn didn't even know how to start dealing with that problem, but she knew it would take a much longer conversation than they had time for now. So she did the wimpy thing and chickened out by changing the subject, while making a silent promise to try and figure it out later. 'We're here. Do you want your necklace now?'

'Yes please!'

Evelyn unzipped Summer's coat and carefully draped the beaded necklace around her, looping it over three times. She was simultaneously filled with gratitude and horror every time she saw it.

They signed in at reception and settled down to wait for Summer's name to be called. Evelyn tried to hide her own nerves, while Summer happily rummaged through the collection of children's toys and books set up in a corner of the waiting room. As much as Evelyn put on a brave face for her daughter, she struggled with doctors too – at least when it was her or someone she loved who was the patient. It was a room very like this one that she'd sat nervously in a few years ago, waiting to hear the news every parent dreaded: her baby was sick, and it was bad. She made an effort to study the room, picking out all the differences between this one and all the others she'd been in recently: the beams and visible parts of the walls and low ceilings were all different, but the large windows, multitude of pamphlets and posters, and screen to announce which patient should go to which room were all far too similar for her comfort.

Eventually the screen lit up with Summer's name, and they walked hand in hand down the corridor.

'Well, hello there, you must be Summer. I'm Dr Macpearson, but you can call me Dr Tom.' He was a smiley, older man with blue eyes that were sharp behind his glasses. What little hair he had left was grey, and he looked friendly and reassuring in his sports coat and corduroys.

'Yup, and you're Jake's daddy.'

'Why yes, yes I am.' Dr Tom laughed. 'And this must be your mum.' He smiled warmly.

'Her name's Evelyn,' Summer replied helpfully.

'Yes, I know. I used to be your Mum's doctor too. It's nice to see you again, Evelyn.'

'You as well.' She shook his outstretched hand which was still warm and firm.

He turned back to Summer, and held his hand out to her too. She shook it, very seriously, and grinned at him.

'I like your necklace. They're bravery beads, aren't they? From the hospital and your other doctors?'

Summer nodded. 'Yes, I've got a lot of them.'

'Yes you do. I know what some of the colours mean, but in case your doctors used different ones, can you tell me what they're for?' He leaned forward.

Summer picked up one of the strands and held it up so he could see better. 'They're all different. The red ones are for blood tests – I've got a lot of them. The blue ones are when I've had to see doctors – I've got the most of them. These funny ones are special – they glow in the dark – and are for radiotherapy, but I was sad because I didn't glow afterward. Not even a little bit. I put my covers over my head to check and everything. The white ones were … Mum? I've forgotten.'

'Chemotherapy.' Evelyn's voice caught in her throat as she choked on emotion. Listening to Summer cheerfully show her beads of courage to the doctor and rattle off all the different procedures she'd been through was agonising. As was the realisation that Summer was right – Charlie had been missing for almost every bead and procedure after the first dozen or so, using work as the excuse. The doctor gave her a reassuring smile and a wink, and she instantly felt a little better.

'I like the purple beads, coz that's the end of treatment, but ...' Summer leaned forward. 'This is the best one.' She showed him the multicoloured heart dangling from the middle of the necklace. 'Because this one means I'm better.'

'I like that one too,' Dr Tom confessed. 'And I bet it's your mum's and Nanny's favourite too.'

'Definitely,' Evelyn agreed wholeheartedly.

'So, how are you feeling Summer?' The doctor took out a pen to make notes.

'OK, thank you. How are you?'

'I'm very well thank you, and very impressed with your good manners. But you're my patient, so I'm very curious to know more about how you're feeling.'

'My head itches, but Nanny says it's from where my hair is growing back. And I still get tired sometimes. It's annoying because I want to go back to school and make friends, and play more, but then I want to go to bed too.' She sighed hugely. 'It sucks.'

'Summer!' Evelyn chastised immediately. 'That is not language I appreciate.'

'Sorry Mum. Sorry Dr Tom.'

'That's all right. I think I agree.' He winked at her, making her giggle. 'I'll tell you what.' The doctor rummaged in his desk and produced a sketch pad and packet of colouring pencils. 'Since we repainted in here, I think my walls are looking a bit boring. Would you like to draw me a picture to brighten it up a bit, while I talk to your mum about boring things.'

'About me?'

'Maybe a little bit, but only the boring stuff, I promise.'

'OK. Do you like badgers?'

'I do. Very much.'

'I'll make you a badger then. A rainbow one.'

'A rainbow badger?' He chuckled. 'That is something I'd very much like to see.'

He turned to Evelyn, and gave her a warm smile. 'Linda's already filled me in on the basics, but I'll need the names of Summer's doctors to get her notes.'

Evelyn produced a large folder. 'These are copies of her treatment plans, and all the correspondence we've received, and a graph tracking her HVA and VMA blood levels – which have been quite reliable measures throughout. Her GP's, consultant's and cancer nurse's contact details are all in there too.'

'Thank you.' He shuffled through the folder quickly. 'I'll make copies of these and drop them back to you.'

'It's OK. I've more at home.'

'From the top then. Neuroblastoma, diagnosed following presentation with ongoing shoulder pain, tiredness, anaemia and sustained, elevated ESR.' He flicked through a few more pages. 'At five years old?' He looked at her over the top of his glasses, eyebrows raised.

'I know. It's quite rare at that age.'

'I kept getting sick and tired,' Summer piped up from the corner where she was drawing. 'Mum kept taking me to the doctor and nagging them until they listened. She saved my life.'

'Where did you hear that?' Evelyn looked at her in shock. She thought they'd protected Summer from knowing how bad things might have been.

'Lizzie told me.'

'Her cancer nurse,' Evelyn explained to Dr Tom. 'Why did she tell you that?'

'Because I asked her if I was going to die, like one of the littler kids did. She said no, because you nagged the doctors until they listened, like you nag me to take my shoes off at home, and because of your nagging the doctors found my tumour in time and could blast it away.'

'Your cancer nurse wasn't wrong,' Dr Tom agreed. 'So, let's go through the rest of these papers.'

# Chapter Three

Summer and Tilly ran ahead, happy in the unexpected sunshine, even though it meant there were limited puddles for the pair of them to jump and splash in. Evelyn laughed at their antics as she stripped off her thick gloves and loosened her scarf. The sun shone brightly in the blue sky, making it warmer than she'd expected, and spring was already starting to fill the air.

She smiled as she watched her two girls bouncing along happily – one a rescue from a rehoming centre, and one rescued from an illness that stole the lives of far too many children – and said a silent thank you to whoever was watching over her. They'd only been in Broclington for a little over a month, but the differences in Summer were incredible.

She paused, and turned her head up to the sky, enjoying the warmth of the sun. All through the woods, for all that it was only February, there were the first, early daffodils, crocuses and buds and leaves that were heralding spring, and the world was coming back to life, bright, beautiful and full of promise of a wonderful year ahead.

She liked the metaphor for her own life as well. Sometimes it seemed only yesterday that she sat in a hospital isolation ward, wearing a mask, gown and gloves while she held Summer's hand as "Santa" waved to her through a window. And other times, like now when Summer was racing around happily playing with Tilly, it seemed as if it belonged to another lifetime. One she was only too happy to leave behind.

Again, she worried about the lack of relationship that Summer had with her father, but tried to put it out of her mind and focus on enjoying the day and living in the moment. That had been one of the things all the other parents, and doctors and nurses had always told her – focus on the moment and try to live in whatever joy there was. And they'd been right.

Tilly had stuck her nose in another hole, investigating something, and Evelyn ran up to her and thwacked her tail gently. She laughed when Tilly spun around and play-growled at her, before racing off, yipping at her pack to follow her.

'Come on,' Evelyn called to Summer. 'Race you!'

They ran and chased after each other, laughing until they were out of breath and rosy-cheeked with joy. Evelyn grabbed Summer around the waist and swung her in the air, making her giggle and squeal with delight.

'So, are you sure you're ready to go back to school next term?'

'Yes!'

'And you liked Mrs Appleby?' Evelyn had liked her when they'd met a few days ago in preparation for Summer's imminent start at the village school, but Evelyn wasn't the one who would be spending every day with her.

'I think so,' Summer mused, 'but she reminded me a bit of Nurse Marie. She wasn't very funny.'

'No, but she was a very good nurse. And Mrs Appleby isn't Nurse Marie. I'm sure if you try your best, she'll be lovely.' She looked around. 'Tilly, c'mere.'

'Tilly, you should listen to Mum. Tilly, come!' Summer rolled her eyes in an expression of such exasperation that Evelyn had to bite back a smile.

The little dog trotted obediently towards her young mistress, before getting distracted and bouncing off in another direction to sniff at something that was probably only interesting to a dog, and stick her nose into yet another hole that looked just like every other one she'd shoved her muzzle in that morning.

Evelyn laughed. 'We're really lucky to have woodlands this close to the house. I think she likes being a country dog, don't you?' She'd barely finished the question before Tilly screeched in pain and shot back towards them, a blur of distressed ginger fur. She dived behind Summer, almost knocking her over in the process, and sat there whimpering and shaking.

'Mum, what's wrong with Tilly?' Summer fell to her knees and hugged the little dog. 'Mum?'

'Come here, girl.' Evelyn gathered her up and gently checked her over. Nothing seemed to be amiss until she reached her front left paw, at which point Tilly yelped and tried to pull her foot away. 'There's a good girl, Tilly. Just let me have a quick look.' Evelyn thought she spotted a tiny puncture wound, but it didn't seem to be bleeding badly.

'What's wrong with her, Mum. Is she going to be OK?'

'Of course she is. I think she just spiked her foot on a bramble or thorn. We'll take her home, clean her foot and have a better look. And probably give her a treat as well. OK?'

Summer pulled a face. 'OK. But I hope she still likes being a country dog. I like being a country girl!'

'I think I missed being a country girl too.' She carefully set Tilly on the floor. 'Come on then, Little Miss Curious. Let's get you home and cleaned up.' She took a few steps, then realised Tilly was still sitting, her hurt paw held just off the ground. 'Come on.'

Tilly took a couple of steps, but her leg collapsed under her.

'Mummy?' Summer's voice was laced with worry, and the fact that she'd gone back to calling her Mummy told Evelyn how scared she was.

'She's probably just a bit sore.' Evelyn forced her voice calm as she tried to reassure both dog and daughter. 'You know how much needles hurt?'

Summer nodded vehemently. 'Even with magic cream they're nasty.'

'Well, a thorn is a lot bigger than a needle. So it probably hurts a bit more.'

'Oh, poor Tilly.' Summer gave her four-legged friend another hug. 'It's OK. It doesn't hurt for long. And you'll be a lot better when we're home and you can have a treat.'

'It's a good thing you're not heavy.' Evelyn cuddled the little dog as she picked her up.


Jake briskly rubbed the belly and chest of the kitten he'd just delivered, trying to stimulate the scrap of fur into taking its first breath of air. The queen – or mother cat – was younger than ideal, and was getting exhausted, so he was glad when her owner brought her in, and he'd been able to intervene. He'd given her drugs to help her push, and fluids, and the first four kittens were already mostly clean and mewling loudly, complaining at their treatment and nudging around looking for their first feed.

But this final kit just wasn't responding. Working quickly, he cleaned his nose and grasped his head before covering him with his other hand and swinging firmly forwards. 'Come on, little guy. Just take a breath. It's only the first one that's hard.' He swung him again.

'Come on.' He hated to lose an animal. Most days, he loved his job, but he had to admit when he lost a life he considered giving it up and becoming a dog trainer, or librarian. Or anything that didn't involve losing animals.

Grimly, he turned the kitten over and gave him a few firm taps across its shoulders before swinging it again. He was rewarded with the tiniest of wet, snuffling gasps, and grinned in relief. He gave the kitten another quick rub, checked he was breathing OK, then held him up for a quick look. 'You arc one lucky little tom.' He tucked him with his mum, next to his brothers and sisters, and breathed a sigh of relief. Another win.

He looked forward to calling the owners and giving them the happy news, and then a not so happy reminder on responsible cat ownership – particularly pertaining to keeping unneutered females indoors when they were in heat. And then, he'd be able to go home and put his feet up.

The surgery phone started to ring while he was cleaning up, and he raced to dry his hands and answer it, at the same time grumbling at his lack of help. Ever since his nurse had gone on maternity leave, he'd been short-handed, but was reluctant to replace her. Erin had worked with him since he'd opened the surgery, and they got on well as friends and colleagues, and he wasn't sure if he'd work as well with anyone else. If he were honest with himself, he'd always gotten on better with animals than humans.

He snatched the phone from its cradle. 'Hello, Badger's Hospital.'

'Still not managed to replace Erin, then?' His brother's voice sounded amused. 'Maybe you could train a parrot to answer the phone.'

34

'I guess the salary would be cheap, at least. You know, cheep cheep!'

Callum groaned down the phone. 'Your sense of humour hasn't improved since we were kids.'

'Well, it's not like I had a good role model.'

'Stuff you. I was funny.'

'If you say so. What's up, Cal?' Jake wandered back into the surgical room, and peered at the kittens. They all appeared to be feeding well, so he left mum to it and settled in a chair.

'Not much, just checking in on you, and wanted to see if you're coming for lunch in two weeks.'

'It's the second Sunday of the month, why wouldn't I be there?'

'Dunno, but Mum called to check I'd be there, which means you have to as well. Apparently there's some big announcement.'

'Intriguing. And you've no idea what?'

'Not a scooby, little bro,' Callum replied. 'But she sounded happy, so that's good. And she's making her spiced apple sponge, so Sarah's excited.'

'You can't blame her. It is a damn fine pudding.' Jake laughed. 'So how is my gorgeous little niece?'

'Four going on fourteen, cheeky, precocious and a total nutter most of the time. Exhausting, brilliant and changing almost daily.' The pride in his brother's voice made Jake grin.

'She still enjoying nursery?'

'She is. I'm not so sure about the teachers, though. Honestly, it's sometimes scary how smart she is. We were running late for nursery last week, mostly because we'd been arguing about how she can't wear her pyjamas out of the house.'

'Why would she want to?'

'Because they're princess pyjamas. Obviously.'

'Silly me. I should have guessed.' Jake laughed.

'Anyway, when I told her we were running late and needed to get moving, she turned around and calmly informed me it was my fault. Because I should have started yelling at her sooner. And that she'd no choice except to wear her pyjamas because of how late we were.'

'That is brilliant.' Jake guffawed. 'So did she?'

'Well. I made her put on some jeans and a jumper as well. So no, not exactly.'

'Dude. She totally got her own way. You're a fully qualified, experienced doctor, partner in a busy GP's surgery – albeit the family one – and you just got played. By your four-year-old.'

'I know,' Callum admitted softly. 'But she's cute enough to get away with it.'

'Speaking of cute … I've just helped deliver a really cute litter of kittens. They'll probably be here until tomorrow. I bet Sarah would just love to meet some cute kitties.'

'I'm sure she would. But you know she'll only bug me to have one. It will be like the chicks all over again. Why do you do this to me?'

'Because I like spoiling my niece. And you do get fresh eggs every day now.'

'And a chicken run to clean. I think I'd rather buy them from the store.'

'Wouldn't be as educational. Or as much fun,' Jake argued.

He hesitated when he heard a car screech into the small yard, and then a door slam. 'Sorry bro, someone's just pulled up. Sounds like I might be getting an emergency visit. Gotta go.'

'No worries. I know how it is. Good luck.'

'Hopefully I won't need it, but thanks.' He headed into the reception, and grinned when he saw Evelyn coming through the door. For a moment, he was inexplicably pleased to see her, and wondered if Summer was with her as he'd love to show her the kittens. But his happy greeting died on his lips when he took in the worry darkening her face and the still bundle clasped tightly in her arms.

'Jake, thank goodness you're still here. It's Tilly.' The door crashed shut behind her, and she looked at the bundle, close to tears.

'Come straight through.' He held open the door to his surgery, glad he'd already finished clearing up. 'On the table please.' He gently peeled away the purple blanket and his breath caught. Tilly couldn't be much further from the happy, healthy dog he'd met a few weeks ago. She didn't acknowledge him, was quivering, and her eyes were glazed over. 'What happened?'

'I don't know. We were out for a walk and she seemed fine. She hurt her paw. I thought it was just on a bramble or something. She didn't want to put weight on it, but seemed OK, so I just scooped her up and carried her back to Mum's.' She wiped her eyes roughly. 'I cleaned her foot up when we got back, which was a bit swollen, and she seemed out of sorts. She didn't want food, and when Summer tried to play with her, she collapsed.'

'Which foot?'

'Her left front.'

'All right Miss Tilly, let's have a look at you.' Even though she wasn't responding, Jake knew it was important to keep her calm. She whimpered slightly as he untucked her paw from the blanket. 'There's a good girl, you're being so brave. Don't worry, we'll have you all fixed up soon.'

He hissed in sympathy as he examined the paw, which had swollen to more than twice its usual size, tugging the skin tight, which was hot to touch. He parted the fur, hoping he wasn't going to see what he was already expecting – and dreading. Though he could feel the adrenaline start to race through his veins, he forced himself to stay calm. 'Where were you when this happened?'

'The woods around the back of the church. What's wrong with her?'

'And she was digging around? Exploring off the leash?' He grabbed the razor from its place on the shelf and buzzed it to check it had power.

'Yes.'

'Sorry about this, Tilly.' He shaved a patch on her other leg. 'I think she's been bitten by an adder.'

'Oh my God.' Evelyn's hands covered her face in horror. 'I thought she was just being a bit of a wimp. If I'd have had any idea I would have brought her straight here instead of going home …'

'She's here now. That's what matters.' He finished inserting an IV catheter into the cephalic vein on Tilly's foreleg. 'I need to get her hydrated.' He connected a hydration pack to the catheter and handed it to Evelyn. 'Hold this please. Keep it elevated like this.' He positioned her hand and arm appropriately. 'Don't squeeze it.'

Evelyn nodded in understanding as Jake slipped his stethoscope into his ears and held the diaphragm against Tilly's chest. He couldn't hold back the frown at what he was hearing. Tilly's heart rate must have been close to one hundred and fifty beats a minute.

'She's what, ten years old?' He grabbed the blood pressure monitor out of the drawer and wrapped it around one of Tilly's back legs.

'Maybe closer to eleven. We were told she was five or six when we rescued her.' She cast a worried eye over the little dog. 'She's bad, isn't she?'

Jake scribbled down Tilly's blood pressure, which was far from the figures he'd hoped for. He forced himself to meet Evelyn's eyes. 'I won't lie to you. Her condition is critical. She's not a very big dog, and she's going into shock.'

'She can't die, Jake. Summer can't lose her best friend. Not now, it's too unfair.' Evelyn was fighting back the tears, and if he'd had time to think about it, Jake might have wondered what she'd meant by "not now", but his entire focus was on Tilly.

'I'm going to give her painkillers and a mild, short-acting sedative to help keep her calm and try to stop the venom spreading any further or faster. And antihistamines to try and bring down the swelling. The fluids you're holding will help with the shock, and we'll get her onto a heating pad too.' He went to pick up his little patient. 'I just need to check her weight for dosage.'

'18.1 pounds. She gets weighed every month with Summer.'

Jake nodded brusquely and drew out the medications, injecting them directly into the line leading into Tilly's leg.

Evelyn switched the bag into her other hand, and rubbed Tilly's ears and nose.

'I need to get her into a cage with a heating pad.'

'Is there an alternative?' Evelyn begged. 'She needs to be kept calm, doesn't she?' She waited for Jake's nod. 'She hasn't been caged since we brought her home. She … she was locked in a crate before she was rescued. It's not fair to her. Even in the car she travels just with a seat belt. Never a crate. If she wakes up in a cage, I'm worried she'll panic. Which will just spike her blood pressure again.'

'OK. I'll get a heating pad, and we'll sit with her on the couch in the waiting room.'

'Thank you.' Evelyn caught his hand in hers. 'Jake, be honest – is this going to be enough?'

'I hope so.'

'But you don't know.' Evelyn sighed. 'I'm guessing there isn't an antivenom for dogs.'

'Not officially licensed, no. But there is one we use off-label. I'm going to make a call. I'm hoping the bigger surgery in town might have some in already, but it's early in the year. Give me a min, and I'll grab the pad and we'll move her together.'

He dialled the number and listened to the phone ring as he grabbed the heating pad and an extension cord, and hoped that his neighbouring colleague would still be there, and have the drugs he needed. He breathed a sigh of relief as the line clicked open to a real-life person instead of the answerphone. 'Hugh, it's Jake Macpearson. I've got a small bitch with an adder bite. Please tell me you've got antivenom in.'

'I think so. Let me check.' Jake heard the fridge open and glass bottles clink as Hugh looked for the drug that might save Tilly's life. 'How small is small?'

'Eighteen odd pounds. Eleven year old Shibu Inu. Nasty bite, got her with both fangs.'

'Nasty.' Hugh clinked some more. 'Vitals?'

'Heart rate up, blood pressure up, non-responsive.'

'Not good. But I have found the antivenom you want. It's last year's batch, but in the fridge, so should still work.'

'It's all I've got.'

'I'll get it over to you ASAP. You can settle up with me later, but you might have to pay a taxi driver for the delivery.'

'Sounds like a good deal. Thanks Hugh.' He headed back to Evelyn and Tilly.

'Come on, girl, you have to get better. Summer still needs you. I still need you.' Evelyn was nose to nose with Tilly, leaning down awkwardly to ensure she was in the little dog's vision, and stroking her forehead gently while still holding the IV bag.

Jake cleared his throat, not wanting to interrupt the tender moment, but still needing to work. Evelyn looked up, and wiped the tears from her eyes.

'Good news.' Jake smiled. 'The antivenom is on the way.'

'She's still not responding.'

'With the shock, and the drugs I've given her, she'll be pretty out of it.' He pumped up the blood pressure cuff, listening through the stethoscope, and glancing at the notes he'd made earlier. 'She's stable.'

'I guess that's about the best we can hope for right now.'

41

'Stable is good. Can you take these'—he handed her the heat pad and cables—'and hold on to the IV bag?' He gently scooped up Tilly. 'Come on, sweetheart. Let's get you warm and comfortable.' He turned to Evelyn. 'Stay close, and try to keep the bag up?'

'Not a problem.' Evelyn nodded, and followed him, matching her steps with Jake's until he sat on the sofa by the reception window, Tilly on his lap.

Evelyn put the heating pad down next to him, and plugged it in on the wall. Jake placed Tilly on it, and tucked her blanket over her before taking the IV bag back.

Evelyn sat down with them, letting her hand rest on Tilly's soft head. 'How long do you think before the antivenom turns up?'

'Maybe twenty-five minutes, or a little less if we're lucky.'

Evelyn nodded. 'I need to call home. There are two people desperately waiting for news.' She unlocked her phone and looked at Jake helplessly. 'What do I tell them?'

'Tell them the truth. She's stable, and she's a fighter. And we'll know more in the next couple of hours.'

'And that's all we know, right now, sweetheart.' Evelyn peered through the glass in the door, to where Jake was still sitting with Tilly. He was such a sweet guy.

'It's OK, Mum. Jake will make Tilly better. She just might be a bit poorly for a little while, like I was. And when she gets home from the doggy hospital, I'll look after her like she looked after me.' Evelyn was touched by the level of faith Summer had in Jake, and prayed that it wasn't misplaced.

'Do you know if Nanny made that call I asked her to?'

'Yeah. She pulled faces and said bad words about Charlie.'

'Charlie?' Evelyn pulled a face. 'When did you stop calling him Dad?'

'Nanny said he's a scumbag, and I'm not scum, so I must be more your little girl than his. I don't think he's been a very good dad, so now he's just Charlie.'

'O … K.' Evelyn drew the word out slowly, trying to work out why her mother would have said something so negative in Summer's hearing. They'd both been so careful to try not to influence Summer's feelings about her father. 'Can I speak to Nanny?'

'Yup. Tell Tilly I love her lots and to do what vet Jake says and get better soon.'

'I will, I promise.'

'OK. Bye. Here's Nanny!'

'Hi Mum.' Evelyn rubbed her forehead in irritation. 'What's going on?'

'I'm sorry, love. Summer overheard me losing my temper with that selfish space-waste you used to be married to. Don't worry, she's in the front room, and I'm in the kitchen now.' She sighed deeply. 'I phoned the insurance company like you asked.'

'Thanks.'

'There's a problem.' Evelyn closed her eyes and waited for her mum to drop the other shoe. 'The policy isn't up to date. Apparently the premiums haven't been paid in months.'

'What? But that's not possible,' Evelyn argued. 'I set it up myself. There's no way I would let Tilly's insurance lapse. It was on direct debit. There must be a problem with the bank. I'll have to call them and get this sorted. I paid in good faith so if there's a technical error they might still honour the policy.' Evelyn's mind was racing; she knew the damage a snakebite had the potential to do to a human – liver, heart, kidneys could all be damaged. And Tilly was a lot smaller than a person. Evelyn didn't even know if the tiny dog was going to survive, but she knew she would do everything within her power to give her every fighting chance.

Her mum interrupted her thoughts. 'Have you considered that it might not be a problem with the bank, so much as one with your account?'

'What do you mean?'

'Was it a joint account?' Her tentative tone made Evelyn freeze. 'It's been a while since he's sent you any money to support Summer, hasn't it?'

'He wouldn't …' She started to argue again before realising that compared to some of the other things he'd done, and risked, cancelling a few direct debits was close to nothing. 'He would, wouldn't he?' She didn't wait for the answer. 'I've got to go, Mum. Thanks.'

Evelyn tapped her details for the joint account – the one they used just for bills and direct debits – into the phone and watched in mounting horror as the screen informed her that her username and password didn't match their records. She took a deep breath and tapped the details in again, this time taking time to ensure she didn't mistype on the small, virtual keyboard. The third time, the rejection screen loaded almost immediately and she swore loudly.

'Bastard!'

Jake looked up in surprise.

'Cheating, greedy, scumbag *bastard*!'

There was a loud thump, like something hitting the wall hard, and a few seconds later Evelyn limped back through the door, her face darkened with anger.

'I'd ask if everything is OK, but as it's clearly not, I'll ask if I can help instead.'

'Not unless you can turn back time and make me less of an idiot.' Evelyn groaned. 'How is she?'

'Not much change.' Jake peered down at his patient.

'She looks so small right now,' Evelyn murmured as she sat down. 'When she's … normal, she's cheeky, feisty, smart and crazy energetic, but right now she just looks so small and helpless.'

Jake gave her what he hoped was a reassuring smile. 'She's not helpless. She's got us.'

The grateful smile Evelyn gave him made him grin properly. He glanced down at Tilly, and knew – once again – that he had to get this little dog well, not just because he hated to lose any patient, but because the thought of seeing Evelyn – and Summer – grieving for their furry family member made his stomach turn even more than usual. For some reason he didn't understand, whether or not they were happy really, really bothered him, even though he knew there was another man in both their lives who should be worried about making them smile. But he couldn't help it.

'You seemed upset after the phone call.' He let the statement hang in the air, not wanting to put any pressure on Evelyn, but at the same time needing her to know that he was there, waiting to lend a shoulder if she chose to use it.

Evelyn snorted in dark amusement. On anyone else it would have been a bit ugly, but somehow the gesture made her seem even more approachable and attractive. 'What was it that gave me away? The swearing or kicking your wall so hard I'm limping?'

'That explains the thump.'

'Sorry.'

'It's a corridor in a vet's surgery. Believe me, it's seen worse than a boot toe. Don't worry about it.' He shrugged. 'Is it anything I can help with?'

'Depends if you're willing to set up payment plans.' Evelyn sighed and shook her head. 'My … ex has turned out to be even more of a bastard than I'd imagined. Sounds like he cancelled the direct debit with Tilly's insurance company, and I'm locked out of our joint account.'

'What an arse-hat move.' Even as he said the words, a small part of him was mentally dancing a jig at the word "ex".

'Yeah. That's a pretty accurate description.'

'Well, you needn't worry about my bill. If you can cover the costs of the drugs, that would be great, but seriously don't bother about the rest.'

'I can't possibly accept that.'

'Of course you can.' Jake was thrilled to have a way to help. 'And you have no choice, because I'm the one writing your bill.'

'Oh my God.' Evelyn's green eyes turned luminous as they filled with grateful tears. 'Thank you so, so much. That's a huge relief.' She gave Jake an awkward hug over Tilly. 'I just, can't thank you enough. Money is a bit tight at the moment, but I thought I had insurance …'

'Like I said. Don't worry about it.' Jake felt a warm glow of pride at being able to help, and take some of the burden off her.

The blare of a car horn and crunch of gravel in the surgery's car park interrupted any reply Evelyn might have given. The antivenom had finally arrived. Jake rushed to the door and grabbed the medicine's bag from the taxi driver, shoving a bundle of notes and thanks at him. Within seconds, he'd drawn out the meds and plunged the needle into the catheter.

Even though they both knew she couldn't respond, Evelyn murmured soothing words to Tilly, running her fingers through her thick, soft fur. Jake watched as the slender digits rippled through the fox-like fur, leaving delicate patterns where they trailed, offering comfort and warmth. As he watched the fingers move, he realised there was a paler ring encircling one of her fingers – where a wedding band was clearly now missing. How had he missed that before?

He checked Tilly's vitals again, and crossed his fingers, hoping this was going to work.

Half an hour later, Tilly's front paw twitched and she let out a tiny whimper. Evelyn looked up, her eyes wide with worry as a huge shiver rippled through the little dog. Jake checked her vitals, and gently tapped the tip of her nose. He grinned when Tilly's nose twitched, and her long pink tongue popped out to lick away the offending sensation.

'I think she's waking up.'

'Tilly …' Evelyn slipped from the sofa to kneel in front of the little dog and be level with her eyes. 'Time to get up, Tilly.' She laughed in delight as the back of the blanket jumped and slipped as Tilly started to wag her tail and wriggle.

This time, Jake's reassuring smile was genuine. 'I think we might be out of the woods.'

'Really?'

Jake checked her vitals again, then nodded. 'Her readings are looking better, and she's certainly looking brighter.'

'I really don't know how to thank you.' Evelyn wiped away tears. 'Did you hear that, Tilly girl? You're going to be all right. Jake's made you better. You can come home with me to see Summer and Nanny soon.' She glanced at Jake. 'When can she come home? Do you need to keep her in for observation?'

'Honestly, I usually would want to keep her here, but I don't want to stress her out in a cage when you said she's had such bad experiences of them in the past. To be honest, I'd been focussed on getting her through these first few, critical hours.'

'What would you do if you kept her in, specifically?'

'Keep her hydrated, keep an eye on blood pressure and heart rate. Possibly more pain killers and antihistamines. Additional sedation if she seemed distressed.'

'If I can borrow your sphygmomanometer, and you can prescribe the meds, I'm pretty confident I can do all that at home.'

'Well, it's not really all that easy. If you get things even slightly wrong, especially with medications, you can do a lot of harm.' He tried not to be condescending, but sending home an animal needing IV medications wasn't something he was ever happy doing.

He was surprised when Evelyn laughed in his face. 'Jake, it's fine. I wouldn't have suggested it if I wasn't confident or competent. I'm a Band 7 Community Nurse. I know she's a lot smaller than most of my patients, but you've already put in the line, and I know how to use that and keep it clean. I know about the importance of adhering to doses, and how to accurately measure meds. But if you're worried, you can measure them out for me into single use syringes.'

'I was a bit patronising, wasn't I?' He laughed.

'Maybe a little, but only to someone with my experience. I'd probably be the same. You have to be, don't you?' She gave him an easy smile that filled him with warmth. 'So what do you think?'

'I think she'll probably be calmer with you than with me.' He ran his hands through his dark hair, thinking.

'You can even come back with me, and check her over and settle her in, if it would make you feel happier about discharging her.' His stomach growled, and Evelyn laughed. 'And if you're hungry, you really should say yes. My mum's a stress baker. Between her and Summer, there's probably enough food for a whole bake sale all cooked up.'

'I couldn't possibly impose.'

'Jake, please. After everything you've done today, offloading some food on you is the very least we can do.' She hesitated and in that moment Jake was worried she'd changed her mind, and realised how much he really wanted to accept her invitation. 'Unless you've got other patients you have to stay here for, or other plans. Which you probably do. Plans, I mean.'

'No, no plans. I've got a litter of newborn kittens here. I'll check on them now, and can check in again in a few hours. It's all I'd usually do anyway. Once they're here and safe, it's really best to leave mum alone to do her thing.'

'OK. I'll give Mum a ring, let her know we're headed back, and make sure Summer knows how to treat Tilly.'

# Chapter Four

Summer was waiting at the door as soon as Evelyn opened it.

'Where is she?' she demanded. 'You didn't change your mind and leave her, did you?'

'Hi Mum, how are you?'

'Hi Mum how are you where's Tilly?' She didn't stop for breath.

'She's with Jake. He's just behind me.' Evelyn knelt down. 'Now remember, Tilly has had a very bad day. She's still feeling really poorly, and it's very, very important that she rests a lot.'

'I know that.' Summer rolled her eyes. 'Nanny said it's like when I got my glow in the dark beads. She needs to get lots of sleep and stay still and not tire herself so the medicine can work and her body can heal.'

'I know you know that darling, but I'm not sure if Tilly does.'

'That's OK, I'll tell her.' She bounced with excitement. 'I'm so glad she's coming home!' She wrapped her arms around Evelyn's waist.

'Me too, sweetheart.' She ran her hand over Summer's head, tousling what had regrown of her hair so far, and enjoying the feeling of it between her fingers. 'Where's your Nan?'

'Upstairs. She's making the cage that isn't a cage.'

Evelyn nodded. It made sense to her.

'I'd knock, but my hands are full.' Jake stood at the doorway, Tilly wrapped in a blanket and snuggled against his chest. For a moment, Evelyn had the strangest feeling of envying the little dog.

'Tilly!' Summer ran to greet them, stopping just short of throwing herself at Jake, and gently petted her dog, before kissing her on the nose. 'You have to be very good, and stay still, and get lots of rest, and do as you're told to make sure you get better. And you really, really have to stay still because you've got an IV line. That's right, isn't it, Jake?'

Evelyn could see Jake's eyes widen in surprise at a child understanding what that meant, but to Summer he just nodded. 'That's right. But not for too long.'

'Good.' Summer smiled and turned her attention back to Tilly. 'After tea, Nanny said we can watch TV. I'll look after you and sit with you to make sure you don't get lonely and sad and we can watch cartoons.' She looked up at Jake. 'She can watch cartoons, can't she?'

Jake nodded, hiding a grin. 'Yeah, cartoons should be fine.'

Summer kissed Tilly's nose again. 'See? It will be like when I come home from hospital, except you can pick the cartoon, and you probably can't have tomato soup and melty cheese.'

'No,' Jake agreed. 'No melty cheese. But if she's hungry, you could try something light and simple, like scrambled egg.'

'OK. I'll get Tilly's teddy from my room, and ask Nanny to make some egg.' She ran up the stairs.

'Where shall I put her?' Jake still held Tilly close.

'Probably her basket in the kitchen is best. We'll be out there, and I can pick up her whole bed to move her if I need to later.'

'Lead the way.' Jake followed her down the corridor. 'So, when you said Tilly is Summer's best friend ...'

'No, I wasn't exaggerating.' Evelyn sighed, knowing what it was Jake was trying to ask without saying the actual words. 'The hair, right? Please don't mention it. It's growing back, but she's still self-conscious about it sometimes, and really hates wearing hats and wigs all the time.'

'I won't, I promise.' Jake's eyes were sincere. 'But actually, it was the IV line comment.'

'Yeah. Not too many kids know what that means.'

'So should I ask, or pretend not to have noticed? Whatever makes things easier for you.'

Evelyn was touched by the sentiment. It had been far too long since someone had thought about what made things easier for her, and she found herself wanting to share more with Jake because of it. 'I don't mind you asking. It's nice that you want to know.' She took a deep breath. Even after the years of fighting it, all the doctors, nurses, teachers and everyone else she'd told, it wasn't easy to say the word. 'It's cancer. Specifically neuroblastoma.'

'Oh.' Jake stooped to lower Tilly into the basket in the corner of the room. He pulled a medicine bag out of his backpack, and produced a hydration pack which he reconnected to Tilly's line, and tucked into the bookcase above her, all the time soothing and telling her what a good girl she was. 'So long as she's happy and still, we might as well keep her hydrated, but she really needs to stay still. Can we block her in somehow?'

'Mum's sorting something upstairs. For now, she'll stay put as long as there's someone with her.'

'OK.' Jake sat down next to the little dog.

'I didn't mean you should sit on the floor.' She was shocked.

'I'm a vet. I'm used to getting down on my hands and knees for my patients. At least your floor is clean.' He laughed. 'Barns usually aren't.'

'Fair enough.' Evelyn sat down at a right angle to him, using her legs to block Tilly inside the square their legs now made.

His feet nudged against hers as he shifted, and Evelyn realised he'd kicked his shoes off at some point, and was touched by the gesture of respect to her family and their home.

'So, how is Summer now?'

'She's doing good, thank you. Her last round of chemo finished a few months ago, and she's making good progress.'

'That's great.' Jake's smile was so genuine that Evelyn felt a warm tingle that surprised her. 'And how are you both settling in to Broclington? It must be strange coming home after so long.'

'It is a bit,' she admitted, again surprised and touched at Jake's insight, 'but as much as living with Mum again has taken some getting used to, it's great to be here. And Summer loves it. She's happier than she's been in ages, and Mum absolutely dotes on her and spoils her.'

'As every nanny should. My mother's the same with my niece.' He hesitated, then let the next words out in a rush. 'You know, if ever you want someone to talk to – someone who isn't family I mean – you know where to find me.'

Evelyn looked up, surprised at the offer and searched his blue eyes, but all she saw there was warmth and sincerity. The level of kindness that Jake had shown her already, and that he was still offering, was incredible. Here was someone she'd spent no more than a handful of hours with, and yet he was showing her more consideration – and kindness – than her ex had in months. She bit her lip as the tears that had been close all day threatened to overwhelm her resolve, this time driven by gratitude. She ducked her head and let her hair fall across her face while she tried to regain control.

'Hey.' Jake rested his fingers on hers, his large hand engulfing hers and falling across her knee as well. She was shocked at the heat through her denim and struggled to look away from the point where their skin connected. For a moment, her mind went somewhere completely inappropriate for a recently separated, still in the process of getting divorced, mother. But for a few seconds, Evelyn pictured that hand sliding higher, and touching other bare skin.

Jake drummed his fingers against hers, making her look up. 'I meant what I said, Evelyn.'

She nodded, unable to speak past the lump in her throat.

'Well don't you two look cosy?' Linda came in holding what looked like parts of a clothes airer with bits of ribbon woven through it, and toys hanging from the bars. She held up her construction. 'What do you think? It was Summer's idea to add the toys.'

'I think it's very clever.' Jake grinned.

'Well, if I had to stay in the corner all day I'd want my bestest toys,' Summer explained from behind her nanny. 'This is Monkey, and Teddy, and Squeaky, and Balley and Chewy.' She pointed to each one of them in turn. 'She knows all their names.'

'She's a very clever, well-behaved dog.' Jake stood slowly to avoid disturbing Tilly. 'Here, do you want me to take that? I'll try to put it round her. Summer, maybe you can help?'

'Yes. What should I do?'

'Just come sit where I was, and talk to her. If you're with her, she'll know she's safe and won't think we're locking her in a cage.'

'OK.' Summer raced to sit next to her furry friend, who shifted to rest her head in Summer's lap. 'Look, she's pleased to see me.' She leaned down to kiss the little ginger head. 'I'm pleased to see you too, Tilly. Now, Jake is going to put your new super special toy holder round you, so you can see all your toys. It's definitely a toy holder and not a cage and I know that coz I'm a kid, and kids know all about toys.' She kept talking as the makeshift "toy holder" was lowered into place around them both.

Tilly looked around with worried eyes, and Evelyn held her breath and prayed that the idea would work and they wouldn't have to sedate the little dog again. When Tilly snuffled sleepily at a toy and gave a tired, amused snort and flopped her head back down on Summer, Evelyn finally relaxed.

'Well, that seems to be a success.' Linda grabbed the kettle off the side. 'Now who's ready for a cuppa, and something to eat? Summer and I have been cooking most of the day.'

Jake looked up, his blue eyes sparkling with amusement as he met Evelyn's gaze. She gave him a half-shrug – it was exactly what she'd predicted. But she hadn't expected the butterflies that took flight in her stomach when Jake winked at her.

Without breaking her gaze, Jake smiled. 'A cup of tea would be great, if it's not too much trouble.'

Linda flicked the switch on the kettle. 'If I had to row a boat to India, pick the tea myself and grind the leaves by hand – it wouldn't be too much trouble. Not after what you've done for us today.' She popped the lid off a metal tin. 'Chocolate chip cookie? They're all home-made.'

Jake waved goodnight for the third time and headed back to his car, his bag filled with more home baking and his heart warm. As she'd promised, Evelyn was completely competent in managing Tilly's needs, and he had no concerns leaving the meds with her – along with his phone number. And he'd made her promise to call him in the morning. Though he'd never wish illness or injury on any living thing, he was glad of the excuse to swap numbers with Evelyn, and speak with her again. Soon.

As he climbed into his car, the curtains in the cottage window parted, flooding light out into the dark and highlighting Summer's small frame as she waved happily. Jake held his hand up in farewell – for the fourth time. He had to admit, he'd had a really good evening – a far better ending to the day than he'd expected when Evelyn had raced in, clutching Tilly to her chest. He'd been shocked when he'd first seen Summer without a hat and was horrified and stunned to learn she'd been so ill, so recently. She was such a happy, outgoing little girl that it was painful to imagine what she'd been through in the past months – and all the more incredible that her nature was sunny and warm. Sunny, warm Summer. He smiled at the thought as he gave her another wave before pulling away.

But it was Evelyn who'd made him feel so at ease and at home. He had no difficulty talking to her like he did with a lot of people. His brother wasn't wrong when he teased him that he dealt with animals better than he did people. But Evelyn made him feel so relaxed that his words tumbled out happily and his usual feelings of unease melted away. She really was amazing, and he was convinced that it was her positive, soothing nature that enabled Summer to be so cheerful in the face of everything she'd been through.

And yet, with levels of empathy that surprised Jake for anything without fur, feathers or scales, he could see a deep sadness and the weight of incredible worry darkening Evelyn's beautiful green eyes. It was so unbearable to him that he'd immediately offered her a friendly shoulder whenever she needed one – and he really hoped that she'd take him up on his offer. Every time she smiled, it lit the room up a bit more, and he wanted to be responsible for making her smile that brightly as often as she'd give him the chance to.

He pulled into the Badger's Hospital car park and went to check on the kittens who'd made such a noisy, chaotic entrance earlier that day. He spoke softly to them as he turned on the light and checked them over. The mother cat glared at him tiredly, but once he'd tucked all her kittens back where they belonged, she went back to ignoring him and returned to the important task of nuzzling and feeding her new family.

He smiled as he turned the light back off. The little guy whose arrival had been so dramatic was doing well, and would be going home with his brothers and sisters tomorrow. Between him and Summer's little Shiba Inu, that was two good saves today, and Jake dearly loved the days when all his patients went home happy and with a positive prognosis.

He wished every day could be so positive, and filled with so much laughter.

# *Chapter Five*

'Are you sure you're ready for this?' Evelyn watched Summer with concern, wondering if she was looking a little pale, as she skipped up to the village school. Tilly trotted happily by her side, not showing a single ill effect from her adder adventures a few days before.

'Yes, Mum.'

'And you're feeling OK?'

'Yes, Mum.'

'You could stay off another week if you wanted. I'm sure Dr Tom would be happy to write a letter.'

Summer stopped her skipping walk, causing Tilly to complain as she unexpectedly jerked the leash. 'Sorry Tilly.' She slipped her hand into Evelyn's and looked at her with such seriousness and maturity that her heart ached for when Summer was still a baby who she could wrap in a blanket and protect from the world. Before she'd gotten ill.

'Are you even listening?' Her daughter stamped her foot in frustration while Evelyn tried desperately to rewind the conversation.

'I'm sorry darling, I didn't hear you.'

'I said I don't want another letter from a doctor. I want to go to school and make friends, and be a normal kid. Please Mummy?' she wheedled.

Evelyn's heart squeezed. How could she possibly say no? 'Of course, darling.' She knelt to straighten Summer's collar. 'But you will promise to tell Mrs Appleby if you start to feel even the tiniest bit tired?'

'Yes, Mum. I promise.' She wrapped her arms around Evelyn's neck and gave her a tight squeeze. 'You don't have to worry. I'm better now. And Dr Tom said I could go back to school. I'll go to school, and Tilly can look after you. And Nanny will be home from work at the retirement home after lunch, so you don't have to worry about being lonely, OK?'

Evelyn nodded, not trusting herself to speak. Somehow, between all the treatments and medical appointments, she'd missed her daughter growing into a kind, considerate and mature little girl. And now, looking at her in her school uniform, so smart and grown up, and comforting her, Evelyn felt a pang of sadness for everything she'd missed.

But Summer was watching her expectantly, and needed to know everything was OK, so Evelyn took a deep breath and forced on her brightest of smiles. 'Of course, sweetheart. You don't have to worry about me.' She placed a kiss on Summer's forehead. 'Do you want me to walk you in?'

'It's OK.' Summer shrugged and handed over Tilly's leash. 'I remember where to go.'

'You're sure?'

'Yes.' She didn't go as far as actually rolling her eyes, but Evelyn could hear it anyway.

'All right, sweetheart.' She gave Summer a quick hug and just about forced herself to let go rather than hang on like she really wanted to. 'Have a lovely day. Remember to be yourself because you're awesome, and everyone will love you.'

'Be good, Tilly. No more sticking your nose in snake holes.' She skipped through the school gate and headed for the main office – exactly where she was supposed to go. 'Bye Mum!'

Two hours later, Evelyn had cleaned the already tidy kitchen, hoovered the already clean floors, folded the washing, and arranged, then rearranged flowers, and flicked through everything on TV. Twice. She rummaged through the cupboards, looking for something to do, and was glad when her fingers closed around the virtually empty, rustly bag that held Tilly's dental sticks. Glad to have something to do, she whistled to Tilly. 'Want to go for a walk? We need to go buy you some more toothbrushes. Shall we go and see if Jake sells the ones you like?'

Tilly's skipping run to the front door matched Evelyn's own enthusiasm. A walk would do her good, and it was always good to support local businesses, especially those run by a kind, caring, friendly man who made her daughter laugh.

But as soon as she entered Badger's Hospital and Jake smiled at her from behind the reception desk, Evelyn knew she was lying to herself. It wasn't just Summer and Tilly who Jake made feel better – he worked wonders on her too.

'Hey, how's my favourite snake wrangler?'

'She's good, thanks.' Evelyn was instantly cheered by Jake's presence, and found it impossible not to grin back. She had to remind herself that he was just being professional and was probably this friendly with all his patients and their owners. At least that was what she tried to tell herself as he knelt to pet Tilly, and glanced up at Evelyn from beneath his wavy fringe, sending her heart rate up a couple of notches.

'So, what can I do for you two lovely ladies today?'

'Toothbrush chews for her ladyship here.'

'I'm sure we can sort them.' He held his hand out to Tilly. 'Paw please, m'lady.' She obediently held up her foot for Jake to examine, while Evelyn bit her bottom lip and tried not to giggle like a schoolgirl.

'What do you think?' Evelyn asked, though she checked Tilly's foot every day and thought it was healing well.

'Healing up perfectly.' He laughed as Tilly fell to the floor and rolled over playfully for a belly rub.

'Tilly, you're a dreadful flirt.' Evelyn mock scolded, while thinking she could understand the urge.

'You can't blame her. I'm irresistible to any woman with fur.' He gave her another fuss. 'So where's your other girl today?'

Evelyn's mood plummeted as she instantly started to worry if Summer was all right. She knew she was safe in the school, but worried she'd push herself too hard and wear herself out trying to fit in and make friends. 'She's at school. First day.'

'Wow.' He gave her a look of such understanding that Evelyn found herself wondering if he could read her mind. 'So, how are you doing with that?'

Yup. Definitely reading her mind, Evelyn thought as she replied carefully. 'She's really pleased to be back. And can't wait to get on with making friends and having a normal life again. She's not had that for quite some time. She'll be fine, I know she will.'

'Of course she will,' Jake agreed as he stood. 'But you didn't answer my question.' He held her gaze with his. 'How are you doing with Summer being back at school?'

Evelyn felt like all the air in her lungs was trying to escape at once. Even her mum – wonderful as she was – had only seen Summer's return to school as a good thing, yet here was Jake, knowing the exact right questions to ask. 'It's not the easiest day. I keep wandering around looking for things to do, and ways to keep busy.'

'You could come and have lunch with me.' Jake made the offer easily, yet Evelyn felt herself hesitate. She was only just finding her feet in Broclington again, and was still settling Summer into her new "normal" life.

'Aww, come on.' Jake nudged her elbow with his. 'Save me from my soggy cheese sandwich. Have you been to The Brockle's Retreat yet?'

'The pub in the square? No, not yet. At least, not since I've been back.' Evelyn wavered, really wanting to say yes, but still questioning if she should. 'What about Tilly?'

Jake laughed. 'This is Broclington. If businesses round here didn't welcome dogs, they'd lose half their customers. They even have a dog menu there, though I can't say I fully approve as there's a lot of sausage on it.' He laughed as Tilly sprang to attention in a perfect begging pose. 'See, I told you I'm irresistible to every furry female. I know exactly how to keep them happy. But what about you? Can I convince you to let me buy you lunch?' He gave her another cheeky grin and Evelyn found herself thinking that Tilly wasn't the only girl around who found the vet hard to resist.

She smiled. 'No, but I'll buy you lunch. It's the least I owe you.'

'We can argue over the bill later. Just give me a minute to close up, and grab her ladyship's dental chews.'

Jake laughed as Evelyn pushed her plate away and leaned back, defeated. 'That was delicious. But I'll explode if I eat another bite.'

63

Jake gave the half-uneaten slice of treacle tart a wistful glance. Evelyn must have caught his look, because she slid the plate over with a smile and shrug. 'Help yourself. Shame to let it go to waste.'

'I shouldn't, but I will.' He felt her eyes travel over his chest and down to his waist. This was interesting, and he wondered if her eyes would have tracked even lower if it hadn't been for the table in the way. She glanced up, caught him watching, blushed and looked away.

So he dug into his extra dessert and watched Evelyn's fluster with amusement. She had a crumb of pastry just in the corner of her top lip, and he watched it in fascination, wondering what Evelyn would do if he were to reach over and brush it away, touching her lips in the process. He wondered what her lips would feel like, whether they'd be sweet and sticky with gloss or velvety and smooth.

He smiled as he took the last bite, and watched as she tucked her golden hair behind one ear. Tilly was napping happily at her feet, filled with sausage and mash from the doggy menu, not to mention a few chips she'd shamelessly begged from a nearby table. Evelyn finally looked relaxed and happy, and Jake was thrilled that he'd been the one to help put a smile back on her face.

'I should be getting back. I've got surgery starting in half an hour.' He admitted reluctantly, not wanting to break the cosy spell that the crackling fire and ancient beams created, or give up the chance to spend more time with Evelyn.

'Oh, of course you must.' She caught the eye of the girl who'd been serving them, and made the universal "squiggle in the air" sign to ask for the bill, before giving Jake a bright smile. 'Thank you. This has been lovely, but I've taken up far too much of your time already.' She reached down to untie Tilly, but Jake leaned forward to grab her hand.

'Don't do that, Evelyn.'

'Do what?' She gave him a bemused look.

'Don't put on some bright, not-totally-real smile.' He didn't give her a chance to reply. 'I hope you meant that you'd had a lovely time, because I have, and if I didn't have patients arriving shortly, I'd be asking you to spend more time with me. Right now.'

'Oh.' Evelyn blushed, and turned away to hide her reddening cheeks as the waitress arrived with the bill.

While she fiddled with her bag, trying to untangle it from Tilly's leash, Jake pulled out a couple of notes and tucked them inside the little leather folder holding the bill. There was no way he was letting her pay. He already knew she wasn't working after time off to look after Summer, and even if that wasn't the case – he wasn't the kind of man who let a woman pay when he asked her out to eat.

'Jake, I said I'd pay.'

He shrugged in a way that he hoped was nonchalant and shot her one of his best grins. 'If it means that much to you, you can pay next time.' And he really, really hoped there would be a next time.

'OK,' Evelyn replied slowly. 'The next one's on me.'

Jake gave himself a mental high-five as he held the door open for her.

'Thank you,' she murmured as she stepped through, so close that for a second Jake got a whiff of her perfume – something light and fruity and fresh.

They fell into step easily, strolling back towards the surgery and pausing every so often for Tilly to stop and sniff a particularly interesting plant or bit of wall.

When Evelyn's toe hit a bit of the pavement pushed higher than the rest by a tree root, Jake automatically caught her, his hand wrapping around her delicate forearm. Without thinking, he drew her closer.

For a moment Evelyn stiffened, and Jake froze, worried that he'd done the wrong thing and misread her earlier blushes and signals. But after a dozen or so heartbeats, she relaxed and shifted her arm into a more natural position, tucked into the crook of his.

Jake breathed out slowly, taking extra care to keep his breath even and trying not to do anything stupid – as he was so apt at doing in situations like this. But Evelyn's arm, wrapped around his, made him feel protective and excited at the same time. Even through their coats, the warmth and weight of her hand tucked into his elbow, wrapped slightly around his bicep, made him feel warm from head to toe.

Except, that instead of feeling worried and trying to figure out what to say, and how to act, and questioning his every move, Jake found that with Evelyn he just felt … calm and at ease. And he didn't want to let her go. The realisation shocked him. If he added together all the hours they'd spent together – and with some of them she was still his client – it probably didn't total a full day, and there was Summer to consider, yet he wanted to spend more and more time with her in a setting where there was definitely no ambiguity about whether it was a date or not!

They both slowed as they reached The Burrow's, and Jake hoped that it was because she was as reluctant to end their time together as he was. He slowed even more as he walked into the car park, and gave her a warm smile as he slowly withdrew his arm to dig out his keys and unlock the surgery.

Evelyn's hand caught on his arm as he reached for the door handle, and as he looked into her bright green eyes, he felt a frisson of excitement as she smiled up at him.

'Thank you. I know you're busy, and I really appreciated today.' She gave him another warm smile that he felt in the depths of his stomach. 'I really needed a friend today. It meant a lot.'

Jake's stomach sank at the word "friend". Was that really all she saw him as? He was convinced he'd seen something more in her playful glances, so he cleared his throat and tried anyway. 'I was hoping to see you again … in a maybe more than friendly way.' When she didn't answer, he carried on. 'The thing is, I really like you, and I think you like me, and I'd love to take you out and see if there could be something between us, because I've really, really enjoyed the time we've spent together.'

Evelyn chewed on her bottom lip.

'Please, say something,' he begged, in agony.


Evelyn stared into his bright blue, kind eyes and tried to find the words to explain. 'I like you too, Jake. But I'm not looking for anything right now. My ex is still legally my husband, even though we've not been together in months, and Summer has to be my main priority. I can't just start running around having fun and being irresponsible.'

Jake stepped closer, and Evelyn felt another blush rising. He looked down at her with such kindness in his eyes that she started to question her reply.

'You do know, Summer already likes me.' He grinned cheekily. 'And come to mention it, so does Tilly.

So if you like me, and Summer does, and even your dog does, why couldn't we spend a little more time together?'

'Summer …' Evelyn began.

'From what you've told me, and what I've seen, Summer is a happy, bright, resilient, healthy little girl.' He covered her hand with his, and gave her another smile that melted her resolution, and forced her to look away in confusion. 'And I know she's your top priority, which is exactly as it should be. But Evelyn'—he waited until she looked up at him—'I think she's wonderful, and I think you're pretty wonderful too.'

'That's really kind.' It had been so long since a man had paid her a compliment that she wasn't sure how to take it.

'I'm not trying to be kind. I'm trying to ask you out. And apparently making a bad job of it.' He ran his hands through his hair.

'No, no you're not doing a bad job.' Evelyn felt a flush of guilt at Jake's morose look.

'I just … thought that a bit of fun and irresponsibility might be good for you.'

'You're right, I've not had much time for fun lately.'

'Then let me help with that.' Jake took another small step towards her, until Evelyn could catch a whiff of his clean, slightly spicy scent. 'Let me help you put that beautiful smile back on your face more often.'

Evelyn had to look away from Jake's gaze which seemed to let him see her thoughts. The nearness of him jumbled her mind, but she didn't want to step away, which confused her even more. 'I don't know what to say,' she admitted in a soft whisper.

'Say yes. It's just a date. At least I hope it's a date.'

Evelyn smiled and nodded. 'OK. Yes.'

'Brilliant. I'll call you this weekend,' Jake promised.

'OK. But give me a few days warning please? I need to make sure my mum can watch Summer, or arrange for a sitter.'

'Don't worry. I've not forgotten Summer,' Jake reassured her. He gestured to the door. 'I should get going.'

'Yeah.' Evelyn looked down at Tilly who was stretched out on the ground, looking bored. 'C'mon Tilly. Time to go home.' She hesitated for a moment. 'Jake?'

'Yes?' He turned back.

Before she could change her mind, Evelyn leaned towards him. The roughness of his stubble tickled her lips as she pressed a kiss to his cheek, her hand resting briefly on his strong shoulder. 'Thank you.'

She walked away quickly, Tilly skipping happily at her heel, as she wondered what she had been thinking that made her agree to a date. She liked Jake. He was a wonderful, kind, attractive man, but she was still married for goodness' sake, and she had to focus on making sure Summer stayed well. She'd just have to find a polite way to turn him down when he called.

As she turned the corner, she brushed her fingers against her lips where they still tingled.

# Chapter Six

Jake inhaled the warm, homely scents of roasting meat and spiced apple pudding as he hung up his jacket and put away his keys. When he was younger, he'd often complained about these enforced monthly gatherings, wanting to spend his Sundays in a pub with his friends, or with whatever girlfriend had been the feature at the time. But now he understood his mum's point of view, and why she'd fought so hard to get them all together, at least once a month, along with whatever friends, relatives and stragglers she gathered. It was too easy to let a few busy days turn into weeks and suddenly months could drift by without seeing some of the people who meant most to you.

He surprised himself by wondering what Evelyn and Summer would make of these haphazard gatherings, then shook his head at his own foolishness. He'd only just convinced Evelyn to go on a date with him, and here he was planning introductions to his family.

'Uncle Jakey!' Footsteps raced across the hardwood floors and a small, warm body slammed into him.

'Hi Sarah!' He grabbed his niece as she flung herself at him and threw her up in the air, making her squeal with delight. He tossed her over his shoulder and held her there, squirming and giggling as he headed to the kitchen.

'Someone lost something?' He grinned at Callum, his older brother.

'Nah, don't think so.'

'Shall I keep it then?' He tickled Sarah until she wriggled so much he had to fight to hold on to her.

'Put her down before you drop her.' His mother rolled her eyes as she kissed him on the cheek. In almost the exact same spot where Evelyn's lips had landed earlier that week. He'd tried to call her the day before, but had to settle with leaving a message. But he could be patient. He understood she'd been through a lot lately, and appreciated that she needed time to come to terms with it all. And he would wait for as long as she needed.

'Jake?' His mother was calling him. 'I asked how your week has been?'

'Sorry.' He dropped the squirming Sarah carefully to the floor. 'I'm miles away.'

'I can see that. Anything I can help with?'

'Hmm?' he replied, still distracted.

'It's got to be a girl.' He hadn't even noticed his sister, Kimberly, sitting in the corner folding napkins. 'Look at the silly look on his face.'

Sarah gasped up at him. 'Have you got a girlfriend, Uncle Jakey?'

'Yeah, have you got a girlfriend, Uncle Jakey?' his brother mimicked.

'Knock it off, Cal.' Jake shot him a glare over his daughter's head, before bending down. 'You know, Sarah, men and women can be friends.'

'Yeah, but they can be girlfriend and boyfriend too.'

'What do you know about girlfriends and boyfriends?'

'I've got a boyfriend.' Sarah poked out her tongue. 'His name's James and we hold hands and sit together and he lets me eat his crisps at lunch. He says my hair is pretty.'

'It is pretty.' He patted her on her silky, dark head while he shot a look at his brother. 'A boyfriend?' He mouthed the words at Callum, who just shrugged.

'Enough about boyfriends and girlfriends and who has them and who doesn't.' Mum wiped her hands on her apron. 'I'm dishing up. Sarah, go see if your granddad has finished in the garden and tell him dinner is ready.'

'Yes, Granny.' She skipped off happily.

'Speaking of boyfriends, where's Jon?' Jake shot the question at Kimberly. 'I was looking forward to seeing him.'

'Don't even talk to me about that arse-hat,' Kimberly all but growled.

'OK, OK.' He held his hands up in defeat. 'Sorry for speaking.'

'Sorry too.' She shrugged. 'Just a bit raw still.'

'Aww, sis.' Jake gave her a big hug, and let her rest her head on his shoulder. 'Do you want me to beat him up?'

'No violence that could end you up in jail please.' Their Mum spoke as she pulled a sizzling pan of roast potatoes out of the oven. 'Plus, I'm disappointed in you. You're a vet. Surely you have access to lots of disgusting things. You shouldn't need to resort to violence.'

'True,' he agreed with a laugh. 'You want me to put a flaming bag of crap on his doorstep? You know I'd do it for you.'

'What worries me, is I think you're only half-kidding.' Kimberly shook her head. 'Anyway, enough about my horrible love life. Am I right about you?'

Jake didn't feel the silly smile that must have lit up his face, but the others saw it.

'Ha! Look at that stupid expression.' Cal laughed.

'You do look happy, love.' His Mum put the joint of beef on the table. 'Are you seeing someone?'

He blew out a long sigh. 'Yes, maybe. I think so.'

72

'Oh, Jakey, do Daddy and I need to give you the talk about when boys and girls like each other?'

'Stuff off!' He stuck his tongue out at his brother. 'I just meant it's really early days.' He ran his hands through his hair. 'There was something I did want to talk to you about, but if you're just going to be a jerk, I'll risk asking Dad.'

'Ask me what?' Tom sauntered into the big kitchen and placed a kiss on his wife's cheek. 'Smells wonderful, love.'

'A medical question, but it's sort of about one of your patients.'

'Don't bother then. You know the answer. It's confidential.' He helped his granddaughter onto her booster seat. 'Ask your brother – in the abstract if you can. And preferably wait until I'm out of hearing until you talk about it please. I'm not comfortable with it, and it's a conversation I would prefer to avoid.'

'Of course.'

'So what's this all about?' Kimberly asked. 'Why's it so important that we're all here today?'

Jake watched as his parents shared a loving look, and felt a twinge in his stomach. He hoped that one day he'd be in the type of relationship where he could share so much with someone with a single glance.

'Julie and I have an announcement to make.' Jake's dad grinned round the table at them all, while his mum glowed with happiness. 'We've made a decision. We're going to Africa.'

Confused silence descended over the table, eventually broken by Kimberly. 'I'm sure we're all really glad to hear that, but does a holiday really need a family meeting?'

Tom laughed. 'Not for a holiday, but we'll probably fit in a safari and some sightseeing at some point. We've signed up for Doctors Without Borders. Me as a doctor, obviously, and your mother will be running the clinic.'

'When? For how long?'

'What do you mean you're going to Africa?'

'What's going to happen with the surgery?'

'All right, all right.' Julie held up her hands. 'Initially we've been asked to go to Eswatini. They've got viral pandemics, including HIV and TB, and are setting up a new clinic. They need help, and we're it. The actual building is still under construction, and we're expecting it to be finished by autumn. We're aiming to get there as they're bringing in equipment, which should be around mid-September. We'll be there for a few months, after that, we're not sure. We might end up staying longer, if it agrees with us.'

'But what about the surgery?' Callum asked. 'You're not closing it down?'

'The family legacy? Of course not.' Their father was aghast.

'Actually, Callum love, we were thinking it might be time that you took a more active interest in managing the surgery. You're already a partner, but we think you're ready to take on more. Like all the management.'

'Me? Really?'

Kimberly tutted in annoyance. 'Obviously you. My degree hardly sets me up to run a medical practice. And while I'm sure Jake could manage it, I don't think Dad's patients would be too happy with his approach to taking temperatures. Tails up!'

'Enough!' Tom held up the knife he'd started carving the beef with. 'Your mother has cooked this lovely meal for you all, and I'd thank you to remember the family rule – no medical procedure discussion at the table. And how Jake takes his patients' temperatures is definitely straying into that territory.'

'To be fair, I do use auxiliary and aural methods too.'

'Jake. Change the subject please. No work talk at the table.'

'Sorry. Can you pass the horseradish please?'

Callum caught him by the door as they were pulling on coats and Sarah was having extra hugs in the kitchen with her grandparents and aunt. 'What was that "medical question sort of" about one of Dad's patients?'

'I don't want any specifics, exactly, more just to check a few things.'

'OK.'

'Eight-year-old girl. She's had neuroblastoma.'

'Wow, that's rare in an eight-year-old.'

'So I've been told,' Jake replied grimly. 'She finished the latest round of chemo a few months ago. She had a bad reaction on the last cycle, but apparently it worked and she's cancer free.'

'That's good then. So what is it you want to know?'

'Are there any restrictions on the things she can do? Any special considerations or anything?'

'How do you mean?'

'Is there anything she can't do?'

'Like activities and stuff?' He waited for Jake's nod. 'Is she back at school?'

'Yeah.'

'In that case, not really. Her doctors – and Dad – must be happy that she's recovered enough that she's not immune-compromised any more. She might get tired more easily than her peers, and might be a little more prone to motion-induced nausea. Some patients get changes to their eating habits, neuropathy – especially in the fingers and toes – and obviously there's the hair loss. She might have increased sensitivity to cold and extreme heat. But no, I wouldn't say there's anything she really can't do, so long as she feels well enough. If she were my patient, I'd probably advise her parents to let her get back to normal as soon as she can, and just try to make sure she gets plenty of rest and a good diet.'

'OK. Pretty much what I thought then.'

'Jake? What's this about?'

'The woman you said I was getting silly looks over? She's got a little girl, and she's been sick.'

'Wow bro, that's really complicated. Are you sure you want to get involved with a woman who has already got a kid, and one who's been so ill at that?' He shrugged self-consciously. 'I don't mean to sound negative, but it's a big thing you're talking about, and I've got to ask.'

'It's all right, I get it. I'd probably ask the same if it were you. We're good.'

'So, are you sure?'

'If I'm totally honest, no. It's crazy, we've not even been out on a proper date, but I can't stop thinking about her. I'm already going out of my way to make her smile – to make both of them smile. I find myself thinking about them all the time. Even coming in here today, for a few seconds I was wondering how they'd fit in. Is it ideal? No. But Cal'—he took a deep breath before trying to put into words the thoughts that had been driving him crazy for weeks—'I think I really like her. Both of them. They've been stuck in my mind since I met them. I don't ever remember reacting to someone like this.'

Callum laughed and wrapped his arm around Jake's shoulders. 'You've got it bad, bro.'

'I think you might be right.'

'Sorry, what was that? Did my ears deceive me? Did you, my younger brother, just admit I was right about something?'

'I said might, you giant pain in the arse.'

'Close enough.' He shifted his arm, dragging Jake down into a headlock and ruffled his hair.

'Gerroff!' Jake elbowed him non-too gently to make him let go.

'Awww.' Callum let him wriggle out and patted his cheeks patronisingly. 'Jakey-wakey has got himself a girlfriend.'

Jake laughed, refusing to let his brother's antics wind him up. 'You know what Callum? I really do hope you're right.'


Evelyn sat in the waiting room, and glanced at the clock again: thirty minutes later than when their appointment should have been over by, and they were still waiting. She peered outside at Tilly, who was clearly bored and was stretched out in the surgery vestibule, apparently asleep.

'I'm bored.' Summer flopped dramatically over Evelyn's lap. 'So bored I might die of boredom. Will it be my turn soon?'

'I hope so.' Evelyn looked at the clock again, and then wondered why. It wasn't like she really had anywhere to go, or anything special to do. She sighed. She was bored too, and not just with waiting for an overrunning appointment. She was incredibly grateful, after so many years of worry, to have the opportunity to actually *be* bored, but she wasn't very good at it. And what should have been an appointment of no more than a couple of minutes to draw blood had turned into a test of patience for both of them. She glanced at Tilly again: for all three of them.

Eventually, Summer's name flashed up on the screen, and Evelyn hustled her down the corridor and through the open door.

'I'm really sorry to have kept you waiting.' Tom Macpearson apologised while pulling out the test vials, needle and tourniquet strap that made up the phlebotomy kit. 'Our usual nurse left us last week, and our locum has let us down. So us doctors are picking up that work too.' He rolled up Summer's sleeve and slid the strap into place, pulling it tight.

'Ouch.'

'Sorry.' He tapped her arm a couple of times, trying to get the veins into a good position. After a few more taps, he frowned. 'Are your veins usually this tricky?'

'Don't know.' Summer shrugged.

'It sometimes takes a couple of attempts,' Evelyn added. 'It's a sequelae of the chemotherapy, but her consultant is optimistic that she'll grow out of it.'

'OK. I think I've got one. Little prick.'

'Ow! Ow! Ow!' Summer sniffed and glared accusingly at the doctor.

'Sorry. Let me try again.'

'OW!'

'I'm sorry, I'm struggling to find a good vein.'

'It's all right, Summer.' Evelyn pulled her daughter's head against her shoulder and fought the urge to shove Dr Tom away from her. 'It'll be over in a few moments.'

'Can't you do it? Please Mummy?' She pulled her arm away from the doctor.

78

'No sweetheart, I'm sorry but I don't have privileges here.'

'Please?' As usual, Summer's tears broke her heart, and she looked helplessly at Tom.

'You're a phlebotomist?' Tom raised an eyebrow in question.

'Community nurse. Band 7.'

'And your registration is still current?'

'Yes.'

While Summer's face was still tucked against her shoulder, Tom slid the tray half an inch towards her, silently offering her the opportunity to take the needle, or say no and let him continue. She gave him a grateful smile. As much as she loathed plunging needles into her daughter's perfect skin, she didn't want to see Summer stressed out any more.

So she pulled away from Summer to look at her. 'Left arm please.' She switched the strap over and tapped the spot that she knew often worked first time. 'What's your favourite treat?' She cleaned the spot with an antiseptic wipe.

'Brockle cake.'

'Nah. Too easy.' Evelyn shook her head. 'Pick another.'

'I like Nanny's caramel banana cake.'

'Spell it please.' She picked up a fresh needle and slid the guard off.

'C. A. R. E. M. A. Ow!' She yelped as Evelyn slid the needle in.

'Sorry sweetheart. You were at A.'

'A. L. Space. B. A. N. N. A. N. A. Space. Cake.' By the time she had finished, Evelyn had filled each of the three, small canisters.

'And what topping?'

'Ice cream!' Summer grinned. 'I. C. E.' Evelyn slid the needle carefully out, holding a little wad of cotton wool over the entry hole to stop any bleeding. 'C. R. E. A. M.'

'Hold this tight.' Evelyn placed Summer's own fingers over the cotton wool, and accepted the tape from Dr Tom.

She slid the tray back to him, and he stuck the appropriate label on each vial, before securing them in the sample bag. 'Impressive.'

'I've had practice.' Evelyn shrugged easily.

'Do you have a minute for a quick chat?'

'Yes, I think so. Is something wrong?' Her eyes flicked to Summer.

'No, not at all. But I think I have a proposition you might be interested in.'

'Summer? Will you go and check on Tilly please? Don't leave the surgery though, and stay in sight of the reception.'

'Do I still get Brockle cake and ice cream for being good?'

'Yes, I think we can just about manage that.'

'OK.' Summer raced from the room, eager to escape.

'So what's going on?' Evelyn crossed her legs and tucked her hair behind her ear.

'As I said, potential proposition that might be of interest to us both – but with no pressure. With Summer doing so well, and back at school, have you thought about going back to work?'

'To be honest, I hadn't yet. It's been a really stressful period, and I didn't want to commit to anything too soon.'

'Well, you already know we're short a nurse and that it's causing us havoc here. You're obviously better at phlebotomy than I am. Did you have any specialisms?'

'My team did a bit of everything.' Evelyn shrugged. 'But we specialised in hospital step-downs and re-enablement. To the point that we merged with the home care team.'

'Can I ask why you left? Was it just the relocation?'

'Actually it was before that. The merger was just before Summer got really ill, and there wasn't a need for two full-time team leaders. The other manager was a Band 7 too, and had just got married and bought a house. And with Summer being so ill, the offer of redundancy was timed quite well for me.'

'Re-enablement is a big part of the community here. Would you be interested in working with us?'

'How many hours are you thinking?' Evelyn was surprised at the offer, but more surprised that her immediate reaction wasn't to say no. Tom was right: Summer was happily back at school, and Evelyn had been a lot happier, and starting to feel bored, and she was planning on staying in Broclington. At least for the foreseeable future.

'As many hours as you're willing to give us – up to full-time.'

'I don't think I'd want to come back full-time just yet.' Evelyn shook her head.

'But what about part-time? Maybe school hours?' He gave her a hopeful smile, and for a moment she could see exactly where Jake got his good-natured cheerfulness from. 'You don't have to answer now, but would you at least think about it? It'd be doing me – and the community – a big favour. And if you're planning on staying around Broclington for a bit longer, I can't think of a better way to settle back in than helping care for our residents.'

'I'll think about it,' Evelyn promised, already tempted. All of Tom's points were good ones, and she couldn't deny that the money would be very welcome.

'Why don't you let me know in a few days? When I call with Summer's test results – which I'm sure will be just fine – I'm assuming that's part of your hesitation.'

Evelyn nodded. Any parent would understand. 'So, three to five days then? Depending on how busy the lab is.'

'Of course.' He held out his hand and gave her a warm, firm handshake. 'It's been nice talking with you. And seeing you work. I really do hope you say yes.'

'I will think about it, I promise.'

'Good.' He held the door open for her, and she headed down the corridor.

Before she opened the door to the reception, she could already hear Summer's excited tones as she showed off Tilly's latest trick of dancing on her back legs and turning in circles on command. Evelyn smiled. Village life definitely seemed to suit Summer, and she was slowly turning into a bright, confident, happy child.

Her smile grew even wider when she saw who was the audience for Summer's latest performance. Almost as soon as she stepped through the door, Jake looked up and met her eyes and gave her a warm smile.

'Hi, how are you?'

'Good thanks. Yourself?' She had to resist the urge to step closer to him.

'Pretty good too. Just dropping off some stuff Mum wanted.' He glanced at the bag on the floor, being investigated by Tilly. 'Snout out, nosey girl.' He laughed and nudged her away.

'What did Dr Tom want, Mum? Was it about me?'

'No, sweetheart. It was about me.'

Summer leaped up and flung her arms round her mum's waist. 'You're not sick are you? Please tell me you're not sick!'

'No, no.' Guilt accosted her and she bent to reassure Summer, cursing herself for the throwaway comment. 'He wanted to ask me if I'd work for him.'

'Like what you did in Northumberland?'

'A little bit like that. What do you think about that?'

Summer pursed her lips while she thought. 'Would you work late lots?'

'No. Dr Tom said I could pretty much pick my own hours. So I could take you to school, work for a few hours, and then pick you up.'

'I think you should do it. You like being a nurse. And I worry you get bored when I'm at school.'

'I'll have to think about it, and talk to your nanny.'

'Do it, do it, do it, do it!'

Evelyn laughed. 'I guess I've got a new job, then.'

'Congratulations.' Jake gave her another delicious smile. 'I suppose it's too short notice to offer to take you out to celebrate.'

'I haven't said yes, yet,' Evelyn argued, while wondering why she was hesitating.

'But you will.' Summer tugged on her hand until Evelyn bent down again. 'You should say yes. Jake's very nice and I think he likes you.' Her whisper was far louder than Evelyn would have liked, and she looked up at him over the top of Summer's rapidly growing curls.

From the laughter in his eyes, she guessed he'd heard every word. 'I don't know about celebrating. I haven't exactly said yes yet, and I doubt I can arrange a sitter for Summer.'

'You forgot Mum. We were going to watch the dancing on TV with Nanny tonight, and teach Tilly more tricks. We can record it for you so you can go out with Jake. Nanny won't mind. And I promise I'll be good for her.'

'I'd really like you to say yes.' Jake almost echoed the words of his dad a few minutes earlier and Evelyn wondered what it was about them both that made her agree – or consider agreeing – to things she'd planned to avoid.

'All right. If my mum is happy to watch Summer …'

'Of course she is! I'm her little angel!' Summer interrupted.

'… then yes. I'd love to go out with you to celebrate.'

'Fantastic.' Jake's blue eyes sparkled. 'I'll pick you up around seven?'

'Sounds good.' Evelyn smiled back, feeling a little bit sparkly herself.

# Chapter Seven

Evelyn stared at her meagre wardrobe and wondered again what on earth convinced her to agree to this. She had nothing to wear on a date, and there was good reason for that: she was a mother who was technically still married. The patch of pale skin still encircled her ring finger, evidence of where her commitment to another man had sat for years. That the marriage was only a technicality awaiting the final paperwork to come through didn't change the fact that her daughter had been so ill recently. No, Evelyn shook her head. She'd just have to cancel.

Summer bounced into the room and landed on the bed in a fit of healthy, happy giggles, closely followed by Tilly. Evelyn smiled as she watched them wrestling on the bed, not even caring that she'd have to make it all over again. Summer was behaving like any other mischievous, normal, *healthy* little girl, and that meant more to Evelyn than any tidy room or household rule ever could.

'Mum …' Summer rolled to sit on the edge of Evelyn's bed, swinging her feet back and forth as she fixed her with a serious look. 'If you don't hurry up, you're going to be late.'

'I'm thinking about not going,' Evelyn admitted.

'Mum, you have to!' Summer was outraged. 'You told Jake you would, and that was like a promise. And you always tell me I have to keep my promises.'

'I do tell you that,' Evelyn agreed reluctantly.

'And Jake will be sad if you don't go. And that isn't fair.'

Evelyn turned to study her daughter. 'You really like Jake, don't you?'

'Yup. And so does Tilly, don't you?' As if she'd been listening, Tilly yipped in response.

Evelyn sat on the bed next to Summer. 'Do you understand what tonight means?'

'I think so.' Summer nodded seriously, once again looking far older than her years.

'Can you tell me?' Evelyn needed to know for sure.

'It's a date. Because you and Jake like each other and want to see if you want to be boyfriend and girlfriend. Which is like holding hands and kissing and sometimes spending lots of time together and having adult sleepovers. Without kids.' She petted Tilly's head. 'Or dogs.'

'How do you know all this?'

'Some of my new friends have mummies and daddies who don't live together and have girlfriends and boyfriends instead. One girl has two mummies. That's interesting, isn't it?'

'Yes, it is.' Evelyn smiled. 'I'm not saying it's going to happen, but would you be OK if Jake wanted to be my boyfriend?'

'I think so.' Summer chewed her bottom lip thoughtfully. 'Charlie isn't ever going to move in with us and Nanny, is he?'

Evelyn pulled Summer against her in a hug. They'd talked about this before, but it didn't make it any easier. 'No, darling, I don't think he is.'

'Then I think you should see if you want to be boyfriend and girlfriend with Jake. He's nice, and he makes you smile. And I like him better than Charlie's girlfriend.'

'Yeah, I like him better than her too.'

'Can I help you pick pretty clothes?'

Evelyn gave her daughter a tight squeeze and kissed her on the head. 'You know what? I think I could really use some help.'

'Awesome!' Summer leaped off the bed and started pulling open drawers.

Evelyn almost jumped out of her skin when the doorbell rang. Summer dropped the hairbrush she'd been "helping" with, and raced out of the room. Tilly peered at her quizzically from the bed.

'Oh, go on then.' Evelyn shook her head as the dog raced out of the room and down the stairs to greet her new buddy as well, yipping excitedly before she even reached him. It seemed everyone was excited to see Jake. Her stomach fluttered as she peered into the mirror and smoothed her hair flat. If she was honest, she was excited too, but the nerves were so bad that her fingers shook slightly.

It had been well over a decade since she'd gone on a first date, and it wasn't something she'd ever planned on doing again. She took a deep breath, hooked her bag over her shoulder, and grabbed her jacket off the bed. She gave herself a final once over in the mirror, wondering again if tightly fitting jeans and V-neck jumper over a silky camisole was a bit much.

But Jake was already downstairs waiting for her, and that meant he was alone with Summer and her mum, who would no doubt be being their overenthusiastic selves. If she didn't get a handle on her nerves and go down soon, Jake would probably have been stuffed with fresh apple cinnamon muffins and co-opted into Summer's latest game. There was nothing for it. She needed to metaphorically put on her big girl panties, act her age, and go greet her date for the evening.

*Date.* The word sent a chill of anticipation over her skin, and she smiled at herself in the mirror. With her hair in soft waves over her shoulders and fully made-up, she didn't look bad. And her mum was thrilled to be having a "Super Awesome Nanny and Summer and Tilly" night in, and the two of them had been excitedly planning and baking half of the day.

Maybe she could relax, and enjoy herself tonight. In fact, she probably needed to. If one of her patients had been through the types of stress she had recently, Evelyn would have been the first to remind them about self-care, and how they needed to take time for themselves. That decided, she straightened her shoulders and headed down the stairs.

She paused outside the living room door, and ran her fingers through her hair again as Jake's deep voice and laughter echoed through the wood. She pushed the door open quietly, curious to see what they were all up to. Her heart filled with warmth as she watched Tilly dance in a circle at Summer's command, shamelessly showing off for their guest, who sat on the pouffe, laughing as he doled out treats and praise.

'Hi.' Evelyn stood at the door, suddenly feeling shy.

'Hey.' Jake grinned up at her, and struggled to his feet, hampered by Tilly and Summer who were still crowding him. He stepped towards her, then hesitated as if not sure of what to do or say next. For a horrible moment, Evelyn wondered if he'd changed his mind and was regretting asking her out.

Summer tugged on Jake's hand. 'I think Mum looks really pretty, don't you?'

Jake unstuck his tongue from the roof of his mouth. He'd already thought Evelyn was pretty, but in tight jeans and a jumper that matched the green of her eyes, and her hair falling in loose waves, she was stunning. Her lips were glossy and pink, and made him think things that were incredibly inappropriate while her daughter was hanging on his arm.

'Yes, I think she looks really, really pretty.' He smiled at Evelyn who blushed, her cheeks pink, which made her eyes seem even more vivid.

'You know, you could stay here and play more. And watch the dancing with us,' Summer wheedled by his side.

He felt Evelyn's eyes on him as he bent down to talk to Summer. 'How about if I promise we can play another day? If your mum's OK with it.'

'Of course she'll be OK with it.' Summer rolled her eyes at him, and he struggled not to laugh at her. 'But you could stay now, too.'

'I could,' he agreed. 'But I think your mum looks too lovely to stay in. And what about your special night with popcorn and dancing with your nan?'

'Good point.' She flung herself at Evelyn and gave her a big hug and a kiss, and he found himself smiling at the picture they created. 'Hurry and go, Mum. Have fun!' She kissed her again.

'Not that I'm not loving all the attention, but what's this for?' Evelyn asked as she hugged her daughter again and was treated to another onslaught of kisses.

'I'm saying goodnight now, so you won't worry about coming home early to put me to bed.'

Evelyn laughed, and the sound made Jake smile. He was hoping to have lots more opportunities to hear that laugh and wanted to be part of making her light up with so much happiness and joy.

'Are you sure you're OK with this, Mum?' She shot her a worried look.

'Of course.' Linda wrapped her arms around her granddaughter. 'We've got lots of fun planned. You go have a good time, love, you deserve it.'

'Well, I guess that's me told.' Evelyn smiled at him.

'Thank you for this, Linda,' Jake added.

'No need to thank me for spending time with my favourite granddaughter.'

'Nanny, I'm your only granddaughter.'

'Then obviously you're my favourite!' She looked up at Jake and Evelyn. 'And don't worry about coming back too early. Relax and enjoy yourselves.'

'Thanks Mum.' Evelyn placed a kiss on her mum's cheek, another on Summer, and rubbed Tilly's ears. 'Be good girls.'

Jake held the door open for her. 'Shall we?' He got a whiff of Evelyn's perfume as she brushed past him and headed to the front door where she stepped into a pair of heels that were so high they brought her almost to his height. The perfect height for him to lean in and brush his lips against hers, and see if they tasted as sweet as they looked.

'Ready, then?'

He cleared his throat, and forced himself to stop focussing on her glossy lips. 'Yes. I've booked us a table at a nice restaurant in the next town over. The pubs here are good, but I thought something a little nicer maybe, and the food at The Old Mill is fantastic. And then after that, if you're not too tired, there's a couple of films that look good on at the cinema, or we could just go have a few drinks somewhere. What do you think?'

'I think that all sounds lovely, and I'm happy to just play along with whatever you want.'

He zapped his car unlocked, and held the door open for her. 'You know, I meant what I said. It wasn't just because Summer prompted me. I really do think you look beautiful.'

'Thanks.' Evelyn flushed again, but less than the last time. 'You scrub up well too.'

Jake grinned to himself as he shut the door, and had to make sure he didn't skip round to the driver's side and give away his excitement at the prospect of a full evening – alone – with such a beautiful woman.

'It's about a twenty-five minute drive, so feel free to fiddle with the radio.'

'Honestly, anything that's not Disney songs or bubblegum pop is fine.'

'You don't like Disney songs?' he asked as he carefully pulled out into the street.

'Not after the twentieth run of them this week.' Evelyn grinned. 'Even with children, I'm not sure anyone in their thirties should know every single lyric quite as well as I do.'

'I could probably give you a run on some of them. My niece, Sarah, is currently obsessed with Cinderella. She makes me act out half the scenes with her. Apparently I'm her favourite Prince Charming.'

'I can see that.' Evelyn smiled at him in a way that made him have to really focus to concentrate on the driving.

He held her door open again when they reached the restaurant, and was again treated to a whiff of the fresh, fruity scent that floated from her hair. When his hand automatically fell to the small of her back to guide her towards the door, he was thrilled that Evelyn momentarily leaned into his touch.

Within minutes they were seated at a window table and reading the menus while Evelyn sipped a glass of wine and he nursed his one beer of the night. She sighed happily and sat back, watching fairy lights twinkle off water that shimmered a few feet from the window as she toyed with her wine glass, tracing a finger absent-mindedly around its rim. Jake watched her fingers move, transfixed by their delicate touch as the candlelight danced against her skin, making it seem almost translucent.

'Thank you for this, Jake.' Her voice was quiet, and huskier than usual, and he found himself leaning in to hear her more easily. 'I can't remember the last time I felt so relaxed.'

'You're more than welcome.' He chinked his glass against hers. 'And thank you for finally putting me out of my misery, and agreeing to a date.'

Evelyn laughed and shook her head. 'It still seems so strange, thinking that I'm on a date.'

'Why? You're kind, caring and beautiful. Who wouldn't want to date you?' Jake laughed in disbelief.

'My ex-husband, for one.'

As soon as the words had escaped, Evelyn wished she could take them back. She hadn't meant to ruin what had promised to be a lovely evening with a man she was really attracted to, but somehow her bastard ex had stuck his selfish, inconsiderate self into her life again. 'I'm so, so sorry.'

'It's all right.' Jake took a long drink of his beer, before fixing her with that bright blue gaze that seemed to look straight through to her soul. 'He's a big part of your life and past. If it helps, I think I can understand a little bit. Callum, my brother, is a single dad and Sarah's growing up without her mum around. Without telling you his business, his ex wasn't very good at being a mother, so chose not to be. The family help out wherever we can, and Sarah's amazing. But the thing is, as much hurt as his ex caused, Callum's not going to forget about her just because they're not together anymore. She's the reason Sarah exists. And it sounds like what happened with your ex-husband is a lot more recent, so it's got to be in your mind still. You can't just forget about him.'

'No, as much as I'd sometimes like to forget we ever happened.'

'So, now you've brought him up, is it a good time to ask why that is? You can tell me it's none of my business and I won't be offended, but can I ask what happened?'

'I'm not sure there's ever really a good time for these conversations.' Evelyn sighed sadly. 'I might as well tell you the sordid details and then he can well and truly butt out.'

'You don't have to, if you don't want to.'

'I know, and I appreciate that. But you've asked, and you deserve to know.' She took a deep glug of her wine.

'Sometimes, I still feel like I'm married to him, like it was only a few days ago that we were happy together.'

'But it's not, is it?'

'No.' Evelyn snorted with dark humour. 'It's much, much longer than that since I was happy with Charlie.'

'Charlie? So that's his name.' Jake nodded grimly.

Evelyn fell silent, wandering back in her memories to a time when they'd been happy, and before Summer had gotten sick.

'So what happened?' Jake prompted her gently.

'Honestly? He screwed up in the worst possible way. It's never easy when a child gets sick, and people handle it differently. I know some couples who became even stronger and pulled together because of the experience, and others who could barely stand the sight of each other.'

'And that was what happened to you and your husband?'

'No, actually'—Evelyn shook her head—'it wasn't anything like that. I was so focussed on helping Summer and making sure we did everything we could to support her treatment, making sure she got the best treatment, ate the best diet, got enough rest. Between that and working as a community nurse, well my whole life became a bit like a medical drama. I think Charlie felt left out.'

'He couldn't really blame you for that.'

'You'd think not, but apparently he did.' Evelyn shrugged. It didn't hurt as much as it used to. 'The chemo was really hard on Summer. It caused neutropenia – her immune system was virtually non-existent, and we had to live completely clean around her. It wasn't quite full quarantine, but it was close because any infection could have been really dangerous.' She took a deep breath and concentrated on keeping her anger in check. She might not be hurting any more, but the anger was harder to let go. 'Charlie and I had already been drifting apart, and he'd been less and less interested in Summer – he didn't come to any of her appointments, barely asked about them and didn't want much to do with her when she was sick – which was a lot. I think maybe he was trying to protect himself, or something.'

'Pretty damn selfish.' Jake frowned.

'It gets worse. Charlie screwed up. In the worst possible way. Turned out his shag on the side had an infection – tonsillitis. To them, it was nothing more than a bit of an annoyance, but to Summer?' Evelyn felt her throat tighten with emotion as her bottom lip started to tremble.

Jake pushed his napkin into her hands and let his fingers rest over hers. The gentle touch and quiet patience gave her the strength to carry on.

'She developed neutropenic sepsis. It's what happens when you get an infection after chemo has wiped out your immune system.' She was so used to explaining the terminology that she briefly forgot he'd understand the medical jargon. 'We nearly lost her.' The words brought angry sourness into her mouth. 'All because he couldn't keep his trousers zipped up!' She shook her head, trying to clear the memories. 'A one-off mistake I might have been able to forgive – given the stress we were both under. But it wasn't just a one-off. It was a sustained affair – a dirty, secretive little relationship that nearly cost my baby her life. When I found out how she'd gotten sick … let's just say I reacted badly. And I don't regret a single word I said.'

'Wow. I'm not really sure what to say.'

'Bet you regret asking now, don't you?'

'Not if it helps you, I don't.' He squeezed her fingers reassuringly, and warmth trickled up her arm.

'It gets worse,' Evelyn warned. 'I can stop now.'

'If it's part of your life, and Summer's, then I'd like to know – if it's not too painful for you.'

Evelyn squeezed his fingers back, and smiled when his thumb rubbed over her knuckles. 'She got pregnant. And Charlie, being the selfish dick he is, left us for her. Not that I would have wanted him back, but he wasn't there for Summer any more, and that was unforgivable to me. And the fact that this all came out just before Christmas somehow made it all the worse.'

'How so?'

'Christmas is the most magical time of year, when you get together with the people you love the most to celebrate just being together. It's a holiday built around bringing light into the darkness, when God gave hope to the world. It's all about kindness and love. Someone who wants to be that petty and hurtful and cruel is never good, but to be like that at Christmas? That's especially low. I almost think someone who would do that is beyond hope. Charlie certainly seems to have been. All of them were.'

'All of them?'

'Summer's grandparents.' Evelyn shook her head, hating to even give them that title.

'They didn't stay in contact with you?'

'Oh, they did.' She grimaced. 'It would have been better if they hadn't. They never really welcomed me into the family. Not really. Charlie and I were young when we met, maybe too young. But we fell in love, and when I was offered a job in Northumberland, he moved up north with me so we could start our lives together. I think, on

96

some level, they always blamed me for taking their son away.'

'That's ridiculous.' Jake shook his head.

'Yup, but that's the way it always was. They wanted someone better than "just a nurse" for their precious son. To be honest, I think they were thrilled when we started to have problems, and encouraged the split. I think champagne might actually have been popped to celebrate when the divorce proceedings started.'

'Wow.'

'They stayed in contact just long enough to question my fitness as a mother, and then cut me and Summer out of their lives. Maybe it was easier to pretend the sick little girl in the hospital bed just didn't exist rather than face the reality of Summer's illness. To be honest, I was never that close to them – I always felt like the outsider in their family. But it hurt Summer.'

'And your ex didn't try to intervene? To stand up for you and Summer?'

'No he bloody didn't! He never did when it came to them.' Evelyn growled, gripping her glass so tightly she was surprised it didn't break between her fingers.

'I'm so, so sorry you both went through that. He didn't – *doesn't* – deserve either of you. None of them do.' The sincerity in his eyes caused her to catch her breath.

'That's really kind.' She ducked her head, letting her hair fall across her face in a curtain.

'I'm not being kind, Evelyn.' He waited until she looked up. 'I'm being honest.' He looked at her with such openness and honesty that she had to look away again and change the subject.

'So, why are you single?'

He shrugged and released her hand as he reached for his beer. She found herself immediately missing the contact.

'No big story there. Just haven't really found the right person to put up with me yet.'

'Put up with you …' Evelyn laughed. 'Do you really take that much putting up with?'

'If you believe my siblings, yes. They often tell me I get on better with animals, and I'm not entirely sure they're wrong. I'm usually quite awkward around people.'

'You're not awkward around me,' Evelyn argued.

'You haven't noticed? Well, give it time.' He laughed self-deprecatingly and looked up as the waitress approached. 'I'm sorry, we've been talking so much I've hardly looked at the menu. Can we have a minute?'

She nodded and stepped away, leaving Jake grinning sheepishly.

Evelyn hid her grin behind her menu as she scanned through her options. Should she order a starter? She was hungry, but didn't want to put Jake off by looking like a pig, and weren't women supposed to be delicate and ladylike on dates? It had been so long since she'd been on one that she couldn't remember, but she was sure she'd read it in a magazine somewhere – probably in a hospital waiting room.

'I think I'll go with the grilled chicken salad.'

'Really? The steaks are great here.'

'Chicken's fine,' Evelyn replied, already questioning her decision.

'OK.' Jake shrugged. 'Any starters? Sides?'

'Oh no, not for me thanks.' Evelyn heard herself answer while part of her was wondering what she was thinking and saying.

'So your entire meal plan, with wine, is a bit of chicken and some rabbit food?' Jake fixed her with that look again, and Evelyn could feel the colour rising in her cheeks. 'Obviously you should order whatever you want, but Evelyn?' He leaned forward.

'Yes?' She was immediately annoyed at the slight breathlessness in her voice, and hoped Jake hadn't noticed it.

'Is that *really* what you want? It's not the type of food you ordered last time.' When she didn't answer, he pushed the question. 'If you were here with Summer or Linda, celebrating a new job, is that what you'd be ordering?'

'Probably not,' Evelyn admitted.

'So what would you order?'

She pursed her lips, before giving in to Jake's contagious grin. 'Medium-rare rib-eye, mushrooms, jacket potato and green veg.'

'Sure you don't want that?' The glint in his eyes told Evelyn he already knew the answer.

'You're incorrigible.' She laughed.

'Is that a yes?'

'Yes, please.' She continued laughing. 'And maybe split an order of the onion rings?'

'Finally! The real you.' He laughed, rattled off the order to the patient waitress, and turned back to Evelyn. 'Would you do me a favour?'

'I owe you more than one favour, Jake.' Evelyn remembered the joy on Summer's face when Tilly finally recovered.

'Do me this one, and we'll call it even. OK?' He waited for her nod. 'Don't take this the wrong way, but would you just try to relax and be yourself? Eat what you want, drink what you want, say what you want and don't worry about offending me. I like you, Evelyn. I want us to have fun tonight, and not worry about trying to impress each other. Or anything else. OK?'

Evelyn took another swig of her drink while she considered Jake's request. It was so different from the perfectly coiffed and polished behaviour her ex had preferred that his request was alien. But Jake seemed so honest and genuine that she found herself nodding. 'OK.'

Jake watched as Evelyn ran her spoon around her dish and scooped out the last bit of chocolate mousse that clung to the edges. 'That was absolutely delicious.' She licked the last morsels from her spoon with such open, unabashed enjoyment that Jake had to swallow hard and remind himself he was a gentleman. For a few moments he'd been glad they were in a public place, because it made it that much easier not to grab her and kiss her as thoroughly as he wanted to.

'Would you like anything else? A coffee, maybe?' He'd enjoyed every moment with her so far, and really wanted to continue their date.

'No, I'm all right thank you.'

'Film?'

Evelyn wriggled slightly in her chair. 'I think I'd rather head back to Broclington, if that's all right with you?'

'Of course, whatever you like.' He signalled for the bill, trying to hide his disappointment.

'I'm just going to freshen up.' Evelyn stood and grabbed her bag. 'Don't you pay the bill. This one's on me.'

'Absolutely not. I asked you out, there's no way I'm letting you pay.'

'Please Jake, I owe you this.' She rested one hand on a slim hip, and her lips came together in a small frown that he instantly wanted to kiss away.

'You're not going to win this one, Evelyn. So thank you for your offer, but no.'

'Thank you.' She placed a quick kiss on his cheek and sashayed to the ladies' room, with Jake's eyes tracking her movement.

He could still feel the slight tingle of her lips against his cheek as he settled the bill, and tried to work out how to convince her to stay out a little longer. Obviously she'd be thinking about Summer, but even she had pleaded that Evelyn shouldn't race home. He planned on doing everything he could to extend this date.

He smiled and stood as she came back to the table. 'Ready?'

'Yes.' She smiled back, and he tried not to notice that she'd reapplied whatever it was that made her lips look so glossy and kissable.

She slipped her hand through his arm as they headed to the door, and he felt a flush of warmth at her touch. 'Are you sure you want to go home now?'

Her forehead crinkled in a way that made her look even more adorable. 'I wasn't planning on going home just yet. Unless you're trying to get rid of me already?'

'No, not at all.' He fumbled over his words. 'But you said you wanted to head back to the village …'

'Because I wanted to relax and have a few drinks with you. Somewhere you can join in too, if you want, and not worry about driving us back. Which I really appreciate by the way.' She squeezed his arm. 'I was thinking if we drove back to yours, we could drop your car off and walk to The Brockle's Retreat, and then share a few drinks. What do you think?'

'I think that sounds like a plan.' It really sounded like perfection, but he didn't want to come on too strong and scare her off by admitting that.

Evelyn paused at the garden gate, and took a moment to sniff the collar of the coat Jake had insisted on wrapping around her shoulders, over the top of her light jacket. Though she'd protested that he'd be cold and she was fine, the weight over her shoulders combined with his slightly spicy scent made her feel warm and comforted in a way she hadn't felt for a very, very long time. And she didn't want the feeling to end. Her fingers were still laced through Jake's, though she couldn't remember when their hands had sought each other out.

'I've had a really good night.' She turned to face him. 'Thank you.'

'You're more than welcome. I've really enjoyed myself too.' He stepped closer to her, and Evelyn felt warm from head to toe as she met his gaze.

'I should go in,' she admitted reluctantly.

'You probably should.' He stepped even closer until there was barely an inch between them. 'I want to see you again. Will you say yes?'

Evelyn's heart thudded in her chest so loudly that she was amazed Jake couldn't hear it. Her breath caught in her throat as he leaned down, so close that she could feel his breath tickling her lips in the most delicious way.

'Please say yes.' She could see the smile in his eyes in the light of the streetlamps. 'Say you'll let me take you out again.'

'Yes, please.' Evelyn smiled, her voice barely a whisper.

'Thank goodness,' Jake breathed. 'I'm not sure what I would have done if you'd said no.' He reached up and gently stroked her cheek while watching her closely. After a few seconds he cradled her face between his hands and leaned in to brush his lips against hers in the sweetest and most delicate of kisses. He pulled back and studied her for long moments, looking for something in her eyes. He must have found whatever it was, because he leaned in and kissed her again, gently teasing his lips over hers.

Evelyn groaned slightly and parted her lips as Jake intensified the kiss. Her hands slid up his back and her fingers slipped into his dark hair, burying themselves in the silky locks as she pulled him closer and pressed tightly against him.

'Wow.' He broke the kiss reluctantly and rested his forehead against hers, his hands still cupping her face as he caught his breath.

'Yeah.' She bit her lip to try and keep from giggling like a silly schoolgirl, and reluctantly let her hands slide down his neck and shoulders to rest on his forearms. She had to bite back a whimper of complaint as he slowly let his hands drop as well, and stepped back slightly, leaving her feeling cold.

'I really should be going. And you should probably be getting in.' His eyes sparkled with amusement. 'Before I give in to the temptation to do something undignified, and give your neighbours something to really gossip about.'

'I guess nothing changes in village life,' she replied, thinking that maybe she wouldn't mind being the topic of local gossip, especially if it involved more kisses like that.

'Yeah.' He laughed. 'Goodnight, Evelyn.' He leaned back towards her and placed a sweet and gentle kiss on the corner of her mouth.

'Goodnight,' Evelyn whispered against his cheek before shrugging off his coat and handing it back to him. She walked up her mum's garden path, still feeling his kiss on her lips, let herself in, and gave a shy wave. As she closed the door, she could have sworn she saw him do a fist pump into the air. She shook her head, smiling, as she took off her shoes. She was already missing the way he so carefully held her – like she was something incredibly precious.

It was a feeling she thought she could get used to.

# *Chapter Eight*

The belch echoed around the table, and Summer covered her face. 'I'm so sorry.'

'That's pathetic.' Jake took a gulp of his drink, and let rip with a much louder, far ruder sounding burp.

Summer stared at him in open-mouthed shock, before cracking up laughing.

'I don't know which one of you is worse.' Linda shook her head as she helped Evelyn clear away the plates and stack them in the dishwasher.

'He is!' Summer giggled. 'His was bigger and on purpose. Mine was just a little oopsie burp.'

'Whereas mine was a proper manly one.' Jake poked his tongue out, making Summer giggle even harder. Evelyn watched as they laughed and teased each other, and said a silent prayer of thanks to whoever it was who sent Jake into her life. It had only been a few weeks since he'd convinced her to go on a date with him, and he had somehow easily slipped into their lives like he was supposed to be there.

Though she'd initially worried about how he and Summer would get along – and introducing a "friend" after a couple of dates, Jake had reassured her every step of the way. He already knew Summer, and made it very clear he understood they came together, as part of a package deal he seemed only too happy to welcome into his life. Summer adored him, and he appeared to adore her, making extra effort to arrange some outings for both of them.

Some, but not all. Evelyn bit her bottom lip remembering the last very adult-only date where Jake had easily tucked his arm around her shoulders, pulling her close, while they shared popcorn and kisses and failed miserably to watch even half of the movie they'd gone to see.

'Come on.' Linda held her hand out to her granddaughter. 'Let's you and me give your mum and Jake some peace and quiet.'

'But Nanny …' Summer's bottom lip immediately popped out, threatening a bout of full-blown stubborn temper.

'But nothing, young lady.' Linda wasn't going to stand for any nonsense. 'Come on. I'll let you pick something to watch on TV.'

'Whatever I want?'

Linda sighed. 'Yes, whatever you want.'

Summer jumped down from the table. 'I'll get Sing-Along Frozen.' She raced into the living room.

'Oh good.' Linda deadpanned, following. 'I don't think I've seen that in at least four whole days.'

'Thank you, Mum.' Evelyn shot her a grateful smile as she stood, firmly closing the kitchen door behind them.

'Hi.' Jake's strong arms slipped around her waist.

'Hello.' She melted into his kiss.

'I've been waiting to do that pretty much since I got here.' He grinned. 'Summer's great, but can you please try and beat her to the door next time? It's been driving me mad that I couldn't kiss you hello properly.'

'You shouldn't have told her you were bringing dessert. Brockle cakes are her new favourite thing.'

'Oh, so you're saying I deserved this torture?' He raised an eyebrow. 'You do know your daughter has told me you're ticklish?' He wiggled his fingers threateningly.

'No, I didn't, but please don't.' She stepped out of his embrace and produced a folded paper from the kitchen drawer. 'I wanted to give you this. Sorry it's late, but now I'm working, I can do this.'

Jake furrowed his brow as he unfolded the cheque. '£775? I don't understand.'

'You wouldn't tell me what Tilly's bill was after the snakebite, so I called my old vet, and your colleague who provided the antivenom, and took the average. You'll tell me if it's more?'

'No I bloody won't.' Jake tore it in half and slammed it onto the worktop. 'I told you at the time you could cover the cost of the supplies and you've done that.'

'But I owe you the money,' Evelyn protested. She was proud, and wanted to pay her way.

'What type of boyfriend would I be if I charged you?'

'Boyfriend?' Evelyn stared at him, the heat taken out of her pride.

'Well, we're dating aren't we? What else would you call me?' He gave her a smile that melted away the rest of her arguments, and stepped towards her.

'Absolutely wonderful. Handsome. Adorable. Sexy.'

'I think I like that last one the best.' He held his arms open to her.

She stepped into them, looked up at him and placed a kiss on his lips, before becoming more serious. 'There's something I want to ask you.'

'Anything.' Jake shrugged easily, apparently happy to offer her the world. Which made her decision even easier.

But she still licked her lips nervously. 'I was wondering what you're doing Friday.'

'This Friday?' Confusion clouded his eyes. 'I thought we were taking Summer to the new Disney thing.'

We. Evelyn loved how he said that, and how he automatically included Summer in things. 'I meant after that.'

'Dunno. Probably just head home. Might watch a bit of TV, or read a book if my eyes are going too square for more screen time. Maybe give my old mate a call – I owe him a catch-up.' He grinned. 'Unless you've got a better idea?'

'I thought, maybe I could come over, and maybe stay with you?'

'Yeah, should be fine.' He shrugged easily. 'I'll just have to dig out some bedding for the spare room. Is Summer having a sleepover or something?'

Evelyn sighed. For someone so incredibly smart, Jake was really good at completely missing the point sometimes. 'I wasn't exactly thinking that I'd be in the spare bed, Jake. More likely yours?' She watched the huge grin spread across his face as realisation dawned. 'So what do you think?'

'Hell, *yes!*' He pushed her back against the door and kissed her thoroughly, trapping her between his warm arms, the solid wood, and the very solid masculinity of his body. 'On second thoughts, why wait? I'll throw you over my shoulder and carry you off right now.'

Evelyn giggled, but had to admit she was incredibly tempted. She could barely remember the last time she'd had sex at all, let alone good sex. And something about the way he kissed her, and drew reactions she'd all but forgotten from her body, told her sex with Jake would be very, very good. She mentally cursed herself, wondering why she'd left the newly arrived black lace and silk in its discreet delivery wrapping upstairs, and was wearing basic beige.

108

He ran kisses down her throat. 'Just say the word, Evelyn.'

'I can't.' She shook her head, trying to remember why she was refusing him.

'Mum?' They jumped apart guiltily. 'Are you and Jake coming to sing with us? It's nearly the best song!'

'I'll be in in a minute,' Evelyn called back.

'I don't know how the hell I'm going to make it to Friday,' Jake complained, hunger still burning in his gaze.

'It's a couple of days. We've been dating for weeks and you've survived.'

'Yeah, but I didn't know you were thinking about this.' He groaned. 'Go through, see if you can't buy me a few minutes.' He looked down, and blushed.

Evelyn couldn't help but follow his gaze. She gulped. Suddenly Friday seemed far too long away.

Friday had taken far too long to arrive, and now it had, Jake was in hell. The torment had been going on for hours. He'd sat in the darkness with Evelyn, his leg and arm brushing against hers each time either of them shifted in their seat, intensely aware of her every move and the promise of what lay ahead. And painfully aware that Summer sat in the next seat over, eyes wide as she stared at drama unfolding on the big screen. Even while he was thinking about what he planned on doing to her mother later.

'Please, Jake,' Summer had begged when they were back home, making him feel worse than ever. 'Will you please read me a story before you go?'

'Summer, I think Nanny wanted to read to you,' Evelyn replied, trying to give him an escape route.

But Summer pleaded, and he'd been helpless to say no. He was completely wrapped around her little finger. As he'd thrown her over his shoulder, fireman style, her squeal of delight pushed everything else away and he was filled with the strange mix of joy and fierce protectiveness he usually associated with his niece, Sarah. Somehow, when he'd not been expecting it, Summer had wormed her way into his heart as well.

So he dutifully read the story she requested, tucked her in tightly, and patted a section of the duvet flat for Tilly. All while feeling Evelyn's eyes on him from her spot on the landing.

When Summer's eyes finally drifted closed, he snuck out of the room, cringing at every creak of the old house.

'You really are wonderful with her.' Evelyn stood on tiptoe to place a soft kiss against his lips. 'You didn't have to take the time to read to her, but I'm so glad you did.' And she'd taken his hand, and lead him down the stairs, where he came face to face with Linda.

'Thanks for this, Mum.' Evelyn kissed her mum's cheek then reached for her coat, leaving Jake standing there awkwardly.

'Yes, thank you Mrs Matthams. You have a good evening.' He cringed, realising that she knew exactly what type of evening he had planned. *With her daughter.*

She headed back towards the living room, but paused at the door. Without looking round, she called to him. 'Remember Jake, a gentleman always puts his overcoat on.'

For a moment, he wondered if anyone had ever actually died just from embarrassment. His brother or dad would probably know, but it was starting to feel like a real possibility.

'Mum!' Evelyn hissed, blushing furiously.

'What?' She turned to look at her daughter, her eyes wide with faux innocence.

'Umm. Nothing.'

'I'll see you sometime tomorrow. Goodnight.'

Jake hung his head, burning with embarrassment. A moment later, Evelyn's cool fingers cupped his face.

'It's just us now.' She studied him with such openness that he hesitated, nearly changing his mind. Until she pressed her lips against his, and his mind went blank to everything except for the feel of her body against his and the heat of her lips.

She eventually pulled away, leaving him gasping and craving more. She held his keys out to him, and though he'd no idea where she'd got them from, he seized them gladly.

The drive back to Badger's Hospital, and his flat above, seemed the longest it had ever been. Though the clock appeared to be counting the minutes as usual, each one stretched into agonisingly long, awkward moments. All the fumbling, bumbling nerves – that he never usually felt around Evelyn – reappeared, and he found his knuckles clenching tightly on the steering wheel as he wracked his mind for something – anything – intelligent to say.

And what was he supposed to do when they got to his flat? She'd already made it clear what she was expecting, what she wanted, but was he supposed to just pounce on her the second he unlocked the door? Or would they sit and make awkward small talk until she thought he was the biggest clot on the planet and wouldn't want to ever see him again, let alone sleep with him.

He bit back a groan as the gravel of his surgery crunched under his tyres, and he pulled into his usual parking spot. Now he couldn't even decide whether to go through the surgery, or walk up the outside stairs to the private entrance. His fingers white-knuckled on the steering wheel, and he jumped as Evelyn placed her hand over his, and gave him a warm smile.

'Shall we go up?'

Oh hell. He was crazy about this woman and needed to not screw this up. 'Sure.'

She stepped out of the car, lifted her bag onto her shoulder, and headed up the outside stairs, making the decision for him. She leaned casually on the railing at the top, waiting for him to unlock the door and let them both in.

Evelyn had to force her fingers to let go of the railing and walk casually into the flat. She'd been there before, but tonight the cosy bachelor pad felt different. Everything did a bit. She shook her head at her silliness.

'OK if I use the bathroom?'

'You know where it is. Make yourself at home.'

Evelyn let herself into the small room and rested her hands on the cool, solid ceramic of the sink. She looked up, and smiled at herself in the mirror as she let her hair down and fluffed it around her shoulders. It was a bit strange, having to make a plan to have "adult time" with the person you were dating – but everything had to be planned when you were a parent.

She looked down at herself, wishing she'd planned her outfit a little better. The stretch jeans that had been perfect for a Disney cinema date now seemed like an awkward barrier she could do without, but the idea of going out in just her underwear, or the silk and lace cami tucked into her overnight bag just felt wrong as well.

The butterflies in her stomach were turning aeronautic stunts worthy of the Red Arrows, and she struggled to catch her breath. It had been years – over a decade – since she'd been intimate with anyone other than her ex, and she was a *mother* for goodness' sake. The stretch marks had long ago faded to silvery lines that would forever tell the story of how she'd carried her daughter, but they were still there, and though she was slim, bearing children changed women's bodies. And she really, really hoped Jake wouldn't be disappointed.

Because as nervous as she was, she really did want to do this. She glanced around the room, hands on hips, while wondering what to do. She smiled when she spotted Jake's dark blue dressing gown hanging from the back of the door. Perfect.

It was the work of a few moments to remove her boots, peel off the jeans and the rest of her clothes, and snuggle into the fleecy fabric. Unsurprisingly, it smelled of Jake and the familiar fragrance both comforted and excited her, sending frissons of desire through her body. Jake was an amazing kind and generous man who made her toes curl when he kissed her, and tonight she was finally going to get to do a hell of a lot more than kiss him. And that thrilled her.

Buoyed by her newly found confidence, she tied the dressing gown loosely around her waist and sauntered back into the living room.

The look in his eyes told her she'd got it right.

'My dressing gown has never looked better.' His appreciative grin filled her with warmth and blasted away any last doubts she might have had.

'I find boobs help make most things look good.'

Jake burst out laughing. 'Come here and let me kiss you, you beautiful woman.'

She stepped into his arms and let her hands slide up his back, feeling his muscles flex and contract beneath her fingers as he tilted her head towards him. The heat from his lips was scorching as he kissed her deeply and pulled her more tightly against him, crushing her against his chest. She melted into him, turning liquid at the fire that raced through her veins, filling her with excitement and hunger.

When she pulled away to reach for his shirt and pull it out of his belt, needing to feel his bare skin, he actually growled. She laughed, burying her face in his chest.

'You think I'm funny, huh?' He looked at her, his eyes dangerous.

She tried to smother the giggle, but couldn't stop the happiness that bubbled from her lips.

Jake bent down and scooped her up, easily tossing her over his shoulder the way he had threatened, laughing along with her as he finally carried her to his bed.

Jake held her tightly against his chest, stroking her hair and back while he waited for his heart rate to return to something resembling normal. She shivered against him, and he dragged the covers from where they'd been kicked to the floor to wrap around them both.

Evelyn sighed and snuggled closer against him, resting her head on his shoulder as she threaded her leg back through his. She tilted her face towards him and landed a kiss on his neck that sent all his blood rushing south again, making him feel like a teenager.

'Well that was worth the wait,' she virtually purred against his skin, and the vibrations gave him shivers of delight as she nuzzled against him, placing soft kisses down his neck which sent his pulse – and other things – rocketing.

'If you keep doing that, you won't have to wait long to go again.'

She chuckled against his neck. 'Promises, promises.' She pushed herself up onto her elbow and leaned down to kiss him again. Her hair fell around his face and hers, surrounding him with her delicious scent as he pulled her tighter against himself. He welcomed her into his arms, meeting her kiss with one so full of passion that it stole his breath away. When she pulled back, he took advantage of the movement to roll her over, where her hair splayed out on his pillows.

'You really are incredibly beautiful, Evelyn.'

'I'm already naked in your bed, Jake. It's not like you need to chat me up.'

He pushed her hair to one side so he could rest his forearms on the pillow and cradle her face in his hands. 'I mean every. Single. Syllable.'

Even in the dim light her eyes sparkled at the compliment and he could see her lips curve in a smile that was half seductive and half pure happiness.

'I love this smile,' Jake confessed in the near darkness. 'And I'm going to do everything I possibly can to keep you wearing it, for as long as you'll let me.'

'Oh, Jake. You don't have to make me promises like that.'

'I know. But I want you to know your happiness matters to me.'

'Thank you.' Evelyn gave him a sweet kiss, before giving him a cheeky grin. 'So you want to keep me happy, do you?' Her hands wandered south and he had to bite back a groan.

'Absolutely.'

'And you'll do anything … I mean *anything* to please me?' Still her hands wandered lower, drawing lazy patterns across his skin that deliberately, teasingly didn't quite reach the place he most craved her touch.

He grinned down at her, captive between his arms. 'Oh, yes. Why? Did you have some special requests?'

'I might do.' She giggled as she lifted herself up to mould her body against his as she kissed him deeply, sending blinding desire crashing through him.

Evelyn groaned at the irritating chirruping that had dragged her from her delicious dream, and snuggled against the warmth by her side. When the chirruping started again, the warmth shifted beneath her and she forced her eyes open. Her sleeping fantasies met with the waking world and for once it was as perfect as her dreams. Nearly. It would be if not for the buzzing and bleeping phone.

'Any chance you can silence that?'

'I'm sorry. That ring tone is for the surgery. Go back to sleep.' He snatched the offensive device from the bedside table. 'Good morning, Badger's Hospital, Jake speaking. How can I help?'

Evelyn pulled the pillow over her head, refusing to acknowledge that the magical night was over. It was uncharacteristically selfish of her, but – just for a few moments – she wanted the world to bugger off and leave them both alone so she could pull him back into bed and spend a few more hours not worrying about being a mum, or a daughter, or a nurse, and could just enjoy being Evelyn for a bit.

'Hi.' Jake sounded confused, and she eased one corner of the pillow up to hear more clearly. 'How did you get this number? Really? That was very clever thinking.'

Evelyn put the pillow back under her head, where it belonged, and tried to smooth out her hair. It didn't sound like an emergency call that would have Jake snapping into super vet mode and rushing away. If anything, it sounded like a cheerful chat. She strained to make out what he was saying, but he'd obviously stepped further away to give her some quiet. Maybe their morning together wasn't over before it had begun.

When she heard Jake's footsteps, she rolled over to greet him, and smiled to see him wrapped in the same dressing gown she'd borrowed the night before. She was surprised when he offered her the phone. 'It's for you.'

She accepted it tentatively. 'Uh, hello?'

'Hi Mum! Did you have a good sleepover?'

Evelyn felt her cheeks starting to burn as Jake quietly left the room and closed the door behind him. 'Hi, sweetheart.' She tried to keep her voice steady. 'Yes I did, thank you. Are you and Nanny and Tilly all OK?'

'Of course we are. We're going to have breakfast, then go to the park, then come home and bake fairy cakes. You should bring Jake for some fairy cakes later. I'll even make some not pink ones for him because he's a boy. Do you think he would like that?'

'I'm sure he'd think that was very nice.' Evelyn glanced at the phone screen. 9.15? She couldn't remember the last time she'd slept so well or so late.

'You're not too grumpy, are you Mum?'

'No sweetheart, I'm not grumpy.'

'Are you sure? Because you do get grumpy in the morning, and you always say you don't sleep well when you're not in your bed.'

'I'm not grumpy. I promise.'

'Good. Because I love you even when you're grumpy because I know you'll stop being grumpy soon, but Jake probably doesn't know that.'

'I'm not grumpy, Summer.' Evelyn flopped back on the pillows, trying her hardest to not be "grumpy" with her precocious child. 'Summer, where's Nanny? Does she know you're using the phone?'

'She's making me breakfast. We're having dippy eggs.'

'That sounds very nice. But you know you're not supposed to use the phone without asking.' She couldn't believe her mother would have given the OK on this call without good reason.

'Unless it's really important,' Summer argued. 'And this was very important.'

'I think we need to have a little chat about what is really important and what isn't,' Evelyn started.

'Oooh, I've got to go. Nanny is calling. And you know my eggs have to be runny. Bye Mum!'

'All right sweetheart. Enjoy your dippy eggs. Be good for Nanny.' Evelyn realised she was talking to herself and Summer had already hung up.

The door opened and Jake backed into the room, holding two steaming cups.

'I am so, so sorry about that.' She sat up in bed, pulling the covers high, and shoved the pillow behind her back.

'For what?'

'For Summer calling and waking you up.'

'She woke you up too.' He laughed. 'Besides, I don't mind.' He sat on the edge of the bed and leaned forward to place a kiss on her lips.

Evelyn tried not to flinch away, horrified at the thought of how bad her morning breath would be.

'Here.' Jake handed her a steaming mug of coffee.

She took a small sip, and the hot sweetness made her smile. 'Perfect, thank you.'

'It should be. I followed the instructions.' He laughed again.

'I don't understand.' She took another sip of the coffee and sighed happily. Manna from heaven.

'Summer told me. She wanted to make sure I knew that if you were grumpy it was because you wanted your coffee, and you didn't mean it. I didn't want you to be grumpy, so I asked if she knew how you liked your coffee.'

'Oh no.' Evelyn covered her face with her free hand. 'I'm so embarrassed.'

'I actually think it's kind of adorable.' He wriggled on to the bed next to her, and held up his arm so she could snuggle back against him. 'Besides, dealing with the "grumps" is one of my specialist skills.'

'Oh really?'

'Not all of my patients are pleased to see me, you know.'

'Are you comparing me to a dog?' Evelyn kept her voice flat, not letting him know what she was thinking.

He studied her for a moment, before clearly deciding she was trying to wind him up. 'You know I treat cats too.

And wildlife. And sometimes the prettiest, most exotic of beautiful birds.'

'You treat farm animals too.'

'Yes, but I'm not stupid enough to compare you with a cow.' He placed a kiss on the end of her nose and the gesture was so sweet that Evelyn wanted to grab him and drag him back against her. Instead, she smiled and took another sip of her coffee.

'You're much more like an exotic bird. Or a cat maybe?'

'A cat?' She watched him carefully.

'Well, you do seem to purr when being petted right.'

'Flipping heck.' Evelyn choked on her coffee, spluttering in what she assumed must be the most unflattering manner ever. 'I can't believe you just said that.'

'I was trying to be cute, maybe even a little suave,' he complained, with such a pout that Evelyn laughed even harder.

'I'm sorry.' She pushed the cup into his hand, and doubled over with a fit of the giggles.

'I actually thought it was pretty good, as lines go.'

'You think that's good?'

'I think even if my lines are bad, I'm good at other things.'

'Oh, really?' Evelyn grinned teasingly. 'What type of other things might those be?'

'Well, there's this.' He put the cups on the bedside table and pulled her towards him and peppered kisses down her neck, making her shiver. 'And this.' He brushed his hands lightly over her ribs, sending goosepimples racing after his touch. 'And this.'

'Getting better, I suppose.'

He tangled his fingers in her hair and lifted her mouth to his. 'And then there's this.' He whispered the words against her lips, before capturing them in a kiss that cleared every thought from her mind except for him.

# *Chapter Nine*

Evelyn dropped her bag in the hall and helped Summer to wriggle out of her coat. 'Quick, quick, upstairs and change please. We're running late. Nanny said she's left your favourite dress on your bed.'

'It's not my fault.'

'I didn't say it was.' Evelyn chased her up the stairs. 'I know I was late picking you up, but my appointments ran late. And if we're quick, we can still both be ready before Jake gets here.' She wanted to do her best to be on time, even though she knew Jake wouldn't mind them being a little late, especially when it was because of work. His patients might be mostly feathered, furred or scaled, but he was used to the unexpected issues that sometimes cropped up when you were responsible for the health of another person – or critter!

'Are you two nearly ready yet?' Linda called up the stairs a few minutes later.

Summer thundered down the stairs, and Evelyn bit down the urge to yell at her to be more careful and remind her to slow down. She didn't want to start a squabble with her daughter just before a major village event – the first since she'd become a working member of the community.

She hadn't been to one of Broclington's Spring Flings – the kick-off event for the May bank holiday weekend and the start of summer – since she was a teenager, and she was a mixture of nerves and excitement. She'd spent almost all her free time with Jake, and while she'd obviously met people in the village, she hadn't spent much time socialising.

She shimmied out of her work uniform and rushed to the bathroom.

Less than ten minutes later, Summer had exhausted what little patience she had, and had thumped back up the stairs to hammer on the door.

'I'm coming, I'm coming.' Evelyn dashed back to the bedroom, wrapped in a fluffy towel.

'*Muuuuuum.*' Summer drew out the name into a grumbling moan. 'I don't want to be late to the party.'

Evelyn let her hair down and gave it a good brushing. The bun she'd had it coiled in while working had left it wavy, and quick work with a brush made it look a little neater. It would have to do. 'I'm moving as fast as I can. Can you grab my green dress from the wardrobe please?'

'The one with the slippery shiny material?'

'Yes. What do you think?'

'You look pretty in it. I think Jake will like it.'

Evelyn pursed her lips and turned to look at Summer. 'You know you shouldn't wear a dress just because you think a boy – or anyone else – will like it, right?'

'Of course.' Summer rolled her eyes like Evelyn had just announced that grass was green. 'You wear it to feel pretty. Like a princess.'

'Just checking.' Evelyn turned back to the mirror, feeling reassured.

'But I still think Jake will like it.' Summer grinned at her in the mirror. 'Can I have some make-up?'

'OK,' Evelyn relented. 'But only a little bit.' She flipped open an eyeshadow palette. 'What colour do you want?'

'Dunno.' Summer peered at the tiny colours. 'Which is the most sparkly like my dress?'

A few minutes later, as Evelyn was applying her own sparkly eyeshadow, and Summer was debating on which shoes best matched her mum's outfit, there was a knock at the door. Summer jumped on the bed to peer out of the window, ignoring Evelyn's complaint.

'It's Jake!' She raced out of the room. 'Hurry up, Mum!'

Evelyn shook her head and smiled at herself in the mirror. Sometimes, she thought Summer was as excited to see Jake as she was. As she carefully threaded her earrings into their holes, she sighed happily. She'd never expected to meet someone like Jake, and the fact he got on so well with Summer filled her with happiness.

She fidgeted with the forest green silk of her skirt and pulled a face. It was the dress her mum had suggested she wear, but she felt horribly overdressed. The last time she'd been to one of the spring dances she was sure she'd been in a far-too-short miniskirt and lacy vest top. Though she'd been a teenager heading off to university at the time.

She'd last worn the green silky number now swishing around her knees to a friend's wedding, and it seemed far too cocktail-like for a dance in the village hall. She knew that her mum, along with her WI friends, had taken charge of some of the events, but the step up from miniskirt and trainers to cocktail dress and heels seemed a step too far.

She headed down the stairs, concentrating on each step in her sparkly, best going-out heels. 'Mum, are you sure I'm not overdressed?'

Jake's admiring whistle made her look up. 'For what it's worth, I think you look perfect.'

'You like?' She turned a quick twirl on the large corner step.

'Very much.' His smile thrilled her. Despite what she'd told Summer about not dressing to impress Jake, she did love the admiration in his eyes.

'Thank you.'

'I'm going to be the luckiest man there tonight, with three beautiful ladies on my arm.'

'Three? Thanks for the compliment, but you've counted one too many.' Linda adjusted her yellow scarf, and pinned it with a sunflower broach. 'I'm being picked up by your mother. All the WI ladies are going together.'

'You're not coming with us, Nanny?' Summer stuck out her bottom lip.

'Nope. I'm going with my friends, but we'll see each other there.'

'Are you sure, Linda? My car is plenty big enough for three. And I'd be delighted to be your escort too.'

'Pah. You and your flattery.' She swotted his arm playfully. 'It's all arranged, and us WI girls are arriving a little later – we've still got some organising to do with the food.'

'If you're sure?'

'I am, thank you. Now you take care of my girls, and I'll see you all there later.'

Jake offered an arm each to Evelyn and Summer. 'Shall we go, then?'

After watching what her mum did, Summer copied Evelyn's action and slipped her hand into the crook of Jake's elbow and smiled up at him. Evelyn's heart melted a little bit more at the sight of her boyfriend – she still got a thrill from the word! – interacting so sweetly with her daughter.

Jake felt a flicker of pride as he walked into the decorated village hall, one hand resting protectively in the small of Evelyn's back and the other wrapped around Summer's young fingers.

'Wow.' Evelyn looked around the beautifully decorated room. Summery flowers and garlands had been woven in amongst the ancient beams, and were interspaced with small painted jars tied with ribbons that twinkled with candlelight. The huge doors at the end of the hall had been flung open into the courtyard that was covered by a marquee, strung with flowers. Swirled around a temporary dance floor were large tables, draped with crisp white linens and glistening with reflections from the army of glasses and cutlery that sat waiting on them. Posies of flowers that matched the ones hanging from beams sat in jam jars at the tables' centres, tied with ribbons that complemented the swathes tied around the chairs.

'It's so pretty!' Summer sounded awed.

'Wait until it gets dark,' Jake told her. 'They turn on all the fairy lights and it looks like something out of a story.'

'I can't wait!' Summer jumped up and down with excitement.

'I'm sure we'll find something to amuse you until then.' Jake grinned at the excited little girl. 'There's all the food, and music and dancing, a fashion show, and the silent auction and meat raffle.'

'What's a meat raffle?'

'Like a normal raffle, but you get prizes like sausages and bacon.'

'Yum! Try to win the bacon, Mum, then we can have cheesy bacon sandwiches!'

126

'Sounds good to me.' Jake turned to the lady selling tickets. 'Three strips please. And if you can make one of the tickets the bacon winner, all the better.'

The woman laughed and pulled off the tickets as Evelyn reached for her purse.

'Please, let me.' Jake had already produced his wallet to pay for their tickets.

'Thank you.' Evelyn gave him a smile that was worth a hundred raffle tickets.

'Thank you, Jake,' Summer agreed without being prompted. She pulled away, and for a moment Jake felt a little saddened. 'Can I go play with my school friends?'

'Of course you can.' Evelyn smiled. 'But promise not to leave the hall. And stay in sight please. OK?'

'OK. See you later Jake.'

'Have fun!' He grinned at her as he slipped his hand back round Evelyn's waist and snuggled her against his side.

'She really is amazing.' Evelyn watched as Summer darted off through the already busy room and started chatting animatedly with a group of children.

'She takes after her mum.' Jake gave her a squeeze as she rested her head briefly against his shoulder.

'So what do you want to do? Would you like a drink, or a quick wander first?'

'I think a wander. The last time I came to Spring Fling, it was nothing like this. I can't believe how much everything has changed. It's so beautiful and professional.' She leaned towards him and lowered her voice. 'I'm actually a bit surprised they still have a meat raffle alongside all this elegance - it's quite a juxtaposition.'

He laughed. 'There was talk about stopping it one year, but there was so much outcry from the community that they didn't dare. You know, I'm surprised you didn't know all of this, given your mum's on the organising committee, along with mine and half the Women's Institute.'

'She said they'd made a few changes, and that they raised more money than they used to, but I hadn't imagined anything like this.' She gestured around the whole room. 'It's beautiful. I'd worried about being overdressed, but now I think I might be underdressed.'

Jake stared at her in surprise. Had she really no idea how beautiful she looked? The silky green fabric followed the curves of her torso and swirled around her shoulders in some complicated, drapey design that seemed to barely cling to her creamy skin, before dropping into a skirt that swished around her lovely legs and whispered as she moved. The dark green emphasised the colour of her eyes, and made her skin look creamy and touchable and he already wanted to place kisses along the neckline of the dress and screw the silk up in his fingers. He swallowed hard. 'You look absolutely perfect.'

She blushed prettily, and reached out to smooth the lapels of his jacket. 'You look good too. I like you in a suit.' At that moment, with the sparkle in her eyes, he would have promised to wear a suit every day.

'It's a bit different than the usual scrubs or jeans vet uniform, I'll give you that.' He guided her around the edge of the hall, his hand against her lower back, letting her take in the room.

'So, what's the charity this year? Do you know? I'd like to have a look at the silent auction and probably put a bid or two on.'

'We've got two. Half of the funds raised will be going to the church to modernise their heating system, and the other half to help refurbish the women's refuge for the county.'

Evelyn looked at him, eyes wide. 'That seems … ambitious.'

'Not really. The Christmas Tree Dance last December raised nearly £30,000. There's no reason to think this Spring Fling won't be as successful.' He smiled as she gaped at him in amazement. 'Since the WI took over the organising, these events have been really popular – and successful. The tickets for this one sold out in three days flat.'

Evelyn gaped at him. 'Mum never said they were *that* successful. I had no idea. How did you get tickets?'

'I might know someone with connections.' He gave her a cheeky wink.

Evelyn lurked at the back of the hall by the silent auction lots, took another sip of the dangerously moreish spring punch and waved back to Summer. She was jumping around with a group of other children, bopping vaguely in time to the music, and it thrilled Evelyn to see her so easily fitting in. She turned her attention to Jake who was still talking at their table with his brother, and then surreptitiously added her initials and a very specific bid to one of the auction lots, and slipped it into the envelope. £775 was quite a lot for a check-up and weekend of dog sitting, but since Jake had already refused her attempts to pay him back for treating Tilly, she'd make a donation against his name and auction lot instead.

When she looked back up, Jake was watching her, and she waved and wound her way back through the crowd to their table.

'Hey.' He took her hand and placed a kiss on it as she sat down, then wrapped his fingers around hers in a gesture so easy and intimate that she had to hold back a sigh of contentment. 'Did you find anything good to bid on?'

'Maybe.' She certainly wasn't going to tell him.

A few moments later, Summer stomped back to the table and flung herself down in a seat, a dangerous pout on her face.

'What's wrong, sweetheart?' Evelyn reached across the table.

'Nothing.' Summer snapped in a tone that said everything, as she folded her arms, pulling away from the comfort Evelyn offered.

'Oh.' Jake looked at the dance floor, and Evelyn followed his gaze.

For a few moments she didn't understand, until she spotted Callum and Sarah, and her memories caught up with her. It seemed that, along with the meat raffle, the tradition of the "Daddy Daughter Dance" had been kept. 'Summer, I—' She stopped at Jake's hand resting on her arm.

'I think I can fix this,' he whispered, his breath warm against her cheek and ear. 'Can I try?'

'Please, yes.'

Jake stood, and cleared his throat before kneeling by Summer. 'I know I'm not your dad, but I'd like to think we're good friends. I'd be honoured if you would share this dance with me.'

'Really?' Summer looked at him, her eyes glowing with hope.

'Really.' He held out his hand, and Evelyn found herself holding her breath.

Summer pulled a face. 'I'm not very good at dancing. I never learned how.'

'That's OK.' Jake grinned. 'I'm not very good either. But maybe we can be not very good together.' He beckoned, encouraging her to wrap her fingers around his. 'What do you say? Will you be my Cinderella for a dance?'

Summer pursed her lips and regarded him seriously. 'I think Mum should be your Cinderella properly. But you can practice dancing with me first.'

'OK. You can be my teacher then. Shall we?'

'Yes please.' Summer took his hand and virtually skipped to the dance floor with him, leaving Evelyn to dab at her eyes with a napkin. Jake had known exactly how to make Summer feel better, and hadn't hesitated to lead her to the dance floor, bending himself like a pretzel to dance with her, and make her feel as special as she deserved. It was more than Charlie had ever done for Summer. And Evelyn was beyond grateful to Jake for it – she remembered her own Daddy Daughter Dances with such fondness, and she was glad Summer wasn't sat on the sidelines watching her friends. There weren't words enough to thank Jake for that.

She watched them as Jake whirled Summer around the floor, picking her up and spinning her every so often, which made her giggle. And treating her like the special princess she was. Evelyn whipped out her phone to take a couple of pictures of the two of them together, wanting to record the magical moment for prosperity. When she zoomed in on the two of them, she could see that Jake was smiling down at Summer.

When Summer bounded back, bubbling and full of excitement, Evelyn's eyes locked with Jake's. 'Thank you.' She mouthed the words over her daughter's head.

'Thank you.' Jake kissed Summer's hand, sending her into peels of giggles. 'That was a lovely dance,' he told her seriously.

'I think you should take Mum to dance now.'

'I think that's a lovely idea.' His eyes flicked up to Evelyn's again. 'What do you think? Would you like to try your luck on the dance floor with me?' He held his hand out to Evelyn.

'Don't worry, Mum. I'll stay here. You go be Cinderella.' Summer grinned at them both. 'And Nanny is here.' She pointed to where the WI were setting out the most delicious looking cakes, pastries and desserts.

'I'd love to.' Evelyn slipped her hand through his arm and they made their way to the dance floor. As soon as they cleared the table, Jake spun her around and pulled her into an embrace. His hand was burning through the silk of her dress as he ran his fingers down her back and fitted his palm into the small of her back. Her hand fitted snugly into his as he whirled her around the floor, swaying in time to the music.

When the music changed to a slower, more romantic pace, he pulled her closer until she was pressed tightly against him. With a contented sigh, she folded her arms around his neck and rested her head happily against his shoulder.

'Are you enjoying yourself?' Jake's voice was low and vibrated through her.

'Hmm, yes,' Evelyn purred against his neck, enjoying the simple pleasure of being so close to him, and everything feeling so comfortable and easy. The punch, Jake's masculine scent, the lights and music combined to make her feel slightly giddy and she relaxed into the feeling. Summer was happy, healthy and well; she was working again, and she was spinning around, safe and secure in the strong arms of a man who appeared to adore her – and Summer.

She twisted her fingers in the fabric of his shirt and rested her head against his shoulder again. 'Thank you.'

'For what?'

'For dancing with Summer. For dancing with me. For looking after Tilly, and making me feel like someone special.'

'You are someone very special.' He stroked a stray curl away from her cheek, and she tilted her face up to look at him. His lips came down warmly on hers, and his arms tightened around her waist as his tongue slipped between her lips. After a few moments, he pulled away and gave her a smile that made her insides melt.

'Just thank you for everything. I can't remember the last time I felt this happy.'

Jake looked down at Evelyn and happiness – and something far deeper than that – bubbled in his chest. He'd never felt like this about anyone before, and he was still amazed that someone as spectacular in every way as Evelyn would even give him the time of day – let alone everything she'd already happily given him.

'Do you think your mum might be persuaded to look after Summer a couple of weekends from now? There's an event in Birmingham that I'm going to, and I'd love to take you with me. We could make a weekend of it. And if I drove, and didn't have anything to drink, it would mean we weren't much more than an hour away, if you needed to get back for any reason. Not that I think you would.'

Evelyn slipped her hand up to cup his cheek. 'That is an incredibly sweet offer, and I love that you've stopped to think about how I'd feel leaving Summer too. I'm sure Mum will be happy to spend a weekend with her. And Summer will probably be thrilled too.'

'You don't even want to know what the event is?' he teased.

'I hadn't thought to ask,' Evelyn replied honestly. 'I just liked the idea of spending time with you.' She blushed slightly, endearing her to him all the more. 'But now I'm intrigued.'

'It's another fundraising event, to support taking art and classical dance into the wider, urban community.'

'Wow, that sounded almost rehearsed,' Evelyn teased gently.

'To be honest, it is a bit. I feel like I've been hearing about it all year. I'm supporting a friend. He's an Event Designer.'

'That's not a term I've heard before.'

'I think he's created the role himself, to be honest. It seems to be something between an event planner, a graphic designer and an interior decorator with all the stress and craziness that involves. From what he's told me, it's part gala, part show. I just did as I was told and paid for the tickets.'

'Just to support your friend. That's so sweet.'

'It'll be better with you by my side. And I'd like to introduce you to Nick. He's practically family – and you've already met all the others.'

'That sounds lovely. Let me know the dates, and I'll ask Mum,' she promised happily.

But it was a promise she'd never be able to keep, because a couple of days later, Summer collapsed at school.

# Chapter Ten

Evelyn pulled her car into the parking bay, and took a deep breath as she looked up at the looming green and white building of the hospital. The cheerful colours of the logo did nothing to lift her mood, and the glossy metal and glass did nothing to reassure her as she strode through the far too familiar corridors. Her uniform helped her fit in, even though she was only wearing it to reassure Summer – lying to her that she was just at work, while really she was far, far north, about to have a conversation that made her stomach churn and palms sweat. She'd told no one where she was going.

Evelyn had been running on automatic since the call from the school. Her blood had run cold as the teacher explained, in a shaking voice, that Summer had seemed fine most of the day, but seemed distracted and a little out of sorts after lunch, and then collapsed at carpet time.

Evelyn didn't feel like she'd warmed up since. If anything, the cold had sunken deeper with every blood test, scan and investigative procedure Summer had undergone. Some of them were with Tom Macpearson at the surgery, and others at the local hospital, with all the results carefully collated and sent to Mr Khan at the Great North.

When he'd called her yesterday to offer her an appointment – a week ahead of the one she'd originally made – she'd felt as if she'd frozen solid. Of course he hadn't said anything over the phone, and there was every chance the earlier appointment had just been the result of a cancellation or a scheduling change. But she'd known him for so long, and been through so much of Summer's treatment with him, that she thought she'd heard something in his voice – a hesitation or note of forced politeness perhaps – that had set her so far on edge she was barely hanging on.

The colourful cartoons and cheerful uniforms seemed too bright and too forced as she sat shivering in the waiting room, desperate for the appointment to start and at the same time dreading it. After what could have been minutes or hours, the consulting room door finally creaked open, and Evelyn felt her pulse start to stutter and race.

'Evelyn.' He'd called her by her first name since the very first appointment when she'd told him that with the amount of time they were likely to spend together, they should be on first name terms. 'Come on through.'

'How bad is it?' Manners be damned, she couldn't wait a second longer.

'It's not good.' He sighed hugely and took his glasses off. 'The original tumour is gone, but there's another one, this time in the spinal cord.'

'But she had blood work recently. It all came back fine,' Evelyn argued, knowing they must have made a mistake. Summer couldn't possibly have a tumour in her spine. 'You have to be wrong, Imran.'

'I'm sorry, Evelyn. I checked the scans myself. It's there.' He shook his head sadly. 'It must have been residual cells. We knew this was a risk when we couldn't complete the last carboplatin cycle.'

'So we'll go back to the cyclophosphamide, or the cisplatin.'

'Evelyn, we talked about this at the time.' He kept his voice calm and patient. 'The cisplatin is basically chemically the same as the carbo. The reaction could kill her outright. And we only started on the platinum therapies when the phosphomides stopped working.'

'But it's a different tumour.'

'We've looked at the biopsies and ran the sensitivity tests. It's in a different place, but it's the same cancer. I'm sorry, Evelyn.'

'So we'll operate.' Evelyn made her mind up. Summer would be fine. She'd been fine before.

'I've consulted with the surgeons to be sure. They don't believe they can safely operate.'

Evelyn shrugged. 'No operation is safe, I understand that.'

'Evelyn.' He leaned forward and took her hand in his, and Evelyn looked down, surprised at the gesture. 'I need you to hear me, even though I know you don't want to. The surgeons aren't happy to operate.'

'So we'll do radiotherapy to shrink the bastard thing and then take it out.'

'Evelyn.' The hand squeezed and she yanked her fingers away like she was being burned and jumped out of the seat as angry realisation hammered its way in.

'Don't say it, Imran. Please don't say it. After everything we've got her through, you can't say it.' She backed away from him, already heading for the door, but he beat her to it, and rested a hand against it, preventing her from escaping and running as far and as fast as she could.

'Evelyn, you know whether I say the words or not, that nothing changes. If words alone could change this, I'd have said them all years ago.'

'Please no.' Her words were choked by panic and tears, and blinding anger at the unfairness of the world. 'Please, don't say it.'

'I'm so sorry, Evelyn. I don't think there's anything else we can do.'

'You don't think?' She pounced on the word.

'Evelyn, I'm so sorry, there's nothing that will work. We discussed her case …'

'Summer. You've known her long enough to use her bloody name.' She refused to have her daughter reduced to a case number. Her beautiful, loving, sweet, and wonderful, happy daughter. 'And there's always trials.'

'She's not eligible for any of the ones I would have recommended. Her age is against her.'

'How can her age be against her? She's eight years old!'

'Which is old for neuroblastoma. You know that, Evelyn.'

'But there must be something,' she argued, begging.

'I personally led the discussion around Summer's diagnosis at the Expert Consultant's Board yesterday morning. Just before I called you. I'm sorry, Evelyn, but everyone was in agreement.' The words swirled around Evelyn, barely making sense. They sounded like something out of a nightmare. They *were* out of one of her nightmares – the kind that woke her up in a cold sweat at 3 a.m. Surely it was a nightmare that she would soon wake up from.

She closed her eyes tightly and waited to wake up.

'Evelyn?'

Suddenly it felt like there wasn't enough air in the room to fill her lungs, and she couldn't breathe. Her limbs turned to jelly and her knees gave way. Imran manhandled her into a seat before hitting a button on the wall, and pushed a bundle of tissues into her hands. But Evelyn was barely aware of where she was any more. All

139

she could focus on was the ice-cold terror that numbed her mind and froze her heart. She was going to lose Summer. Her baby was going to die. She fought to breathe and felt a hand on her back, pushing her lower as she started to feel like she was drowning and the room span around her.

'Just breathe, Evelyn. Just breathe.'

How could she when she knew what was coming? What the following months could bring. Months? The thought triggered a question. One she didn't want to ask, but didn't know how to avoid now it had occurred to her.

'How long?' She forced the words between teeth that had started to chatter.

'Evelyn, you know we can't ever put a timeline on things like this, they're too individual ...'

She managed to find the strength to look at him. 'You know damn well I'm a nurse. I'm in my freaking uniform. I want the medical answer please, not the patient one. *How long*?'

He bit his tongue, clearly not wanting to answer.

'Please, Imran.'

He sighed. 'It's completely individual, but ... I'd say longer than weeks, but not more than months. Maybe six to eight. Although radiotherapy wasn't enough to eradicate the cancer before, as a palliative treatment it could buy a little more time, and improve quality of life.'

'Eight months.' Evelyn folded in on herself again, collapsing against her own legs. Less than the amount of time she'd carried her beautiful baby before she'd even met her. Maybe thirty-five weeks. Her brain carried on, trying to work out how many days and hours that amounted to, but her mind couldn't grasp the figures. It didn't matter. However long it was, it wasn't even close

140

to long enough. If it had been eight years or even eight decades it still wouldn't have been long enough. Deep sobs wrenched themselves from her chest and agony poured down her face, blinding her as she cried. They weren't even out of May. Six to eight months meant Summer might not even live to see Christmas.

The door whooshed and thumped closed and something clattered on the table, but Evelyn wouldn't have noticed a herd of elephants if they'd paraded through the room in pink tutus.

A pair of gentle hands pulled her upright and wrapped her in a hug. 'I'm so, so, sorry.' Lizzie, who had been Summer's lead nurse and co-ordinator since they'd first been referred to the hospital. She'd been there for almost every bead, every treatment, every worry and question. It made sense that she'd be with Evelyn now.

There were soft murmurs and the door whooshed and thumped again, but Lizzie waited patiently, rubbing soothing circles on Evelyn's back while she sobbed and hiccupped helplessly. When she finally started to calm, she sat up and scrubbed her hands across her face. Lizzie pushed a cup of tea into her hands. It wasn't steaming any more, but it was still warm, and sweet, and something she could focus on to try and stop her hands from shaking so badly.

'I don't know what to do, Lizzie.'

'What do you want me to tell you?'

'The truth.' Evelyn took a breath and steeled herself for Lizzie's response.

'You do whatever you need to. You go home, you hug your daughter, you cry, and you work on making the best memories you can in what time you've got left. You make these last few months special. You make them matter.'

'But it's not long enough. And it's not fair. It's not supposed to be like this. No parent is supposed to watch their child die.'

'I know. It's the worst thing anyone can ever go through.' There were tears in her eyes as she placed her hand over one of Evelyn's. 'But I promise you, you won't go through this alone. Whatever happens, we'll make sure you have every bit of support you need.'

Evelyn nodded numbly, not knowing what to say. Not that there were any words which could help.


Jake yelped and snatched his hand away from the mixing bowl as his mum rapped the spoon against the back of his knuckles. 'I've told you before, stick your fingers in my cake mix at your peril.'

'I know, but your cake mix tastes so good I can't resist.'

Julie laughed at her son as she dolloped the mix into a baking tin and handed him the bowl to lick out, as if he was a kid again. 'It's not that I mind the early morning visit – you're always welcome here – but why are you here? It's rare to see you this early in the week. Is everything all right at the surgery?'

'Yeah, it's fine.' Jake sat down at the table, and placed the bowl in front of him after giving it a few cursory swipes.

'So what's going on? Is it something I can help with?' She placed two steaming mugs in front of them.

Jake fidgeted with his for a moment before taking a deep breath and letting the words tumble out in a rush.

'When do you think it's too early to tell someone that you love them?'

Julie froze, her cup in mid-air. 'I think your dad and I first said that to each other a month or so after we started seeing each other.'

'Only a month?'

His mum chuckled at the memory. 'Things were a little different when your father and I first started "stepping out". I take it this is about Linda's daughter?'

'Yes.'

'And you're sure about this? She's a lovely, lovely girl but with everything going on with her daughter, there's a lot to consider.'

'I know, Mum. And I'm sure. I think I love her. Them.' He sighed and ran his hands through his hair. 'I felt like my heart stopped for a few seconds when I heard Summer had passed out. I find myself thinking about them all the time. How I can make them smile, events I can plan, ways I can help. I see something that makes me smile, or sad, and I want to tell Evelyn. And when a client brought in a litter of puppies for their first inoculations, I actually asked if I could take a picture so I could tell Summer all about them because I knew she'd love to hear about them. I was going to take Evelyn to Nick's gala next week.'

'You're introducing her to Nick?' Julie understood how much that meant.

'Yes. I was. And I wanted to bring them to one of your Sunday lunches. I was going to ask you about it before everything happened.'

'Wow. You're really serious about her.'

'Them, Mum. I'm serious about them.'

'*Eeeee*!' She clapped her hands together gleefully. 'My baby's in love. I'm so pleased for you, darling.' She jumped up and gave him a huge hug. 'Now we just need to get that precious little girl better again, so everyone can have the happy ever after they deserve.'

Hours later, Evelyn sat at the roundabout into Broclington with her foot poised over the clutch. She couldn't remember huge swathes of the drive home and just followed the satnav, turning when it instructed her to turn, and stopping for a break when she needed to. She hadn't remembered feeling tired, or hungry, or thirsty or anything. There wasn't any feeling that could penetrate the desperate sadness and pain lodged in her chest. She didn't know how she was supposed to go home and face her mum or Summer because she had no idea how to tell them about her day, or the contents of the papers that Lizzie pressed into her hands as she'd left. How was she supposed to tell Summer she was going to die? The words didn't even make sense to her, so how could she possibly explain them to her daughter?

A set of headlights pulling up behind her, and the quick beep of the horn snapped her back into the present. Without thinking about it, she flicked on her indicator and turned left. A few minutes later, gravel crunched under her tyres as she pulled into the car park of Badger's Hospital. Despite the late hour, and the closed blinds, she could see the lights were still on. As she fired off a quick text to her mum, Jake opened the door and waved.

'Hey.' He placed a kiss on her cheek as she pushed past him into the surgery. 'I wasn't expecting to see you tonight. How are you? How's Summer?'

Evelyn bit her lip. Of course he would ask that. Perfect bloody gentleman that he was. But she'd had more than enough conversation that day, and couldn't bear the thought of trying to explain everything, so instead she pasted on a bright smile and turned to face him. 'Is there any chance we can just not talk?'

'What do you mean?' Confusion crossed his face as she stepped towards him. 'Are you all right?'

'I mean, can we just not talk?' She ignored the second question, and instead stood on tiptoes to kiss him. 'Just don't say anything. Please.' She kissed him again, pressing herself against his chest.

He kissed her back, gently at first, then with increasing intensity that matched her own growing hunger. This was what she needed – to feel whole and alive again even if it was just for a few moments. She dragged at his shirt, yanking it out from his jeans, needing to feel the warmth of his skin against hers. He hissed as her cold fingers hit his stomach and traced underneath his shirt upwards to his chest, and down again to wrestle with his jeans.

'Evelyn …' Her name was a groan.

'Hush.' She pressed another burning kiss against his lips and looped her leg over his thigh, shamelessly rubbing against the rough denim stretched taut across his muscles. She nipped at his lips and he grabbed her, throwing her back against the wall and caging her there.

He ran his teeth down her throat and she arched into him as he dragged her skirt up around her waist and ground his hips against hers.

'Is this what you want?' The question was growled from deep within his throat, making her squirm against him.

'Yes, please yes.' She shoved what was left of her dignity – and underwear – aside and moaned as he lifted her leg up over his forearm, and drove into her, his mouth fastened to hers in a possessive, burning kiss.

And finally the ice shattered, and warmth trickled back through Evelyn.

Afterwards, Jake held her on his lap, his arms wrapped tightly around her as she rested her head on his shoulder.

'That was … amazing.' He whispered the words into her hair, his mind reeling.

'Hmm.'

He took a deep breath, and hoped that he'd be able to get the words out in the right order. 'Listen, Evelyn, I've been thinking. I know things aren't going to be easy for a while, and that there are other things – and people – that you need to be focussing on, but I want to be part of your life. Of yours and Summer's lives. And if you'll let me, and if you think it would help, then I'd like to come to the hospital appointment with you next week. Even if I just drive you there, and wait outside, or come in and quietly take notes for you.'

He realised she was frozen still in his lap.

'Evelyn? What do you think?'

'They moved the appointment.' Her voice was strangely thick, and Jake's stomach clenched. 'It was today.'

'And?' When she didn't answer he tucked his fingers under her chin and forced her to look up at him. 'And?'

'And it's back.'

'And?' He needed to hear that Summer was going to be OK. That the life he was half-planning and desperately hoping for with her and Evelyn was going to happen.

'And nothing.' She started to shake in his arms. 'There's nothing they can do. There's no drug, no procedure, no trial. There's nothing. Oh God, there's nothing they can do. I'm going to lose my baby. Jake, I'm going to lose my baby.' She collapsed against him, drenching him with her tears but he didn't care – his own tears were already falling into her hair.

When eventually her tears subsided, he pulled her to her feet, and dried her face. He held her tightly against him, and whispered into her hair. 'I meant what I said, Evelyn, and I need you to know that it still stands – maybe now more than ever. I'm not going to let you go through this alone.'

He was surprised when she shoved him away, wriggling out from his arms, and visibly straightening her shoulders. 'I'm sorry Jake, but this is goodbye.'

'What?' Confusion slowed his response. 'But I want to be here for you. And for Summer.'

'For God's sake, you don't know what you're saying Jake! You don't know how hideous it's going to get!'

'I know I'm not willing to let you go through this alone.'

'Well it's not your choice,' she snapped back at him. 'I don't want to be going through this! My daughter is going to die. Soon. I don't have the headspace for dealing with anyone else. I'm sorry. Thank you for everything.'

'But—'

'But nothing. Please don't make this any harder. We've had fun, and now the fun is over.' She placed a kiss on his cheek then turned on her heel and walked away from him. She hesitated at the door, her hand resting on the handle. 'I'm sorry Jake, but goodbye.'

The door swung shut, leaving him watching as the darkness swallowed her up.

'But I love you.' The words bounced back at him from the cold, dark glass. 'I love you both.'

# Chapter Eleven

'Mum?'

'Yes, sweetheart.'

'Did Granddad go to heaven?'

'Of course he did.' Evelyn tried to keep a smile on her face, though she could feel it starting to quiver.

'Will I go to heaven?'

'One hundred, million percent,' Evelyn told her fiercely.

'How do you know?' The innocence with which Summer asked the question broke what was left of Evelyn's heart into even more pieces.

'Because all good little girls go to heaven, and you're one of the best.'

'At least Granddad will be there to look after me. Do you think he'll remember me?'

'I think he'll be waiting to give you the biggest hug ever.' Evelyn snuggled Summer's blankets more cosily around her, and carefully patted a section flat for Tilly, who watched patiently from her basket in the corner of the room.

'Ready for your night night poem?'

'One more question?' Summer begged.

As if Evelyn could refuse her anything now. 'Of course.'

'Does dying hurt?'

Oh God, please give me strength. Evelyn bit the inside of her lip so hard that she tasted blood. She'd had to answer a lot of difficult questions in the days since her visit to the hospital, but this was one of the worst. 'I will make sure it doesn't. I promise you that.'

Summer nodded, reassured. 'Poem now please.'

'OK, sweetheart.' Evelyn patted the bed, needing to buy herself some time to find some level of control. 'Tilly, come on. Up!'

'All I need to do right now is snuggle in my bed …' Summer prompted her.

'And rest your sleepy head, and close your sleepy eyes …'

'And chase dreams across the skies.' Summer grinned. 'Night night, Mum.'

'Night night, Summer. Night night, Tilly.'

Evelyn made it halfway down the stairs before she was blinded by tears and her knees folded under her. She sat, in the middle of the staircase, rocking back and forth while biting into her own wrist to make sure the sobs didn't escape and upset Summer. Or her mum.

'Come here, my love.' Linda had opened the living room door silently, and was standing in the hall, her arms held open.

Evelyn fell into them, sobbing silently against her mother's shoulder.

'I know, love, I know.' She soothed her in whispers, and gently led her back into the living room.

'I don't think I'm strong enough to do this,' Evelyn admitted, when the latest bout of tears subsided. She winced as she dried her eyes – she'd cried so much over the last few days that the skin around her eyes was red raw, and her nose seemed to be constantly blocked. Her throat hurt, and her heart ached, and it was only going to get worse. She realised now that in a few months she would look back on these awful days with longing, because at least she was still a mother. In a few months' time she would be … she didn't even know what she would be. Probably dead too, because she had no idea how she would keep breathing after she lost her baby.

'We'll find the strength somehow, between us,' Linda promised. 'We have to.'

'I know I have to.' Evelyn rested her head against her mum's shoulder. 'I just don't know how.'

'I know you're not going to want to think about this, but have you managed to get hold of Charlie yet?'

'No.' Evelyn rolled her eyes. 'The bastard's changed his number. None of his social media accounts are active, and his emails are bouncing back. As far as I'm concerned, he's dropped off the face of the planet.'

'What about his work?'

Evelyn shook her head. 'I've left messages. I've tried everything I can think of. We might not be together any more, but he still needs to know what's going on. And have a chance to see Summer.'

'So what are you going to do?'

'I've written to him. Left messages with our mutual friends. Asked the hospital to call him. I even tried to call his parents, and had to leave a message asking them to call me. It's up to him to contact me now.' She wiped a tear from her cheek. 'Summer deserves so much better than him. She deserves better than all of this.'

'You both do, love.' Linda placed a kiss on her forehead. 'You both do.'


Jake waited until he saw Evelyn's car pull out of the driveway, and then gave it a few more minutes before knocking on the door.

'Hello Jake.' Linda looked exhausted with deep, dark circles under her eyes. 'I'm afraid you've just missed my girls.'

'I know. I waited until I was sure they'd left,' he admitted cautiously. He didn't want to lie to Linda, but he needed her on side. 'Can I come in? Please, Linda. I promise I won't take up too much of your time.'

Linda ushered him in the door. 'Can I offer you a drink?'

'That would be nice, but maybe in a minute?' He took a deep breath. 'I need to ask a favour of you, but you can't tell Evelyn or Summer about it. In fact, I'd prefer it if you didn't even mention I'd been here.'

'I don't know.' Linda shook her head.

'Please. I wouldn't ask if it wasn't important.'

'Why don't you tell me what it is first, and then I'll decide.'

'That's fair,' Jake agreed eagerly. At least she hadn't said no. Yet. 'I know that Evelyn keeps copies of Summer's medical records here. I want to see them. Please.'

'With all due respect, Jake. Summer's doctors are some of the best. What do you, as a country vet, think you'll see that's different?'

'I don't know. I don't expect to find anything. But she's pushed me away, Linda.' He gulped in another breath before confessing. 'I've fallen in love with your daughter – and granddaughter – and she's pushed me away. I feel like I need to do something, even if it's just understanding everything better. Please, Linda.'

She watched him for long moments while his heart hammered against his ribcage. Eventually she sighed. 'Do you want tea or coffee? There's carrot cake too. Summer and I made it yesterday, so it's probably still good.'

'I'd love some. And coffee would be great, but only if you're making some yourself.'

'Tell you what, I'll go and get the files for you, and you can put the kettle on. You know your way around well enough. Make yourself comfortable in the kitchen.'

'Thank you.' Jake caught her hand and gave it a squeeze, and for long moments, their eyes met and they shared their joint pain at what the coming months were predicted to bring.

Within a few minutes, Jake was sat at the table surrounded by papers, medical files, treatment records, letters and scan print outs. He pulled out a notepad to jot down the key points, and took pictures of the most important things on his phone.

Evelyn locked the door behind her, dropped her bag and nurse's kit on the desk and collapsed in the chair. Her head ached and was muzzy, and even her hair seemed to be painful. She yanked out the ties holding it off her face and massaged her head, before grimacing. She'd meant to wash her hair that morning, but had overslept. She went to bed every night exhausted and desperate to sleep, but as soon as her head hit the pillow, her mind started to race and she felt like she'd seen every single hour in the night again. When she eventually drifted into a level of unconsciousness that resembled sleep, she was plagued by nightmares that she fought to wake herself from.

Her next appointment wasn't for a few minutes, so she put her head down on the desk.

She jerked awake what felt like a few seconds later as someone hammered at the door. 'Evelyn, are you all right? Someone get the key.'

She rubbed her eyes tiredly, then cursed at the black smears her mascara left on her hands. She'd put it on this morning in an attempt to disguise the red puffiness of her eyes, and her lack of sleep. She forced herself upright, limped to the door, and fumbled with the lock.

'Sorry, I must have dozed off.'

'All right, enough.' Julie took one look at her and snapped into management mode. 'Tom, can you take Evelyn's next patient? It's just a wound check and dressing change. Callum had admin time this afternoon, so can take most of the rest. You'll have to figure the rest out. Evelyn and I are going to the staff room.'

'I'm fine,' she tried to argue. 'You don't need to fuss.'

'I'm sorry, dear, but you're really not.' Julie wrapped an arm around her shoulders and guided her to the small room that served as kitchen, break and meeting room all in one. 'I think it's past time we had a chat, don't you?'

'I guess.'

'No guess about it.' She gave her a sharp look as Evelyn's stomach growled. 'When was the last time you ate something? What did you have for lunch?'

Evelyn yawned as she tried to remember. 'I'm not sure.'

'Breakfast then?' She tutted at Evelyn's shrug, and rummaged in the cupboard. 'Beans on toast it is then.'

'I'm not really that hungry.' Julie ignored her and dropped bread into the toaster, before dumping sugar into the tea she was making.

'I understand that. I imagine your stomach has been in knots for days. Am I right?'

Evelyn nodded tiredly.

'And you're probably not sleeping. You probably collapse in your bed, toss and turn for hours, wander around the house pointlessly, then finally fall asleep in the early hours of the morning, only to have nightmares that

154

shake you awake before you've had a moment of real rest.'

'How did you know?'

'I'm not a doctor or nurse, but I've been in this job long enough to recognise grief-induced exhaustion. I know that you and Jake parted on less than good terms, and that you're making mistakes in your notes, and falling asleep at your desk.'

'I'm sorry. You must hate me.'

'Oh, not at all Evelyn. But I am letting you go.'

Panic filled her. She needed this job. It was the only thing she had left that was normal and healthy. And she needed to have something good left in her life to focus on … afterwards. 'But—'

'No buts my girl.' Julie held up her hand. 'I'm sending you home. At least temporarily. I know you wanted to keep working for as long as possible, but I think you've reached your limit. Consider it sick leave, because if you carry on like this you will make yourself ill. Tom, Callum, me and the rest of the team will be with you every step of the way – and if you want to come back to work with us at some point in the future, there will be a role for you. I promise you that. But right now, you need to go home and look after yourself and your daughter.'

'I don't know how to,' Evelyn admitted as she took a bite of the toast, which was much, much tastier than she had expected.

'Yes you do,' Julie soothed her. 'You've been her mum for her whole life, and you're a brilliant one. You don't even have to think about it, you just do it. Without thought, or worry, or anything but love. Everything else will just happen as it's going to happen.'

Evelyn's shoulders started to shake as tears streaked through her mascara to leave dirty trails of pain on her cheeks. 'I'm sorry.'

'No, I'm the one who's sorry.' Julie wrapped her arms around her. 'I'm sorry you're going through this. I'm sorry there's so little we can do to help. I'm sorry for Linda, but most of all I'm sorry for Summer and you. No parent should ever have to face this.' She rocked Evelyn back and forth, stroking her back while she cried against the unnatural pain that coloured her future. 'It's all right, I'm here. You just cry for as long as you need. I've got you.'

And true to her word, Julie sat there patiently, letting Evelyn cry until she had no tears left.

'Dad?' Jake slammed the front door, barely bothering to clean his shoes before bursting into the living room. 'Dad, are you here?'

'He's upstairs. What's going on?' Julie looked up from her book. 'Is everything all right?' She struggled to stand up from her curled-up position on the sofa.

'I think it might be.' He gave her a hopeful smile. 'But I need Dad.'

'What's all this hollering about?' Tom's heavy footsteps sounded on the stairs and Jake steeled himself for the argument he was anticipating. 'Jake, it's late. Is everything OK?'

'I need to talk to you. About Summer. And I don't want to hear a word about patient confidentiality or anything like that.'

'Jake, you know I can't discuss any patient with you.'

'Dad, please.' Jake wasn't above begging. 'It's more important than I know how to explain. I'm asking you as my dad. Please, please help me.'

'You're asking me to break the law, jeopardise my professional standing, and go against the code of conduct I've worked to for decades.' His face was stern and unmovable.

'Tom, I think we can make an exception. Just this once,' his mother interceded and Jake held his breath, hoping it would be enough. 'He's in love with Evelyn. And Summer. Tom, tell him what he needs to know.'

Tom looked at his wife in shock. 'Julie, you know the rules.'

'You know that I do, and you know that both Jake and I understand what we're asking. But if you turn your son away now, when he needs your help more than ever, you'll regret it for years.'

Tom nodded slowly, his mouth a thin line. He wasn't happy, but was obviously going to listen to his wife.

'Thank you, my darling.' Julie placed a kiss on his cheek. 'I'll get a computer and pull up Summer's notes, and then I'm putting the kettle on. I'm getting the impression this could be a late night.'

'So you really love her?' His dad watched him closely.

'Yes.' As much as he wanted to tell Evelyn before anyone else, he knew his dad would only accept his total, unfiltered honesty at this point.

'OK. What is it you want to know?'

'I've been looking at some trials. Alternative treatments that I think might help Summer.'

'How much do you know about her case?'

'Pretty much everything. Or at least everything that's on paper. I've read her records. More than once,' Jake admitted.

'I thought Evelyn and you weren't seeing each other any more.'

'She wants to concentrate on Summer, and doesn't want to put me through what the next months might bring.'

'Jake.' He rested his hand over his son's. 'If you've really read all the records, you know there's no might or maybe about this.'

'I've been doing some research too.' Jake ignored the comment and pulled a sheath of papers and his laptop out of his bag. 'There are some trials that I think look really promising.'

'I did put feelers out when I first heard the prognosis. I'm happy to take a look Jake, but I'll be amazed if you've found something I, and Mr Khan, missed.'

'I know this is your field, Dad. And I appreciate you looking at these. I'm just a vet. I've probably misunderstood something, but I have to know for sure.'

'You're a good medic, son. I've no doubt you can understand these documents as well as me. The only difference between us is your patients' bites really are worse than their barks.' He rested his hand briefly on Jake's shoulders. 'Show me your top contenders.'

Jake shuffled through the papers. 'These are the ones that I think are most promising.'

He waited, trying to be patient, while his dad flicked through the papers, hmm-ing and aha-ing every so often. Every time he made a noise, or nodded, or scribbled a note, Jake wanted to snatch the papers back to see what it was that he was interested in. And every time his dad frowned, or shook his head, his heart fell a little further. When he discarded the trial Jake had pinned the most of his hopes on, he felt like crying.

'Jake, can you come and help me in the kitchen please?'

'Mum, can it wait? We're a bit busy.'

'No love, it can't. Shift please.'

He grumbled as he left the dining table and the cosiness of the living room to see what it was she wanted, and was surprised to see her calmly sitting at the kitchen table, apparently not needing any help at all.

'What's up, Mum?'

'Your blood pressure, to look at you.' She indicated the stool opposite her. 'I know you're desperate to find an answer, but you need to prepare yourself to accept that there probably isn't one.'

'You think I don't know that?'

'I'm worried you might have convinced yourself otherwise. But I do know that you peering over your father's shoulder, huffing and puffing and flinching every other second is only going to make things worse.' She held her hand out to Jake, and pulled him towards her. 'Your dad's going to do his best. Give him time to read and concentrate.'

'I know.' Jake struggled to keep his jaw from clenching.

'Do you really think you might have found something?'

'Maybe. I hope so.'

'I do too.' Julie smiled reassuringly. 'I really do. And you're a good medic, Jake. If you think you've found something, I'm sure you're right.'

'Thanks Mum. I really needed to hear that.'

'Anytime, love. Anytime. Shall we actually put the kettle on now?'

After more than an hour, Tom strode into the kitchen and dropped Jake's papers on the breakfast bar. He pushed his glasses onto the top of his head and rubbed his nose tiredly. 'Any chance of another cuppa, darling?'

'Of course.' She stood to put the kettle on.

'Well? What do you think?' Jake couldn't wait a second longer.

'There's some good research here, and some interesting trials, but …' He ran his hands through what was left of his hair, mirroring the gesture Jake had long ago picked up from him.

'But what?' Jake's voice was clipped and tense.

'I'm sorry, son. I'm just not seeing what you think you are.'

'You're saying there's nothing?'

'I don't think so.' He shook his head sadly.

'What about the German study?'

'It was interesting, and I think we're only going to see an increase in the use of immunotherapies, but the chemotherapy they are preferencing is similar in make-up to the treatments Summer has reacted to badly in the past. The doses necessary to achieve chemical remission before the immunotherapy can be used, in Summer's case, would be very high. As she's already had failed remission, it would have to be consecutive sequential administration, not contiguous.'

'So the treatment would probably be dangerous.'

'Almost definitely.' He accepted the steaming mug from his wife with a smile. 'Sadly, I don't think they would accept her. In fact, I'm sure of it. She's too late stage.'

'I liked the MRNA one in New York, but I think the roll-out will be too late to help Summer,' Jake mused aloud.

'Agreed.' Tom shook his head sadly. 'But for other children – and adults – in the future, it's potentially very exciting.

'Instead of focussing on the ones that won't work, why don't you tell us which one you thought was most promising, and you and your dad can discuss it in more detail,' Julie suggested.

'The Massachusetts one,' Jake replied, after a few moments of thought. 'If I understood it right, the chemo when paired with the monoclonal antibody seemed to incite less negative reactions, even among patients that had experienced them before. And I don't think Summer's had that type of chemo either – though I'm trying to translate my animal knowledge into human, and American brands into British generic familial.'

'I doubt she would have been given it before. It's a very harsh drug, especially for someone so young, and she's already had circulatory issues.' Tom flipped through Summer's red treatment record booklets. 'The chemo in question – it can do a lot of damage to the point of leaking out of veins and causing damage as it's administered. I doubt it would be possible to give it in high enough doses safely to make any difference.' He closed the book. 'But you're right, she's not been tried on it.'

'What really interested me with that one is that they've already taken patients with recurrent illness, and the combination of their prototype drugs mean they've been able to reduce the inductive chemotherapy doses.

And if she's not had that drug before, it could work, couldn't it?'

'In theory, yes.' Tom's response relieved some of the knot in Jake's stomach.

'So if they lowered the chemo dose alongside the other meds, that would make it safer? Maybe safe enough?'

'In theory.' Tom nodded slowly.

'Have you seen the phase 3 trial results? Even with patients with high risk, stage 4 cancer they're reporting a two-year event-free survival rate above eighty per cent.'

'Really? I don't remember seeing that.' Tom started flicking through pages at a rate that was far too slow for Jake's liking.

'Give them here.' He just about managed to not snatch the papers from his dad, but only just. He skimmed through the papers as fast as he could, looking for the paragraphs he needed.

'Here. 86.4 per cent were event-free two years after they started the trial.'

'That is very, very promising.'

'And you think this drug could work for Summer?'

Tom sighed. 'I'm not an oncologist, Jake.'

'No, but you're very good, and you've looked at her case and the study. I'm asking what you think, Dad.'

'I think I would like to put in a call to Summer's oncologist.' He took the papers back. 'I don't know how this could have been missed …' He continued flicking before freezing over one page. 'Oh.'

'What, what's the matter?'

'Jake, I don't know how to tell you this, but this can't help Summer.'

'But you just said the drugs might work. What have you seen differently?'

'Here.' He circled a section with his finger. 'She's not eligible. She's too old. I'm sorry. That's why I hadn't seen the results on this one. I stopped reading after the dosing mechanisms when I saw the eligibility criteria. I'm so sorry.'

'That's all right.' Jake grinned. 'You think it might work. That's all I needed to know.'

'She's still not eligible. Their cut off is sixty months old. Five years.'

'Why are you smiling, love?' Julie rested her hand on his shoulder, concern etched over her face.'

'I included that one because it's gone into phase 4 trials. It's received the initial approval for use,' Jake explained, his heart soaring with hope.

'And is that good for Summer?' Julie asked quietly.

'It is when one of the lead consultants on the trial has a private practice in Boston where he's accepting patients. Without an upper age limit.'

'Jake …' His father's tone was cautious, gentle. 'We don't know for sure this would help her …'

'No, but you said you liked the chances of it enough to call her oncologist.'

'You did say that, darling,' Julie inputted.

'I did. And I'm still happy to do that. But Jake, this is an experimental treatment – albeit phase 4 – in America. It would cost a fortune.'

'We know what Evelyn earns,' Julie added. 'It would be cruel to dangle an unaffordable hope before her.'

'I'm not going to hurt Evelyn, or Summer,' Jake assured them both, horrified at the thought. Even though Evelyn had cut him from their lives, he understood that she'd done it out of love, trying to be kind and protect him from being hurt. She'd just been too late. 'Money can be found. There's online fundraising and all sorts.'

'He's not wrong,' Julie agreed. 'We've both seen stories in the news where it's been done. How expensive do you think this could be?'

'I'd have to look into it in more detail, and contact the Boston clinic … but I'd imagine it could easily run to two or three hundred thousand.' Tom placed his glasses on the worktop.

'That's what I was thinking.' Jake nodded. 'So we have a plan. You'll call Summer's oncologist, and I'll start trying to work out how we can raise that much money. And when you've been told yes, and when I've figured it out, then I can tell Evelyn.' He smiled broadly, a massive weight lifted from his shoulders. His research and digging had been a tiny flicker of light against darkness that was too heavy for him to bear, and now that flicker was becoming stronger and brighter. He might really have found something that could help Summer.

'If, Jake. The word is *if*.'

'It will be a yes. I'm sure of it.'

'You know what, love?' Julie wrapped her arms around her son's shoulders. 'I believe you're right.'

Tom shook his head. 'You can't know that, darling. Neither of you can.'

Jake grinned back at his dad. 'I've just got a feeling it will all be all right.'

'From your lips to angels' ears.'

# Chapter Twelve

'Oh, I forgot to tell you, Evelyn, I made an appointment for Tilly at the vet.' Linda yawned and rubbed her back as she limped across the kitchen to the kettle. 'She's been itching at her tail a lot, and doing that thing where dogs drag their botties on the floor. I think she might have worms or something.'

Evelyn cast a sharp look at the little dog who was happily chewing on a toy, showing no signs of distress. 'I haven't noticed anything.'

'You've probably just been too busy. I was going to take her myself, but my back is so sore that I'm worried she might pull at the lead and make it worse.'

'What's wrong with your back?'

'I'm sure I told you yesterday. I think I've pulled a muscle or something.'

'Do you want me to take a look?'

'No, it's fine, I've already called the surgery.'

Evelyn pursed her lips together. She couldn't remember her mother complaining about being in pain yesterday, and hadn't noticed her struggling. But then again, she hadn't spotted Tilly's issue either. 'When's Tilly's appointment?'

'In an hour.'

'Mum, that's when I'm supposed to be picking Summer up from school.'

'I know, but I thought it was important and it was the only appointment left. And Tilly does sleep on Summer's bed.' Linda continued to squeeze the teabag against the side of the mug, not meeting Evelyn's eyes.

'You're right, of course.'

'I can pick Summer up from school. I enjoy seeing how excited she is, and hearing about her day anyway.'

'Me too,' Evelyn admitted, while silently wondering how much longer Summer would be able to attend school. Her immediate reaction had been to pull her out, but Summer had been so distraught at the thought of leaving all her new friends, that instead she'd worked with Dr Tom and the teachers to let her stay for a few days a week, letting her have some normality for as long as possible. Even though Evelyn really wanted to keep her at home, wrapped in blankets, feeding her chicken soup – as if it would do any good. Her heart ached with loss every time she left Summer at the school door, knowing it was a few less hours she would have with her baby, but it was what Summer had wanted. So far the radiotherapy and steroids had let Summer feel relatively well, but Evelyn doubted she'd be going back for the summer term. And the thought was agonising.

'Hadn't you better get ready?'

'What do you mean?'

'Well, you've not worn make-up for ages, those jeans have seen better days, and running a brush through your hair wouldn't hurt.'

'Mum, it's an appointment at the vet.'

'With Jake.'

'And?' Evelyn was getting a bit fed up of looking at her mum's back. 'We're not getting back together, Mum. And excuse me for not caring what I look like right now. I've got one or two other things on my mind that are a little bit more important!'

'Suit yourself.' Her mum shrugged.

Evelyn looked down at herself, took in the faded, baggy jeans and fleece and pulled a face. Maybe her mum did have a point. It wouldn't hurt to spend more than ten seconds grabbing whatever she saw first in the cupboard.

And if she looked like she was doing fine, maybe less people would give her the sympathetic, sad, well-meaning glances that she'd come to hate so much. 'Fine! Maybe you're right.'

'If you think so, darling.' Linda gave her a too bright smile, and for a moment Evelyn felt a twinge of something resembling suspicion.

'You do know I'm not getting back together with Jake, don't you? It wouldn't be fair on him. I need to focus on Summer.'

'Of course you do.'

'OK. Just checking.' She reached for her mug of tea, which was a lot darker than she'd usually drink it. 'I guess I'll take this upstairs and get changed. Thanks, Mum.'


Jake tried not to pace the floor, and resisted the urge to check the clock or peer out of the window again. Linda had texted to warn him that Evelyn was on her way, but not especially happy.

'Mate, you're going to wear a hole in the floor.' Nick grinned at him over his coffee.

'Can't help it.' Jake was overwhelmed with anxiety that fought against hope. He didn't know how he was supposed to act around Evelyn when she got here. He was still in love with her – if anything the absence she'd enforced had proven the old adage true and he was crazier about her than ever. He wanted to see her, to wrap his arms around her and make everything go back to the way it had been before Evelyn's last visit to the surgery. Or better, to how it was before Summer collapsed. He couldn't promise everything would be OK, but with the papers laid out on the desk, and Nick's expertise, he felt like it could be a possibility.

'You're making me nervous now,' Nick complained.

'Sorry, mate.' Jake forced himself to sit down, and immediately started tapping the arm of the sofa and drumming his feet on the floor.

'I don't think you were this nervous before you signed the mortgage on this place.' Nick sat opposite him.

'That was just money.'

'A helluva lot of money.'

Jake shrugged.

'You really do love her, don't you?'

'Them,' Jake corrected. 'I love them.' He took a deep breath. 'I think Evelyn might be the one.'

'Wow, mate. I'm really happy for you. Now all you've got to do is pull off this crazy scheme.'

'It is crazy, isn't it?'

'Yup. But my best ideas usually are.' Nick grinned. 'And what we need to achieve here, and the time frame you have, it might just be crazy enough.'

'You really think so?'

'Mate, I know so.'

They both jumped at the sound of the buzzer.

Jake took a deep breath before answering it. 'Hello?' His voice came out slightly hoarse with nerves, and he hoped the intercom system hid it.

'It's Evelyn.' Her voice sounded like music to his ears. 'I thought I had an appointment with Tilly.'

'I'm in my flat. Come right up.' He closed the line before she had a chance to complain, then glanced at Nick. 'Kitchen for you.'

'I dunno,' he teased. 'You ring me up, drag me over here, dump a huge, urgent project in my lap, call in a bro-favour, use up my annual leave and now you want to shove me in the kitchen?'

'Just while I explain things.' He gave his best mate a shove. 'Please?'

'All right, all right. But only 'cause you're an honorary bro. I'll put the kettle on or something. But I warn you, anything tasty looking might get eaten.'

'Whatever. Help yourself. Just go.' He closed the door behind Nick as Evelyn's soft knock sounded at the door. He smoothed his shirt down and his hair back, and opened the door. 'Hi.'

'Thanks for this.' Evelyn gave him a tight smile, her mind clearly elsewhere. And Jake knew exactly where that was, and who it was with.

'Never a problem. Take a seat.' He had to fight the temptation to pull her into his arms.

'I'm not staying, Jake.' The sadness in her eyes filled him with grief, and he had to remind himself why she was here. Even though she didn't know yet. 'I just want to get Tilly sorted.'

'Oh, she's fine.' Jake shrugged.

'Mum said she's been gnawing at her tail and dragging herself along the carpets. She thinks she has worms.'

'She doesn't,' Jake replied.

'And you know that without even looking at her?' Evelyn snapped. 'Sorry, I …'

'It's fine. Please sit down Evelyn. Just for a minute. I need to explain something.'

'Jake, there's nothing to explain.'

'Yes there is. Now will you please bloody well sit down and let me talk?' He bit his tongue, his nerves getting the better of him. Shocked, Evelyn sat down on the sofa. 'I'm sorry, but I know Tilly's fine because she's just the excuse for getting you here. Your mum thought it would work. She was right.'

'You're conspiring against me with my *mother*?' Evelyn's eyes flashed dangerously.

'Yes. But it's for a good cause.'

'Oh really?'

'It's for Summer.' Jake sat beside her and handed her the papers from the coffee table. 'Please don't be mad at me. Or actually, do. I'd rather you were angry with me than your mother. She let me see Summer's notes, but only because I begged and thought I could help somehow, and I know I shouldn't have made my dad talk to me about Summer without your permission, but I didn't want to get your hopes up if there was nothing here because that wouldn't have been fair to you or Summer and—'

'Is there?' Evelyn interrupted his nervous waffle. 'Is there something here?' The hope in her voice was almost painful to hear.

'Yes. We think so. Me, Dad, your mum, Mr Khan and Mr Hazelmire.'

'Who is Hazelmire?' Evelyn shook her head. 'It doesn't matter. What do you think you've found?'

'Hazelmire is a consultant oncologist in Boston. And he's the one who thinks he can help Summer.'

'Are you sure about this?' Her hands were shaking, and he gently reached out and took them in his, praying that she wouldn't pull away.

'I wouldn't be sitting here telling you if I wasn't. Dad looked at everything, and called Mr Kahn's team. He called the American team, and they've reviewed Summer's case. They believe they can help her.' He handed her the file. 'It's all in here.'

Her hands were shaking, making the papers rustle as she tried to read them. 'I can't do this. I'm shaking too hard to read it.'

'It's OK.' Jake nodded, understanding. 'It's a new treatment regime. One that uses new drugs and technology alongside existing ones.'

'So it's a trial?'

Jake nodded. 'Yes, but the results are really promising.'

'How promising?' Evelyn held her breath.

'They've had patients with high risk, stage 4 neuroblastomas. And even for them, they're reporting good outcomes. Their overall results are standing at a two-year, event-free survival rate of eighty-six per cent.'

'Eighty-six per cent?' Her breathing was fast and shallow, her eyes filling with tears.

'86.4 per cent to be precise. And it's just gone to phase 4 trials.'

'Phase 4?' Evelyn's brow furrowed as she stared at him. 'But if it's so well established, why didn't Summer's oncology team know about it? Who is this Hazelmire? Is he even trustworthy?' She was getting agitated.

'I need you to try and stay calm and let me answer.' He waited for her nod. It was tenser than he would have liked, but he couldn't blame her for that. 'It's only gone into phase 4 in the last few weeks. Summer wouldn't have been eligible for phase 3.'

'So the eligibility criteria has changed with the next phase.' She nodded. 'A phase 4 trial. That's good.'

'Not exactly.'

'How not exactly?'

'Not at all, exactly. Summer isn't eligible for the trial.'

'That's why Summer's doctors didn't tell me about it. They knew she couldn't have it.' She snatched her hands away from his, and he instantly felt the loss of her touch. 'Why the hell are you telling me about this? If she can't have it, why bother tormenting me?'

'Because Hazelmire – who was the lead on the trial – believes in the regime so much that he's got permission to take it into his private practice. Summer can have the treatment privately.'

'Do you have any idea how much that would cost? How little chance I have of raising enough money to get her the meds that could save her life?' She was on her feet now.

'We think just over three hundred thousand.' Jake stood slowly.

'Oh my God.' Evelyn choked on tears. 'That's impossible.'

'By yourself, yes.' He took hold of her shoulders. 'But you're not alone.'

'Oh, you're a secret millionaire are you? Are you going to give me hundreds of thousands of pounds?'

'Guess that's my cue.'


Evelyn jumped and span around to stare at the strange man who stood in the now open kitchen doorway, virtually filling it with his broad shoulders. He held a tray filled with cups and a pile of plates and pastries.

'Your snack selection is crap, but I found these in the cupboard. I've already eaten one. They're not too bad. Do you take sugar in your tea, Evelyn?'

'Erm …' She had no idea what to say, or how to act in front of this stranger who must have heard almost everything. She stared at him in confusion, trying to place him. He seemed familiar, and at the same time she hadn't a clue who he was. Tall, broad and muscular, he looked like he could have headed up the English rugby team.

'Evelyn, meet Nick. Nick, Evelyn.' The name clicked immediately, and she glanced over to the close-up wedding picture on Jake's mantle shelf. She must have looked at the picture a dozen times, which is why she vaguely recognised the giant groom.

'Let me guess. I'm not what you pictured when you imagined an Event Designer.' He laughed good-naturedly.

Evelyn looked him up and down, taking in the scruffy jeans, rugby shirt and battered boots. 'Not exactly, no.'

'That's all right.' He gave her a wide grin. 'My competitors spent years underestimating me too!' He held his hand out to her, and she gingerly placed hers in his. 'I'm really pleased to meet you. Jake's been talking my ear off about you for weeks. I feel like I know you already. And I'm so sorry about everything you and your family have been going through.'

'Thank you.' Evelyn was surprised at how gentle his grip was. 'So, I'm not wanting to be rude, but …'

'What the hell am I doing here?'

'Pretty much.'

'You need to raise a lot of money – fast. Planning events that get people to part with their hard-earned cash is pretty much what I do every day. And I'm really good at it.'

'Yeah, but don't you usually raise funds for big charities?'

Nick sighed, his whole chest raising and deflating in a great movement. 'I don't understand why you're arguing with me. Don't you think this treatment could help your daughter?'

'I don't know.' Evelyn felt ready to burst into tears again. It was just all too much. A possible treatment that sounded good – but with a doctor she didn't know, in a strange country. And the hurdle of so much money seemed unimaginably insurmountable. She didn't want to even hope that it could come true. It was all so far away.

'You're scared to hope. To believe that it might be possible, is that it?' His eyes bored into her.

'How did you know?' Her voice was barely a whisper.

'It's like his superpower.' Jake rested his hand on her shoulder, and instead of wanting to pull away, Evelyn relaxed and let his touch warm her. 'He's always been good at reading people.'

'It is useful in my work,' he admitted. 'But that's enough about me for now. This is about you and Summer. And right now, you only need to answer one question. I know you're probably feeling a bit overwhelmed right now, but just focus on my one question.'

'OK.' Evelyn nodded.

'Do you think this treatment in Boston – without knowing anything more about it apart from what Jake's already told you, and without worrying about costs or logistics – is something you'd be interested in for Summer?'

'Yes, of course. It could save her life.'

'So let us show you our proposal, and then you can go home and do your own research and read everything

Jake's prepped for you, and talk to whoever you need to talk to, and then all you have to do is say yes, or no.'

'But you will say yes,' Jake added. 'I'm sure of it.'

'So'—Nick reached for a bag on the coffee table, and pulled out a laptop and a large spiral-bound book—'Jake and I have been talking a lot over the last few days, and this is what we've come up with.' He drummed his fingers on the book. 'He told me your daughter didn't get much of a Christmas last year.'

'No, she was in isolation.'

'Poor little mite.' Nick flipped over the next page of the book to show a beautiful sketch of Broclington village centre, decked out for Christmas, only filled with summery flowers and sunshine as well as trees and tinsel. 'As you can see, I've taken inspiration from that idea.' On the next page Santa was decked out in red shorts and T-shirt and riding in an open-top carriage pulled by snow-white horses. Another page showed a Christmas village on a summer's afternoon, with hot chocolates replaced with ice creams bedecked by candy canes, while the next pictured people dancing and whirling around the marquee she and Jake had danced in so recently. She shook her head, wondering how things could have changed so much since that wonderful night.

Evelyn ran her fingers over one of the last images in the book – a carnival procession, led by a little girl, dressed in Christmas finery and seated in Santa's carriage, her blonde curls shining in the sun. Even from the tiny sketch, Evelyn could see her bright green eyes as she smiled and waved at the crowds. Her eyes welled up again, and she fumbled to wipe them.

Jake pushed some tissues into her hands, and she smiled at him gratefully, before looking back at the smiling, sketched Summer. 'We thought, because she's such a special case, and because he didn't get to visit her last December, that Santa might come early, and bring some Christmas magic with him.'

'Summer's Christmas.' Nick nodded. 'So what do you think?'

'I think it's wonderful.' Evelyn sniffed, touched by the amount of thought and hard work that had already gone into the event.

'We were thinking the best time would be the end of August.'

Immediately, Evelyn started counting. 'That's eight weeks away.'

Jake sat beside her, and took her hands in his. 'I know it sounds a long time away, but Hazelmire's team are confident that it will be soon enough still, and Dad will monitor Summer's condition weekly and liaise with them directly to make sure nothing changes.'

'And we need the time, Evelyn,' Nick added. 'We'll start fundraising this week – if you say yes – and step things up as we approach the August bank holiday, with the final events and Summer's Christmas being that weekend.'

'We're planning to turn the Summer Carnival into a fundraising event for Summer,' Jake explained. 'The council are meeting this week to finalise the charity for the year. We're going to put forward Summer's cause.'

The hope that Evelyn was starting to feel disappeared like snow melting under a downpour. 'But they might not pick her.'

'They will,' Jake reassured her. 'Dad will champion the cause, and half of the fundraising committee is made up of the WI. Your mum and mine are both members.'

'Mine too,' added Nick. 'The WI vote is fairly certain.'

'And as to the rest of the village? You're part of our community, Evelyn. You grew up here, and even though you've only been back a short while, you're already important to Broclington. And so is Summer. You only had to see her at the Spring Fling to know that.'

'And you really think we can raise enough money?' Evelyn turned to look at Nick.

'I really do.' He nodded seriously and she could see nothing but honesty in his eyes. 'I raise funds for charities. I don't do lost causes. I wouldn't offer to do any of this if I didn't think there was a damned good chance of us pulling it off.'

'But it's such a huge undertaking, so much money.' Evelyn was still worried.

'Let me try to explain why I'm so confident.' Nick took a breath. 'Christmas is a truly magical time. It's a chance to leave the stresses and seriousness of everyday life behind for a few hours, and remember the innocent joy of childhood. It's when we gather the people we love the most close, and share wonderful memories and moments that will last the whole year through. We cherish the family we've gathered around us – whether they're family by blood or friendship – and give thanks for all the goodness in our lives.

'It's cosy and warm and built around the concept of kindness to others – that's why we give gifts. We fill the streets with lights to turn the darkness and coldness into something beautiful. Simply put, Christmas brings out the best in people and fills them with hope.'

'And that's exactly what Summer needs,' Jake added. 'And what our fundraising will offer. Hope.'

'And,' Nick finished off the thought, 'I really think people will want to get behind that message.'

Evelyn pressed her lips together tightly, not wanting the hope bubbling in her chest to escape. 'And Tom and Mr Khan really think this will work?'

'They can't promise anything,' Jake reminded her quietly.

'I know that.' Evelyn was impatient.

'But, yes. They're both really hopeful for this. Confident even. And waiting for your call.' He squeezed her hands tightly, and Evelyn felt a rush of warmth as his eyes sparkled. 'So, what do you think?'

'I think I'm one of the luckiest people on the planet.' She reached across to grab Nick's hand. 'And I think I might have just made a new best friend. Thank you so, so much for all of this.'

'So we're doing this?'

'I want to read everything first, and talk to the doctors, but … yes. I think we're doing this.'

'Fantastic!' Nick grinned hugely. 'Operation Summer's Christmas is a goer.'

# *Chapter Thirteen*

Jake could feel Evelyn's tension beside him as they sat in the council meeting, waiting for the usual humdrum village business to be finished. Her whole body was tense, and his fingers were going numb from where she squeezed his hand so tightly. But he wouldn't have moved for anything. Well, anything short of the three hundred thousand pounds they needed for Summer's treatment.

Within hours of the nerve-wracking meeting in his flat, Evelyn texted him a single word: yes. She'd spoken to his dad – who'd called him almost the same second she'd hung up on him, and spoken with Summer's oncology consultant. Whatever they had said reassured her, and Operation Summer's Christmas was officially going ahead.

In the few days since, Nick, true to his word, started a fundraising campaign – launching a website and started prepping press releases. He'd met Summer, and been utterly charmed by her, and arranged for a photo shoot, which she absolutely adored. All he was waiting for now was the agreement from the village council to officially make Summer's cause their charity of the year, before he would start contacting every journalist, publicist, philanthropist, local dignitary and celebrity in his substantial contacts list.

Beside him, Evelyn shifted, and Jake realised they'd finally reached the vote. Even though he'd assured her again and again that Summer would be picked, he knew she wouldn't be able to relax until it was made official. He could understand the sentiment. Even though he knew it would go in their favour, he couldn't help the nervousness in his stomach. It was Summer's life that depended on how the ten council members raised their hands in the next minute or so. But that was the point. It *was* a little girl's life – and one who was a member of their community. They *had* to vote for her.

He could feel Evelyn start to shake beside him as the motion was read out. Unable to bear watching, she buried her face in his shoulder. Gently, he stroked her hair, trying to offer some level of comfort as he watched the council leaders consider the motion.

The three WI members raised their hands almost immediately. There was no surprise there. And his dad's hand had gone up before the motion was even completed. The Head of the School's Governing board – whose elderly Labrador was a regular patient of Jake's – shot him a wink and raised his hand too. Two more hands went up, and Jake sighed in relief.

'Evelyn.' He stopped stroking her hair, his eyes blurring as he whispered to her. 'You need to look at this.'

'I don't think I can,' she mumbled into his shoulder.

'You have to see this.' He moved her hair to whisper the words. 'Trust me.'

She reluctantly looked up and her eyes widened as she took in the council leads: every single one of them had their hand raised. Her own hand went to her mouth in amazement as Tom lowered his from the vote and started to clap. After a few seconds the rest of the council followed Tom's lead, and he held his hands out to her with a huge smile. Hot, grateful tears streaked down her cheeks as she tried to compose herself, overwhelmed by the support.

'Unanimous,' she whispered the word in wonder. 'Thank you so much.'

'Told you it would be.' Jake gave her a happy squeeze.

'We should let Nick know,' she murmured quietly, not wanting to disrupt the meeting any further.

'Already doing it.' Jake tapped a message into his phone, which pinged in reply almost immediately.

'What did he say?'

Jake showed her the screen. *Bloody awesome. Told you so. I'm on it.*

Evelyn looked around. 'Do you think it would be really rude if we snuck out? I desperately want to tell Mum and Summer the news.'

'I think it will be OK. People will understand,' Jake reassured her. 'Let's just wait a few minutes and we'll slip out between agenda items.'

'OK.' Evelyn giggled. She felt giddy with the relief of the council's decision, and the thought of sneaking out made her feel like a misbehaving schoolgirl.

When they reached the car park, Evelyn was virtually skipping with happiness. 'I can't believe it was unanimous! I know you said it was going to be all right, but I never imagined it would be unanimous. I can't thank you enough!' Without thinking, she swung around and grabbed Jake, and placed a huge kiss on his lips.

Almost immediately, his arms snaked around her waist and he drew her tightly against him as he kissed her back. His lips were warm and so familiar that she felt like she'd finally come home. But as his tongue teased her lips, the clock tower chimed the hour and she felt unwanted reality creep back in, and she forced herself to pull away from him, immediately regretting the cold that replaced his warmth.

But she forced herself to take one step, then another, away from him, and hoped the shaking in her legs wasn't so obvious that Jake would be able to see it. If she was honest, she'd thought about rekindling a relationship with him – how could she not have when he made her feel so treasured and cared for? – but she still stood by her belief that it was unfair to ask any man to take on a sick child. Summer's own father, such as he was, hadn't been able to handle her illness. There was no way Evelyn could expect another man to take on such responsibilities and stress, and possible heartache.

She shook her head sadly to shake the thought from her mind. It wasn't fair to anyone to consider starting a relationship, no matter how much she adored him, and looked forward to every second they spent together.

'Well, I don't know about you, but I'm starving. Fancy grabbing something to eat?'

Now that he mentioned it, Evelyn was hungry. She'd been too nervous before the council meeting to stomach more than a few sips of coffee. 'I should really be getting back. I can't wait to tell them the result.'

'Of course you can't. Good news should be shared. But I could pick up some food and bring it back to yours. We could celebrate.'

'Well …' For a moment, Evelyn was tempted to say yes, but she reminded herself that she still needed to keep distance between them. Right until the moment where he melted her resolve.

'You know, I bet if I gave The Brockle's Retreat a call, the chef would whip me up some of their Badger

Burgers. Summer loves those.' Yet again, Jake effortlessly, and automatically included her daughter in his plans, making her question her resolve.

'You've got that much sway, even with the local pub?'

Jake shrugged. 'They'll do it for any local. But the chef there might or might not have a cat who might or might not be a patient of mine.'

'Burgers would be lovely.' Evelyn pulled out her purse. 'Let me give you some money.'

'Wouldn't even think of letting you.' He waved her offer away. 'You head home, tell Summer and Linda the good news, and I'll meet you there with the food as soon as I can.'

Jake's phone started buzzing with notifications as he walked into the pub and waved to the landlord. He ordered himself a quick half while he waited for the food to be cooked and packed up into one of the many cool bags that were kept in the kitchen just for locals, who staff knew would always return them.

He checked his phone as he sipped his ale. True to his word, Nick had already been hard at work, and Jake was copied in on nearly a dozen emails and social media notifications that introduced Summer's Christmas to the world. The press release was beautifully written and Summer smiled out from the screen, looking completely adorable. He grinned back at the digital version of her, feeling surer than ever that this was going to work.

Less than fifteen minutes later, he knocked at Evelyn's door. He stumbled and nearly dropped the food as Summer threw herself at him, chattering away excitedly.

'Did you hear? I'm going to go to America for special medicine! It's so special you can only get it one place in the world, so I'm going to have to get on the biggest plane ever and fly there which will take a whole day and we'll have to sleep and eat and use the toilet on a plane in the air. How crazy is that? And Mum says you can see the clouds from their tops instead of their bottoms. It's going to be amazing!'

'It sounds pretty cool,' Jake agreed as he swung her up onto his hip.

'Oh, I didn't tell you the best bit.' She squealed with excitement, making Jake wince. 'The doctors said they're going to make me all better. And then when the cancer is gone again, they have more medicine to make sure it never comes back. And it works on almost everyone. Isn't that brilliant?'

'It really is.' Jake struggled to get the words out past the lump in his throat.

'And before I can go, we have to raise loads of money, so we're going to have Christmas in summer … for me! And I'm going to be a Christmas princess!'

'That sounds amazing.'

'I've missed you, Jake.' She placed a kiss on his cheek that melted his heart as fast as the cheese on the burgers.

'I've missed you too, Summer.'

'And … we'll have to live in Boston for months. I'll miss my friends, but it's OK, because I would have missed them when I was dead. So I don't mind missing them for a little bit if it means I get to keep them for years.'

'That makes sense.' The lump in his throat was choking him now.

'But I don't want to miss you again.' Summer snuggled against his neck as he carried her into the kitchen. 'So I think you should come to Boston with me and Mum.'

He saw Evelyn's panicked look, and tried not to feel hurt as he sat Summer down at the table and focussed on dealing with her feelings and question. 'I don't know if I can. I have a lot of animals to look after, and if I came with you, who would look after all my patients?'

'A different vet?'

'Would you be happy if you went all the way to Boston and had to see a different doctor?'

Summer's brow wrinkled as she thought about it. 'Probably not. But will you think about it?'

'I promise I will.' He handed the food to Linda, who wrapped him in a big hug and kissed his cheek in almost the same spot Summer had.

'There aren't enough words to thank you for what you've done for my girls. You really are an angel.'

'It really wasn't that big of a deal.' He tried to shrug off the compliment.

'You and I both know that's not true. Know that you have my eternal gratitude, and that there will never be any favour too big for you to ask. You're as good as family, in my eyes.'

'Thank you.' Jake nodded earnestly, understanding how much it meant for her to say.

'Nanny, Jake, can we nearly eat? I don't want my Badger Burger to get cold and all the cheese to go hard.'

'Badger Burgers?' Linda pulled a face, teasing Summer. 'They don't sound very tasty. Maybe we should throw them away and have a nice, healthy salad.'

'*Noooooo*,' Summer complained. 'They're not real badger. Jake wouldn't eat badger and neither would I. Badgers are too cool to eat. It's just mushroom and cheese. But it's black and white and a bit grey, so it sort of looks like a badger.'

'I guess it does.' Linda studied them as she plated up the meals and handed them around. 'Let me have the bill for these Jake, and I'll pay you back.'

'Nope.' He shook his head. 'You can consider it the first donation to Summer's Christmas.'

'The first of many, hopefully.' Evelyn raised her glass.

'Cheers to that!'

'Cheers!' Summer clinked her glass with all the others.

'Evelyn, if you and Linda have a few minutes after lunch, there's something I'd like to show you.' He tapped the phone in his pocket, thinking how thrilled they'd be to see everything Nick and his team had been working on in the last few days.

'Of course.' Linda didn't give her daughter a chance to respond, and he was a little relieved that she'd not had the chance to refuse him.

When he'd started looking for something that might help Summer, it had been out of love and desperation. Though he'd never said the words to either of them, he knew it was truer than anything he'd felt before. And there was a part of him that hoped that one day soon, Evelyn would let him back into their lives. It was the same part of him that cried out in loss when she pulled away from him, and the part that had been in agony when Summer fell ill again. But even if she didn't, even if all he could ever have with her was friendship, he'd find a way to be happy with that. He'd find a way to be happy with whatever made them happy.

They were midway through the burgers when the phone started to ring.

'Leave it.' Linda shrugged. 'If it's important, they'll leave a message. Let's enjoy our lovely food.'

Almost as soon as the landline stopped ringing, Jake's mobile started.

'Coincidence?' Evelyn gave him a quizzical look as he checked the called ID.

'Nick.' He swiped his finger across the screen. 'Hey mate, what's up?' His eyes widened as he listened to what his best friend was saying. 'Are you sure about this? Wow. That's amazing. No, no, I'm with them now. Hang on, let me put you on loudspeaker.'

Nick's voice was slightly tinny as it reverberated around the table. 'Hey all. So, Summer, I've got an important question for you. How would you like to be on TV?'

She squealed with excitement.

'I'll take that as a yes.' Jake could hear the grin in his friend's voice.

'She's currently dancing around the kitchen,' Jake confirmed.

'Yes, yes, yes! I'm going to be famous!'

'How on earth did you manage this so quickly?' Evelyn leaned forward to speak into the phone. As she did, her top pulled tight, and was tugged lower in a way that made it really hard for Jake to concentrate, and he had to fight to look away.

'I work fast. And my brilliant wife has called in a few of her contacts too.'

'She's a journalist,' Jake explained for the benefit of the others.

'She also asked me to tell you that you can consider this the repayment of that favour she owed you.'

'More than happy with that.' Jake grinned. 'Summer's worth it.'

Evelyn gave him a smile that was worth more than a million favours owed by friends.

'Right-ho. I've got more stuff to send out, and will leave you to enjoy what's left of your day. I just wanted to let you know the good news. And hear your reactions. I'll keep you updated.'

'Thanks, mate.'

'Thank you, Nick!' Summer blew kisses at the phone.

'Yes, thank you so much.' Linda and Evelyn echoed the shared sentiments as Jake ended the call.

'So was it a big favour?'

'No, not really.' Jake lied a little, underplaying that the favour Claudia had owed him related to his saving their wedding day with quick thinking, and an even quicker trip to find the registrar and get them to the hidden country retreat where Nick and Claudia had finally said their vows – just a few minutes later than planned. Remembering the day, and his best friends declaring their eternal love for each other gave him a warm feeling, and he couldn't help smiling at Evelyn and hoping that one day he'd find the courage to tell her how he felt.

Linda must have noticed the look on his face, because she held her hand out to Summer. 'Come on, you. I think it's time to take Tilly for a … saunter.'

'A saunter?' Jake was curious about the hesitation.

'She's really clever,' Summer explained. 'If you use the other word, even if you spell it, she knows what it means.'

'And we try not to get her too excited too soon,' Evelyn added. 'Until shoes and coats are on, it's not fair to tease her. When it comes to … meanders, she's not very patient.'

Jake thought about meandering hand in hand with Evelyn at a glorious sunset and decided he didn't blame Tilly one bit for being impatient.

As soon as the front door closed, Evelyn started to bustle around the kitchen, clearing the plates and generally trying to find any reason not to look at Jake. Kissing him outside the council meeting had been a mistake, but she'd been so happy and relieved, and it had been so natural to throw her arms around him and kiss him that she hadn't even thought about it. It was the moment that her brain had interfered that everything had gone wrong, and she started doubting everything, and questioning Jake.

As if reading her thoughts, he stepped up behind her. 'I kind of feel like we were interrupted earlier.' Even though he was a few inches away from her, she could feel his warmth against her back, and it took everything in her to not lean back against him and let him slip his strong, comforting arms around her. It would have been so easy to relax her guard for a few moments, and let him take some of the pain away.

But she didn't know how to do it. It had been easier when Summer was still healthy, and she didn't have to think about hospital trips, treatments that compromised immune systems and infection risks. But after last time, she couldn't take the risk, with Summer's health, or her own heart. So instead she focussed on rubbing the grease and different sauces off the plates.

'Evelyn.' Jake's hand caught hers as she reached for the dishcloth. 'What is it you're not telling me?'

'Nothing, I'm fine,' she lied, hoping he would back off.

'I don't think you are.' The hurt in his voice was obvious. 'But if you don't want to tell me what's wrong, then there's nothing I can do to make you. But there's also nothing I can do to help.'

Evelyn wavered, her resolve starting to crumble.

'If it makes any difference, I really do want you to tell me.'

'I don't think you do.' Evelyn flung the dishcloth back in the sink.

'I really do.'

She searched his eyes for any hint of deception, but all she could see was honest concern. 'I'm struggling to get my head around it all.'

'That's understandable.' Jake rubbed her back in comforting motions. 'Finding out Summer had relapsed must have been an incredible blow to you. It was shocking enough for me.' He pressed his lips together tightly, his jaw clenched, and for the first time Evelyn considered how Summer's illness had impacted him, and guilt flooded her.

'It's not just that,' she admitted quietly. 'I almost expected it. I dreaded it, feared it, and prayed every day and night that it wouldn't happen, but it wasn't really a surprise. But everything else? I'm struggling to believe it's all real.'

'How do you mean?' He leaned back against the side, a few steps back, but still close enough to reach out easily.

'That this is all happening. That you've found Hazelmire and his team, and that so many people want to help us.

'You still don't get it, do you?' Jake shook his head. 'You're an important part of this village and community.'

'Do you really think so?'

'I know so. It's just how people are round here, and it's because of how you are.'

'I'm just not used to anything like this,' Evelyn shook her head, feeling tears well up again. She scrunched up her eyes to force them back. Lately, she felt raw with emotion and seemed to be crying at every little thing. 'I'm not used to being able to rely on many people. Even Summer's father let us down. Mum helped as much as she could, but her life was here, and mine wasn't, so I just learned to get on with things. And now it seems everyone I've ever met – and more people I haven't – want to help us. It's a bit overwhelming, and it all seems so surreal that I worry I'm going to wake up tomorrow and it will have all gone away, and it will go back to being just me and Summer. And I'm not sure how I would cope with that now.'

'You're not going to be alone.' He stepped forward and wrapped an arm around her shoulders. It was an innocent gesture that could have just been friendly, but Evelyn sensed it could easily be much, much more. 'As long as I have any choice in it, I won't let you be alone.'

'I don't know what I've done to deserve any of this.'

'You're kind, you care about others, and you put them first. You're a wonderful, wonderful person

191

Evelyn.' He answered honestly. 'You know, Nick would say it's karma. You put good energy into the universe and you get good back.' He hesitated, giving her one of the looks that made her think he could read her mind. 'Is that why you've been pulling away from me? Because you think you don't deserve happiness? Don't think I haven't noticed.'

'I'm sorry.'

'I don't want you to be sorry.' He waited until she turned to face him. 'I want you to give me a chance to help fix whatever's wrong.'

'I don't know that it can be fixed,' Evelyn whispered, needing him to know her fears, and hoping Jake somehow had the answer that she didn't.

'I'm not going to let you down. I'm not your ex. For one thing, I'm not that bloody stupid. Or unkind.' He tugged her hand, and she stepped into his arms. 'I'll say it again, Evelyn. I'm not going to let you down. Aren't I proving that right now by being here even after you tried to chase me away? I want to be here for you, and for Summer, for as long as you'll let me. Whatever happens. In whatever way you want. Even if you just want to have some fun with me for a while.'

Evelyn tucked her head against his shoulder, and breathed in his familiar, safe scent.

'Does this mean you might be willing to let me try?' She felt his breath catch while he waited for her answer.

She nodded against his chest. 'I'd like that, but I'm scared. I only just survived what Charlie did to us. But you're right, I do deserve some fun, and being with you is definitely making me happier.'

'Will you please look at me.' He waited until she did. 'I'm not him. Frankly, he was a bastard and an idiot, and if I ever met him, I'd take great delight in telling him that.' He stroked her hair back from her face. 'Evelyn, I'm not going to make the mistakes he did. We were great together, and we could be again so easily. I really, really care about you. And Summer. And if you let me, I'll spend every day trying to prove that. I can't promise I'll always be perfect – you know I can be a clumsy eejit at times – but I can promise to always try. But even if you say no, I'm still going to do everything I can to get Summer to Boston for the treatment she needs.'

'Even if we're just friends?'

'I won't lie. I'd like more than that, but my helping Summer isn't contingent on what happens between us. I'd never put a condition like that on you. I want to be with you again Evelyn, but only if you want to be with me for me. If that makes sense.'

'It does.'

'I'm not asking you for an answer now. You need to take time to think about this. But'—he gave her a wicked grin that turned her knees to jelly—'I'm not going to make it easy for you to say no. I hope you realise that. I'll be in touch to talk about the fundraising, but I'm leaving you with this to think about.' He cupped her face in his hands, stroking her cheeks as he slid his touch backwards and laced his fingers through her hair.

Her breath came on short, fast gasps of anticipation as he leaned down and brushed his lips against hers, tasting her as if she was the most decadent of chocolate. He pulled her more tightly against him, and the heat and energy of his body thrummed against her, making her hot all over. His lips danced against hers, sending waves of pleasure pulsing through her body.

193

When he eventually pulled away, his breathing was as fast as hers. 'I'll see you soon, promise me you'll think about what I've said?'

Evelyn nodded, not trusting herself to speak.

# Chapter Fourteen

'Mum, can I ask you something?'

'Of course you can.' Evelyn tucked Summer's covers more tightly around her shoulders. 'You can always ask me anything. You know that.'

'Why have you stopped having sleepovers with Jake?'

*Crap.* Evelyn regretted her answer. This was not something she wanted to discuss with her daughter. 'It's complicated.'

'Why? Don't you like him any more?'

Evelyn thought back to the steamy kiss Jake had planted on her in the kitchen just a couple of days earlier, and felt the blood rush to her cheeks. 'No, I still like him.'

'So did he stop liking you?'

'No.' That was definitely not the case. He'd made it only too clear how much he still liked her, and she was so grateful for that. To have a man like Jake, who she adored, care about her so much was something she was so, so grateful for. But to put the pressure of long distance on a fledgeling relationship? It was too much to hope – or ask – for. It was probably better for them to just stay friends. And if she kept telling herself that, she might eventually stop missing him.

'Then what's the problem?' Summer demanded, folding her arms over the top of her covers.

'I already told you, it's complicated.'

'It's because of me, isn't it?' Her bottom lip started to quiver. 'It's like with Charlie.'

It was time for that conversation then. She took a deep breath, not wanting to ask it, but owing it to her daughter. 'Why did you stop calling him Daddy?'

'Because he's not my daddy!' Summer growled. 'He's a crap stink head!'

Evelyn wrapped her daughter in a hug, ignoring the bad language. 'Why would you think that?'

'Because it's true!' Summer sobbed. 'Charlie stopped loving me, and now Jake has too. It's the cancer isn't it? Everyone hates cancer, and I have it, so nobody can love me.'

'Oh, sweetheart.' Evelyn rocked her gently and tried to find the words to explain. 'It's not you, it's me.'

'So you *did* stop liking Jake.'

'No.'

'What's the problem then? If he likes you and you like him, and it's not me, then why can't he be here and be your boyfriend and my friend again?' Her tears gave way to anger.

'Summer, if you try to calm down, I'll try to be honest with you.' She took a deep breath. 'I'm scared.'

'Scared of what?' Summer looked at her in amazement, and Evelyn realised she'd never admitted being afraid of anything to her daughter.

'Scared of being hurt again, I guess. Or of you being let down.'

'Oh, is that all?' Summer snuggled back into her bed, seemingly mollified.

'It feels like a pretty big "all" to me.'

'You don't need to worry about any of that.' Summer yawned.

'Really?'

'Yeah. Jake looked all over the world to find a doctor with medicine to help me. And made it so I'm going to be on TV. You don't do that if you don't really like someone.' She gave Evelyn a look far more mature than her years. 'I think he likes you lots, Mum.'

Evelyn smoothed her daughter's hair flat against the pillow. 'You know what, I think you might be right.'

'I know I am,' Summer replied sleepily. 'You tell me not to be scared. That I have to be brave. Why do I have to be brave if you don't?'

Jake pounded the pavement as he turned the corner back to the surgery, forcing his legs to work harder to maintain his speed as he started up the slope that would take him home. Sweat trickled between his shoulder blades and the muscles in his legs complained, but it was worth it to leave some of his frustrations pounded into the ground.

He jumped in the shower as soon as he got home, and tried to wash the thoughts of Evelyn down the drain with the sweat and soap suds, but the efforts seemed futile. Nothing really kept thoughts of her at bay.

The hammering at his door had him racing out of the bathroom, hopping as he dragged his trousers on and ran to open the door. At this time of night, and with that amount of noise, he was expecting it to be an emergency.

He flung the door open, and felt his heart step up a notch when he saw Evelyn standing at the top of his stairs.

'Hi.'

'Hi.' She grinned back, her eyes wandering down his still damp chest. 'OK if I come in?'

'Always.' He stood aside. 'Is everything all right? Summer, Tilly, your mum?'

'Everyone's fine,' Evelyn reassured him.

'I should go and finish drying off.'

'You could. Or …'

'Or?' He felt his eyebrow, and something else, raise.

'Or you could come here and kiss me.'

'Yes ma'am.' Jake's eyes lit up with happiness and hunger as he stepped towards her and slipped his arms around her waist. He teased a trail of kisses down her neck, making her squirm with delight, before placing a sweet kiss on the tip of her nose. 'Not that I'm complaining, but I do want to know. Is this just a booty call?'

Evelyn burst out laughing. 'A booty call? Does anyone even call them that any more?' She struggled to be serious, until Jake leaned down and kissed her firmly, driving the laughter from her lips. 'This is me trying to be brave, and telling you that I want some fun and joy in my life. I'm trying to let you in, Jake, but I'm still scared.'

He gave her another sweet kiss. 'Maybe I can help with that.'

'I think I need it.' Evelyn stood on tiptoes and drew Jake down so she could kiss him, gently at first, but then with growing passion as he pulled her tightly against him.


Evelyn stretched and smiled, luxuriating in the warmth of waking up next to Jake. The sun dappled through the hastily drawn curtains and painted patterns across her eyelids.

'I can feel that, you know.' She didn't open her eyes, not wanting to break the peaceful spell in the room, and admit that it was morning.

'Feel what?'

'You looking at me.' She let her eyelids flutter open, and her smile stretched even wider at the sight of Jake propped up on an elbow and watching her. 'How long have you been awake?'

'Just a few minutes.' He shrugged before leaning down to brush a kiss against her lips. 'You know what I think? I think brave is good. I *like* this fun brave version of you.'

'I definitely agree.' Evelyn kissed him back, before flopping back against the pillows happily. 'What's the time?'

'I don't know.' He tapped the clock on the bedside table, making the face light up, and pulled a face. 'Wow, it's nearly nine. Must be something about you, I never usually sleep this late.'

'Well, I guess you were tired.' She grinned and wriggled closer to him. 'Maybe you wore yourself out.'

'Hmm, can't imagine how.' He snaked an arm around her waist. 'Have you anywhere you need to be for a while?'

'Not until later when I'm meeting Nick to prep for Summer's interview.'

'He invited me too. I hope that's all right.' The nervous look in his eyes was so endearing that Evelyn felt her worries melt away a bit more. They weren't gone completely, but they were starting to fade a little.

'Of course it is. None of this would be happening without you. I owe you a lot.'

'Well, neither of us have anywhere to be for a few hours, so you could start making it up to me now.' He gave her a cheeky grin.

'Hmm.' She pondered the question while running a finger over his chest and making him squirm. 'I guess I don't really have anything better to do.'

He laughed and grabbed her, pulling her underneath him.

'I get to wear make-up?' Summer squealed in delight. 'Can I Mum? *Pleasepleasepleasepleaseplease*?'

Evelyn laughed at the power of Summer's enthusiasm. 'OK'—she glanced at the make-up artist— 'but only a bit, please?'

The woman nodded her understanding, and gave Evelyn a wink. She'd take good care of Summer, who practically leapt into the chair in front of the mirror in excitement.

Evelyn turned to Nick. 'Exactly how big of a favour was this?'

'The biggest. My wife Claudia is a print journalist. She hates to give away an exclusive, but she knew you'd get more attention and raise more money with TV coverage. So she called one of her old uni friends, Meghan, who's a soft news correspondent here.'

'Soft news?' Evelyn didn't recognise the term.

'Fluffy stories. Nice, feel good things. But don't ever let her hear you call it fluffy journalism,' he said. 'So Meghan took the story idea to the weekly editorial meeting, and they liked it so much it's been uplifted to become a studio story.'

'Which is good?'

'It's great,' Jake reassured her.

'I didn't expect all this. I thought it was just going to be a little local news thing.' Evelyn looked around the glossy studio, feeling a bit overwhelmed.

'It was. Then it got uplifted.' Jake shrugged. 'This is going to be great. And just look how much fun Summer's having already. She's loving the attention.'

'She really is.' Evelyn smiled as she watched Summer being fussed over in the make-up chair. 'And she deserves it. I'm just a bit nervous. How many people do you think will see this?'

'Our viewing figures vary a bit from the hundreds of thousands to the millions. But we'd expect somewhere in the higher figures for a story like this, especially if we get some good sound bites for the trail.' A woman with a clipboard and headset came up to them. 'The trail is the bit we fit into the headlines to encourage people to stay tuned in. And a story like this will get a lot of viewers. We're ready to start miking you up. Once you're ready, I'll take you through to meet Natalie, and she'll run through some of the questions she'd like to cover on air with you.'

'Oh wow, this is really happening.' Evelyn grinned at Jake. 'Wait, Natalie like Natalie Rosh?'

'Who else? Are we miking you up as well?' She looked at Jake.

'I hadn't thought about it,' he admitted. 'This is yours and Summer's thing.'

'It's yours too,' Evelyn argued, 'and I think I really need you. I don't know if I can do this any more.' Her breath came in fast gasps as she realised the enormity of what she was about to face: the woman who she'd watched almost every evening was about to interview her in front of millions of people.

'It's OK. You've got this.' Jake wrapped his warm, firm hand around her shaking fingers and gave them a squeeze, before looking over to where Summer was now preening in the mirror. 'Hey, princess. Do you mind if I come with you and your mum when you talk to the news lady?'

'Duh. It was all your idea. Of course you're going to talk. Obviously.' Even from where she was stood, Evelyn could see Summer roll her eyes. Eight years old, going on thirteen. She shook her head in amusement, and then the panic set in again. If she got this right, Summer really could live to see her thirteenth birthday, but if she got it wrong …

'Relax.' Jake waited for Evelyn to look at him. 'We just go and have a chat about Summer and Summer's Christmas, chat about the fundraising a bit, and then they'll edit it into something really good.' He looked to the woman with the clipboard.

'That's exactly it. And we'll do a good job. Our Editor-in-Chief has twins about Summer's age. That's part of the reason he was so eager to help and uplift the story. You'll do great.'

Jake kept his hand wrapped firmly around Evelyn's, tucked just behind Summer who was sat in between them, grinning from ear-to-ear as she was interviewed. She patiently held up her bravery beads necklace and showed them to Natalie, pointing out the most important beads while the interviewer made the appropriate noises.

Eventually she turned to Evelyn. 'So, can you explain what all this is for? Why does Summer need to go to Boston?'

'Very simply, the cancer has returned.' Evelyn tried to keep her voice neutral. 'And this time it's not operable.'

'It's in her spine, right?' She waited for Evelyn's nod. 'So what about chemotherapy and things like that?'

'There weren't that many drugs that the cancer was sensitive to, and Summer developed a bad reaction to some of them.' She hesitated. 'Most of them, actually.

But the doctors in Boston are very optimistic that their new treatment regime could help.'

'How optimistic?'

'More than eighty-five per cent of their patients – all of them under sixteen – are still event free two years after they started the trial.'

'And what does that mean?' Natalie leaned forward.

'Basically, almost all their patients are still cancer free after two years. Summer's last remission wasn't even six months.'

'Wow. That does sound really promising.' Natalie smiled. 'And you need to raise funds.'

'Desperately.'

'And so you came up with the idea of holding a Christmas Festival. In summer. Can you explain how you came up with that?'

'Christmas has always been one of Summer's favourite times of the year, and unfortunately because of her treatment, she spent last Christmas on an isolation ward.'

'I understand it was a close thing?'

'Yes.' Evelyn had to swallow hard to keep the tears at bay to be able to answer. 'It was bad. But Summer's always been a fighter, and she got through it.'

'So you wanted to give her the Christmas that she missed.' Natalie nodded in understanding.

'Exactly.'

'There are some people who might say that the idea of Christmas in August is a crazy gimmick, controversial even. That it won't work. What would you say to them?'

Evelyn's throat constricted painfully. It was the fear bothering her most at the moment; the idea that there was a treatment somewhere in the world that could help her baby, but she might not be able to get her there.

'I think I've got this one.' Jake squeezed Evelyn's fingers out of sight of the camera. 'We have faith it will work. The thing about Christmas is that it's magical. It's when people come together with the people they love the most, and celebrate love and hope. They believe in the spirit of giving and kindness and joy – in Santa. Believing in Christmas is about believing in everything you hold dear. It's believing in the goodness of people, and hope'—he turned to smile at Evelyn and Summer—'and it's believing in love.'

Natalie nodded as Jake leaned forward.

'So, if it's OK, I've got a question for you, Natalie?'

'Of course.'

He fixed her with one of the looks that Evelyn knew so well.

'Do you believe that joy, and hope, and love should be held in your heart all year long? And not just a single day in December? Do you believe there's a place for the magic of Christmas *every single day*? Do you believe in the miracle of human kindness all year round?'

'I think I do.' Natalie nodded slowly, obviously affected by Jake's speech. After a moment she cleared her throat. 'So tell us more about this little place called Broclington, and what Summer's Christmas is going to look like.'

'That's easy!' Summer laughed. 'We're going to have a proper Christmas, but in August.'

'The whole village will be decorated for Christmas,' Jake explained. 'And Christmas in Broclington is still quite traditional. We have carollers, a big tree decorated in the middle of the village – which the villagers

204

ourselves planted over a decade ago, and we add more decorations to every year. And we have the Mistletoe Ball, which is always really popular, Secret Santa gift exchanges across the whole village, and fundraising events that last the week. And this year, because it's Summer's Christmas, we're combining it with our summer carnival and fete, with all the proceeds going towards Summer's treatment.'

'Wow.' Natalie smiled. 'They do say it "takes a village to raise a child" – I guess in this case, it couldn't be more true.'

'That's right,' Evelyn agreed.

'It's what our community does best. Pulling together to help each other.'

Natalie turned back to the camera. 'So there you have it. A community pulling together to give a child the best gift possible – her health – for Christmas'—she gave the camera a warm smile—'in August. We'll be putting more details of this story, and tracking the fundraising efforts on our website. But I think I know what I'll be doing this August bank holiday, and I hope you'll join me there.'

'And … we're off.' The woman with the clipboard waved a hand in the air, indicating the filming was done. Evelyn breathed a huge sigh of relief, and finally relaxed.

'That was fun!' Summer was practically buzzing with energy.

'I'm glad you think so.' Evelyn rubbed her eyes. 'How do you think it went?'

'It was great.' Natalie smiled. 'I don't think it could have gone much better. Your answer'—she gestured to Jake—'about Christmas was really, really good. Inspiring. And I meant what I said. If you think it would help, I'd like to be there to support the cause.'

'That would be amazing.'

'Then I'll be there. With the camera crew. And we'll put the footage on our page, and all the contact details for the organisers.'


Summer made her television debut the next evening, and the emails and phone calls started the next day, and by the weekend there were so many that Nick called an emergency planning meeting. Summer and Linda had been baking all morning, and the little girl was bouncing with sugar and excitement by the time Nick knocked on the door.

'Hi Nick!' Summer ran to greet him. 'Nanny and I made fairy cakes and sausage rolls and cinnamon buns.'

'Sounds good. Lead me to the treats!'

'You found us then.' Jake clasped his best mate's hand and gave him a quick bro hug before introducing him to Linda.

'It's good to see you again, Nick.' Linda shook his hand, clasping it between both of hers. 'Thank you so much for everything you're doing for my girls.'

'You're more than welcome. To be honest, I'm kinda enjoying myself.' He waved to Summer and Evelyn. 'And this spread looks amazing.'

'Oh well, it's the least we could do.' Linda smiled. 'Sit, sit. Help yourself and tell us what this meeting is all about.'

'Yes, you've been pretty cagey about everything.' Evelyn leaned across to help herself to a cinnamon roll. 'You said it was good, but complicated?'

'I did.'

Jake rolled his eyes at his friend. 'All right. Tell them.'

'We are … at capacity.'

Evelyn pulled a face. 'What do you mean, we're at capacity?'

'We've sold out. Every stall at the fete, all the spaces for the carnival floats, every ticket at the Mistletoe Ball. We've sold everything.'

'That's amazing!'

'It gets even better.' Jake knew he was grinning like an idiot, but there was nothing he could do about it, even if he'd wanted to.

'How can it be better than that?'

'Because I've got at least half as many enquiries again,' Nick answered. 'And more coming in. Take a look at this.' He flipped open his laptop, tapped a few buttons and brought up one of the fundraising threads for Summer's Christmas.'

Evelyn read a few of the comments aloud. 'That's a shame, I really wanted to go.' 'More tickets please.' 'Great event, great idea, great cause. How can I get involved?' She scrolled through more comments, her finger blurring on the mouse as her eyes widened in amazement. 'Is this for real?'

'It's real. Did you look at the number of people interested in attending?'

'No. Where's that?'

'Right-hand side of the screen.'

'*Shh* … ugar plum fairies and chocolate drops!' Evelyn's eyes were round with shock, and Jake had to bite back a laugh. He'd had much the same reaction when Nick sent him the link that morning – only he'd not had to worry about little ears hearing profanities.

'What is it?'

'Two thousand seven hundred people have confirmed they're coming. And another, I don't believe this'—she took a huge breath—'another four and a half thousand people are interested. This can't be right.'

Linda stared at Nick in horror. 'How is this even possible? How are we going to manage all these people? We can't have that many people wandering around Broclington. I don't understand how this happened.' She shook her head.

'It was the news report,' Jake explained. 'I'm actually trending on Twitter. It's hilarious.'

'I'm famous!' Summer bounced in her seat.

'Yes you are, munchkin.' Nick grinned at her.

'Do you really think that many people will turn up?' Linda asked. 'Surely some people just click they are going, and don't turn up. It's not like a proper RSVP, is it?'

Nick nodded slowly. 'That's true, but I think more will turn up than won't. And numbers will probably increase too, as people tell their friends about it, and it gets shared more. And not everyone who will come are on social media.'

'So that's what this meeting is for? Trying to figure out how the heck we manage this?' Linda nodded in understanding.

'Exactly.' Nick nodded too. 'Jake and I already started looking at some options. We looked at some of the cities in the region and the numbers they get, and how they manage their visitor figures. Some of the themed events – like the big Victorian Christmas Market had around two hundred stalls and a hundred and fifty thousand visitors last year.'

'But cities are different,' Linda argued. 'Obviously they'd get more people.'

'That's true, Mum,' Evelyn replied. 'But Broclington's fundraising events are already pretty well known locally – you know how fast the Spring Fling dance sells out – and this has novelty value, right?'

Nick nodded. 'And the feel-good factor. If you've got a choice that weekend of a normal summer fete – or Summer's Christmas – a lot of people will choose Broclington just for that feel-good element. Especially because there are probably normal summer fetes going on the weekends before and after.'

'So here's what we're thinking.' Jake pulled out a notepad. 'And what some other places do. Nick thinks he's got enough interest from stallholders that we could extend the fete across two days, which would thin crowds a little bit. We think only the locals would bother to visit twice. And for the non-locals, we could get coaches and run a shuttle service from somewhere. I'm sure one of the farmers won't mind lending a fallow field for cars, to make some extra cash.'

'I've already looked up the long-range weather forecast,' Linda added. 'It's looking really, really good for three weeks' time. If we could get hold of a bigger marquee, we could move the ball to the park and work out of the cricket pavilion instead of the village hall.'

'What if we went even bigger?' Nick grinned, and Jake wondered what on earth he was thinking. 'What if, instead of just a little marquee stuck on the side of the cricket pavilion, we got a huge one that we spanned across part of the park. We could put one over the top of the bandstand, and run it all the way back. And then open the far end up to the evening and have a Starlight Dance too. We could even black the marquee out and fill it with fairy lights. And light all the trees in the park.'

'Wow. You don't think small, do you?' Jake had known what to expect from Nick, but even he was impressed with his best mate.

'Not if I can help it.' Nick's grin had now reached the level of Cheshire cat.

'If we could even get permission to do something like that, we don't have anywhere near enough decorations.' Evelyn sighed into her coffee.

'We don't.' Linda tapped her fingers thoughtfully on the table. 'But I bet we know people who do.'

'Who are you thinking?'

'Well, we already work with other WI groups across the region. I bet they have Christmas decorations they aren't using. And come to think of it, most people won't be using them right now.'

'I think this is going to take a bit more than people's tree lights, Mum,' Evelyn argued.

'I know that. I was thinking about the neighbouring councils and businesses. And I bet Nick has some useful contacts.'

'You know it.'

'In fact,' Linda mused aloud, 'I wonder if we might not be thinking big enough still. We could decorate the whole park and square, and the main street. If we closed it off to cars for the weekend, we could turn it into a proper street festival as well as the fete in the park.'

'What about power for everything?'

'Let me worry about stuff like that.' Nick waved away the concerns. 'If we can set up multi-stage music festivals in the middle of fields, we can manage a few lights in a park. The only thing potentially stopping us would be permissions.'

'Which I can't see being a problem,' Jake replied. 'The village council are already backing you. That's not going to change.'

'So we're going to go for expansion?' Nick asked, as he looked around the table.

'Yes!' Summer was the first to answer, filled with excitement. 'The bigger the better!'

'You heard her.' Jake raised his mug. 'The bigger the better.'

The others clinked their mugs in agreement.

# *Chapter Fifteen*

Evelyn laughed as Summer twirled in front of the mirror, swishing her skirts back and forth. The bridal boutique had called a few days earlier, offering to provide Summer with a dress for the parade and Mistletoe Ball. Initially, Summer had worried and wanted to wear her princess dress, but as Evelyn watched the final dress fitting, she knew she'd been right to insist Summer at least look at the dresses.

The one she picked had a silvery white lace bodice, a pale blue chiffon skirt that was embroidered along the bottom with more lace, and sequins that sparkled as she moved, matching the detail on the blue satin sash.

'Do you like it, Mum?' She met her eyes in the mirror.

'I think you look like a princess. But it's not me who matters. Do you like it?'

'I love it!' Summer twirled some more. 'It's so pretty.'

The shop assistant, Molly, watched her, hands on her hips. 'I don't think you look like a princess. Not just yet.' She picked up a box from the side. 'Everyone knows princesses have crowns.'

Evelyn bit back a smile as Summer held her breath, trying to hold back her excitement.

'Will you stand still, and close your eyes?' Molly opened the box, but kept it angled away from Summer, letting Evelyn sneak a glance. She winked at her.

'Close your eyes, Summer.' Evelyn found she was holding her breath as much as her daughter as Molly lowered the tiara into Summer's golden curls.

Molly tweaked the dress, making sure the belt was straight and the skirt fell perfectly to Summer's ankles. 'OK, you can open your eyes.'

'*Wowowowowowow*! Mum, look! I really am a princess!'

'You always have been.' Evelyn rested her hands on her daughter's shoulders and watched Summer admire herself in the mirror.

'Yeah, but now I look like a princess, instead of just a cancer kid.'

Evelyn gulped, not quite knowing what to say to that, so instead concentrated on fiddling with Summer's curls and tucking them perfectly into the tiara band. 'You look beautiful, sweetheart.'

Her hands shook as she stroked Summer's rapidly growing, silken hair. A few weeks ago she'd given up hope of ever seeing her baby grow up, and now as she stood in a boutique watching her dress in lace, she got a glimpse of a future: maybe, God willing, they would pull this off, raise the money needed, and the treatment would work. And maybe in fifteen or twenty years' time, they'd be in a similar store while she watched Summer pick another lace dress, only that one would be expensive, white, and chosen for the love of her life.

She turned to Molly. 'I can't thank you enough for this.'

Molly nodded, and Evelyn realised her eyes were glassy too. 'We're happy to help. You look beautiful, Summer. And we'll all be cheering you on in the parade.'

'You made me look like a proper princess! Thank you so, so much.'

Evelyn turned to Summer. 'We need to get going home.'

'OK.' Summer had one last, longing look in the mirror before heading back to the dressing room.'

'Wait a second,' Molly called after her. 'I'll come help to make sure you don't scratch yourself on any of the pins. I'll make sure it's ready by next weekend,' she promised Evelyn before following Summer.

The next morning Jake was nursing his first coffee of the day and still trying to wake up, but even half asleep he was buzzing with excitement. He'd been up far too late fussing over his last-minute plans for his own fundraising efforts.

He'd been inspired when he'd seen other people arranging sponsored events, like the postman who was aiming to run a hundred miles in the week leading up to the fete in addition to his usual delivery routes, and decided he had to get involved. But he'd kept it secret from Evelyn and Summer, partly because he wanted to surprise them, and partly because he worried about how successful his idea was going to be, especially because it meant trying to get people up and out their homes relatively early on a Sunday morning!

But he needn't have worried: his patients had more than stepped up, and it was looking like he was going to blast through his initial fundraising target. He checked the time, and headed to the bathroom to get ready. His patients – and their owners – would start arriving in no time.

He was barely dressed before he heard excited yapping from dozens of dogs in his car park. He peered out the window and grinned widely. 'Hi, I'll be right down.' He grabbed the boxes from where he'd left them last night, and balanced them as he locked up. He deposited them at his brother's feet. Callum was standing holding the leash of their parents' elderly Labrador in one hand, and his daughter's hand in the other.

Jake knelt to pet Sooty, and gave his niece a brief hug, promising to see her later. 'Thanks for this, Cal. Just give it a few more minutes for everyone else to arrive, and I'll meet Summer and Evelyn. Make sure everyone has a bag from the top box – they're poop bags, just in case – and those who want it can take whatever from the bigger box.'

'Got it'—he leaned forward—'and Mum and her crew are already at the church hall.'

'Brilliant.' Jake raised his voice and waved to his patients and friends. 'Thank you, everyone, for coming – and for all your hard work so far. We've already raised loads, and I'm sure we'll raise even more. I'll see you all in a bit – I've just got to fetch our unsuspecting guests of honour!' With that, he grabbed a bundle from each of the boxes, and jogged out of the car park.

A few minutes later he was stood in Linda's hall, waiting for Summer and Evelyn to finish getting ready while Tilly jumped around him excitedly.

'Are you nearly ready?' He tried to keep the tension out of his voice, but he really, really wanted to get the timing right for the best effect.

'I'm tired. It's too early,' Summer complained.

'I know it's early, but it's getting so hot that we have to walk Tilly early,' Evelyn replied. 'And then we're going to have a lovely breakfast at the café.'

'It's true,' Jake agreed as he knelt to help Summer tie her laces. 'If you feel hot in shorts and T-shirt, then imagine how hot Tilly feels. She's wearing a giant fur coat all the time. And, she doesn't have nice sparkly

215

trainers like yours to protect her feet when the pavement gets hot, and she can't sweat like we can.'

'Sweat is gross.'

'It can be a bit. But it does keep you cool.'

'S'pose.'

'Here, take a jumper please.' Evelyn pulled on her own cardigan and handed one to her daughter.

'*Muuuuuuum*, it's August. It's too hot for jumpers.'

'It might not be this early.'

'I don't want it.' Summer put her foot down stubbornly, and Jake had to hide a grin as he realised that she'd clearly inherited her mother's morning grumps – the same ones that she'd warned him about.

'How about you just tie it around your waist? That way your mum's happy because you have it, and you're happy because you don't have to wear it unless you want to. OK?' And then he'd be happy because his carefully laid plans might actually work out, rather than being derailed by an argument.

'OK.' Summer tied the jumper round her waist and smiled up at him, all traces of stubborn argumentativeness gone as she slipped her hand into his. 'Come on, Mum. I'm hungry.'

Their timing was perfect. Just as they reached the end of the street, Sarah, Callum and Sooty sauntered past. Jake had no idea where Callum had got it from, but as well as the blue snowflake bandana that he'd expected to see, Sooty was also wearing a clever costume that turned his front half into Santa, complete with a beard and matching red hat. The bells on his collar jingled jauntily as he trotted along, barely limping from the arthritis that Jake knew was in his hips.

'Oh wow. Look, Summer! It's Santa Paws!' Jake whistled to Sooty. 'Come say hi, old man.'

'Aww, he's so cute.' Summer knelt to pet him, and Jake took advantage of her distraction to quickly tie a matching snowflake bandana around Tilly's neck. He held his finger to his lips and winked at Evelyn who shrugged away her confusion. She trusted him, and that knowledge filled him with happiness.

He gestured to the top of the road, and what Summer hadn't seen: over a hundred dogs and their owners all heading towards them, and every single pup was wearing a bandana, or tinsel, or bells or full-on costumes. Pride filled him as he watched them all appear, his patients and customers turning out to support him, and Summer and Evelyn.

Summer looked up, her eyes widening in amazement as she took in the sight. 'There's so many dogs.'

'They're all here for you.' Jake lifted her to her feet. 'We're having a sponsored dog walk to help raise money for your treatment.'

'This is so cool! Mum, how cool is this?'

'Very, very cool,' Evelyn agreed while shooting Jake a look of such love and gratitude that his stomach turned itself in knots. He loved nothing more than seeing her happy, and his breath caught when he realised that there was nothing he wanted to do more than make her smile this brightly every day for the rest of his life. The realisation was like a punch to the gut, and for a moment he let himself consider a future where Summer's hand would tuck tightly into his again and again, just like it was now. And where Evelyn would keep smiling at him the way she was right then.

But within moments, they were surrounded by a pack of excited waggy tails, wet curious noses, and ears being shoved under their hands as dogs demanded attention and greeted them all.

'Shall we go?' Jake laughed as a spaniel dressed in tinsel shoved her nose under his hand. 'Hello, girl. Are you impatient for your walk and breakfast?'

'Are we still getting breakfast?' Evelyn asked.

'Yes.' Jake nodded. 'The plan is we loop around the south side of the village, through the park, past the cricket pavilion, and finish at the village hall – where the WI and Margaret from The Brockle's Paws are putting on breakfast for everyone.'

'This is amazing.' Evelyn gave him a brief kiss before slipping her arm through his as they began to walk. 'I feel like I spend half my time lately saying thank you to you, but thank you again. This really is wonderful.'

'And again, you're more than welcome.' He smiled down at her, glad to have made her happy, and to have found another way to contribute to helping Summer.

That Thursday, two days before the big launch of Summer's Christmas events, was sunny and bright but Evelyn still shivered as she walked across the village to the park. She shoved her hands into the pockets of her hoodie, zipped up over shorts, in a vain attempt to find some warmth.

The enormity of the next few days, and what they meant to Summer's future, was impossible to push to the back of her mind any longer. She'd been overwhelmed by the generosity and kindness of so many people – most of whom had been strangers a few weeks ago – and thousands and thousands of pounds was already sitting in the bank account labelled "Summer's Christmas", but it wasn't enough.

Nick had formally registered the group as a charity, which he assured her meant they would be eligible to claim additional money back through tax relief, but it still wouldn't be anywhere close to enough. Everything was pinned on the activities and events of the weekend, and Evelyn struggled with the knowledge that her daughter's life would be decided over a few hours of a weekend – and that almost the whole event was reliant on the fickle British weather being kind. The forecast was good, but Evelyn was well aware that wasn't always reliable.

And, as if that wasn't enough, the whole event was being set up and run entirely by volunteers. She was gobsmacked, and grateful beyond words, for everything that everyone had done so far. The Broclington community, and so many other people, had been so generous with their time and money. But she still wasn't entirely over the hurt that Charlie had caused her, and how badly she'd been let down by him and his parents. So as much as she tried to be optimistic, she struggled to not expect that everyone would let her down sooner or later. It was that knowledge, that she was entirely reliant on other people, that sent shivers through her veins.

When she rounded the corner to the cricket pavilion her breath caught, choked by the emotion that thickened her throat. Despite the fact that it was so early that even Tilly hadn't bothered to get out of bed before Evelyn left, the park was bustling with people already.

Two young men she didn't recognise were carefully unrolling a huge white canopy which would no doubt pop up into a beautiful marquee within hours. They laughed and joked with three other people she didn't know who were emptying a van of what looked like a giant, wooden jigsaw puzzle. The doors to the cricket pavilion were already open, and more voices echoed inside, so Evelyn went to see what was going on, and where she could help.

'Evelyn, love.' Julie spotted her as soon as she stepped foot into the building. 'Are you thirsty? Come and grab some coffee with us in the bar. We're drawing up a plan of action for the day.'

'Sounds good. Thank you all for being here.' She looked around the rest of the WI ladies, who she felt had adopted her in recent weeks, and was filled with gratitude for everything so many people had already done for her and her family. 'So, how can I help?'

'Up to you. There's plenty to do. You've already seen the boys out front setting up the dance floor and marquee. Nick, and the team from Birmingham should be with us by about 10.00. They've got to collect the truck, pick up all the decorations from the theatre, and head over here. There should be vans arriving from the county council with decorations from our neighbouring villages. It'll be all hands to unload and get them set up. And to get the marquee decorated.'

'So what do we do until then?'

'Plan, and then make breakfast.' Julie consulted her list. 'We've got more volunteers arriving around 9.30. We'll be doing sausage and bacon sandwiches for everyone. Plus veggie and vegan options for those that want them.'

'How many people are you expecting?'

'We're cooking for sixty,' Nancy Snowdon, the school administrator, answered.

'Wow. That many will be here helping?'

'Probably a few more. Some people will eat before they come.'

Evelyn stared at them in amazement.

'And the sparkies should be here by about lunchtime.'

'Sparkies?'

'Electricians,' Nick's Mum explained. 'To run the cables, ensure the generators are set up properly, and sign everything off. Then we've got Environmental Health coming down tomorrow afternoon to sign off everything else.'

'What happens if they don't?' Evelyn asked. 'Sign everything off, I mean.'

'They will,' Julie assured her. 'We're used to running events like this. The only thing that has really changed is the venue because we're using the pavilion instead of the village hall.'

'And we've got the full list of requirements we have to meet as well. We'll just tick off every point as we set up.'

'So, what can I do until Nick and the decorations all start arriving?'

'Help with breakfast. We're going to have a lot of hungry people to feed soon.'


Jake rolled his shoulders back and forth and tried to stretch the crick out of his neck as he stood and looked around the marquee. He'd just finished hammering in the ground pegs the set-up team had given him, and was glad to see the job done as his back was starting to ache from being bent into a pretzel and driving the pegs into the hard, dry ground.

He must have pounded in close to a hundred of the blasted things, while the others had twisted, clicked and snapped the dance floor into place around the bandstand, which was now just brushing against the canvas of the new, temporary roof.

Green garlands and fairy lights were being strung between the supporting legs and poles, and tinsel, baubles, and flowers wove their way around the bandstand. The decorations were all silvers, whites and pale blues, making the place look like a wintery wonderland, and matching the shimmery fabric that was being tied around the tent, and draped from the ceilings.

He didn't totally understand the vision of his mum and the rest of the organising committee, but he was happy to just do as he was told, put things where they pointed, and hang whatever they wanted, wherever they asked. And the result – even though they were far from finished – was already looking beautiful.

He pulled his T-shirt away from his chest and flapped it against his damp skin.

'It's pretty amazing.'

He looked up and was treated to a view of a gorgeous pair of legs, stretching from trainers all the way up to cut-off jean shorts. He was so freaking lucky. 'Yeah, it's pretty cool.'

'Thought you might be thirsty.' Evelyn leaned down, giving him a very *interesting* view as she handed him a tall glass, already dotted with condensation. 'Your mum's lemonade. She's made a vat of it.'

'It is good.' Jake downed half the glass in one go. 'How's it all going?'

'Really good.' Evelyn smiled so happily that suddenly all his aches disappeared in a flood of warmth. 'Once the tables are set up, we'll be virtually done in here. And people have already started work in the park, and the council are putting the lights up through the village centre.'

He downed the rest of the glass. 'So what's the next job on the list?'

Evelyn looked down at the clipboard she'd used as a drinks tray and ran her finger down the list. 'How about helping with decorating the village square?'

'Sounds good.'

Evelyn laughed. 'That's only because you've been in here all day. You haven't seen the trees yet.'

'Trees?' Jake suddenly wondered what he'd gotten himself into.

'This way.' He couldn't help but watch her as she sashayed through the marquee, clipboard in hand, in full organisation mode. Jake followed, thinking that he could happily let her organise him for years to come.

'So, what do you think?'

'I think we've got something really special here.' The words slipped out before he could stop them, and he winced inwardly. He'd promised Evelyn he'd try and help her to find a bit more "joy and fun" in her life. It didn't matter that he suspected he wanted a lot more than that; that was all she was able to offer, and he didn't want to risk putting too much pressure on her, and losing what they did have.

'What?' Evelyn spun to look at him, an odd look on her face.

'Here in Broclington,' he amended clumsily, part of him hating himself for wimping out. 'The whole community coming out to help. All the trees and everything.' He indicated the dozens of trees standing along the square, that were already being decorated by villagers of all ages.

223

'Yes, it really is a special place,' Evelyn agreed, but she still watched him with the odd look.

'So what is it you want me to do?'

'Well, we still need to garland the main tree, and finish decorating the top half. How are you with heights?'

'Not too bad.' He eyed up the fir tree, which was now over twenty feet tall, and smiled at the plaque that was in danger of disappearing beneath its big branches. It was only eight years ago the village had decided to club together and buy a live fir tree to be planted in the corner of the village square for Christmas. It had been lovingly cared for, watered and decorated ever since, and was thriving as a visual representation of the sense of community in the village. 'What do you want up there?'

'The school have been making paper snowflakes, and the teachers strung them all together on ribbon.'

'And you thought the tree our current villagers planted should be decorated by our next generation? Very appropriate.'

'The committee thought so. Plus so many of them are friends with Summer. I think they all liked having things to do to help.' She looked at the floor momentarily, and for a second Jake could see her eyes glistening in the sun. 'Everyone has wanted to do things to help.'

'That's just how we do things here.' He swung an arm around her shoulder, and pulled her in close, revelling in the way she fitted so easily against him. 'So, take me to the snowflakes.'

# Chapter Sixteen

Evelyn bolted awake, her heart thumping as the adrenaline spiked and she tried to work out what was wrong and what had woken her.

The bed bounced, and a soft giggle filled the darkness.

Now more awake, Evelyn slid her hands out from under the covers, and seized the little monster jumping on her. She tackled the monster and pinned her to the bed, half under the covers. 'Have you any idea what the time is?'

'Nope, but it's Christmas day.'

'I suppose it is.' Evelyn smiled as she tucked the covers around them both. 'But it is still really early. And it's going to be a long day. You should try to get some sleep.'

'But I'm too excited,' Summer argued, even as she stifled a yawn.

'But you want to have enough energy to enjoy every single minute, don't you?'

'S'pose.'

'So maybe we could go back to sleep? At least until it gets light?'

Summer gave her a disgusted sigh. 'Ugh. If I have to,' and cuddled against her mother. Evelyn breathed in her daughter's warm, sleepy scent and closed her eyes happily, grateful for the incredibly precious moment. And the chance to get a little more sleep.

An hour or two later, when the sun was finally filtering through the curtains, Evelyn carefully slipped out of bed and tiptoed out of the room. She wanted Summer to get as much sleep as possible. And from the slightly selfish point of view that every parent would understand, but rarely admit to – except after a few drinks and in very select company – she enjoyed a few minutes to herself to sip coffee and just relax before switching into "mum mode".

The enormous importance of the day weighed heavily on her shoulders, and her stomach turned at the thought of food. The fears that had been plaguing her for the last few weeks returned, bringing friends and piling up her stress levels until even the coffee turned sour in her mouth.

She was blown away, and humbled, by all the work that the community had already put into raising funds for her and Summer, and the village did look beautiful. But she couldn't help the doubts and fears that refused to be ignored. Broclington was big – as far as midland villages on the edge of the Cotswolds, they were one of the biggest, but they were still just a village community. The amount of money needed to fund Summer's treatment seemed unsurmountable, especially when it was a village community spearheading the campaign.

She blew on her coffee, deciding she would try not to worry too much. Instead, she would focus on all the positive, fun, and beautiful things happening that weekend. Summer deserved the most magical and wonderful of Christmases, and Evelyn was going to make sure she got exactly that.

She smiled at the sound of feet bouncing down the stairs, rapidly followed by the patter of paws.

'Merry Christmas, Mummy!' Summer crashed through the door, followed by Tilly who skidded across the floor.

'Merry Christmas, Summer.' Evelyn gave her a warm hug before kneeling. 'And Merry Christmas to you too, Tilly.' The little dog ran in circles, barking excitedly. 'Hush.' Evelyn laughed. 'You'll wake Nanny.'

'Too late.' Summer flew out of the kitchen at the sound of Linda's footsteps trudging down the stairs. 'Happy Christmas, Nanny.'

'Happy Christmas, my lovelies.' Linda appeared at the door, Summer cuddled tightly against her side.

'Can we open presents now?' Getting into the spirit of the weekend, Linda had decided to put up her own tree and decorations – complete with gifts!

'How about some breakfast first?' Evelyn asked, not holding out much hope that she'd get Summer's attention long enough for anything even resembling a healthy breakfast. Not that she blamed her. She was excited too. Not that many months ago, she'd spent Christmas morning in an isolation room, in a mask and gloves, praying as Summer fought to hang on for long enough for the antibiotics, corticosteroids, and everything else to work. The thought of seeing her tear through the gifts piled under the tree was exciting.

'Tell you what'—Linda poured herself a coffee—'I've got some breakfast pastries in the freezer. Why don't we put those on and while we're waiting for them to cook, you can see what Santa left. Sound good?'

'Santa's been?' Summer's eyes went so wide that her eyebrows disappeared into her fringe.

'Of course he has.' Linda answered like it was the most obvious thing in the world.

'Are you sure?'

'Well, it is Christmas, isn't it?'

'Sort of.' Summer pulled a face. 'But Annie at school said it's not really proper Christmas, because it's not December.'

'Well Annie doesn't know what she's talking about.' Evelyn forced a smile to hide the scowl threatening to break out. 'Does she, Mum?'

'No, she does not.' Linda pulled her head out from the freezer, clutching the pastries she'd promised. 'But then, maybe her nanny hasn't spoken personally to one of Santa's elves to let him know about our special event.'

If it was possible, Summer's eyes got even wider. 'Did you really?'

'You might say Mrs Clause is a friend of mine.' She shot Evelyn a wink over Summer's head.

'Can we hurry up? I really, really want to see what Santa brought!'

'OK, OK.' Linda arranged the food carefully on a tray, and popped it into the oven.

Evelyn laughed as daughter and dog raced into the living room, squealing and barking with excitement. 'Friends with Mrs Clause, huh?'

'And why not?' She poured herself a coffee and held her hand out for Evelyn's cup. 'I thought this might be one of the last Christmases, you know, while she's young enough.'

Evelyn nodded in understanding, worrying how long it would be until someone like Annie stole the magic by bursting the Santa bubble.

'Mum, Nanny! Come on!' Evelyn smiled. The next Christmas didn't matter. For now, Summer believed, and that was enough. And after everything the community had already done for them, she was starting to believe too.

Jake surveyed the trees and decorations lining the square with a satisfied grin. It was the final thing to check, and everything was either ready, or nearly ready for the weekend's festivities and fundraising.

The vans and cars with all the stallholders were already trundling into the recreation ground to set up their wares and the festive fete. The Santa's village, which would lead to the grotto in the newly decorated library, was set up and just awaiting the arrival of the village's "elves". And Mr and Mrs Clause, who would be accompanied by some deer, courtesy of a few calls made by the local vet.

The cricket pavilion and marquee were set up, and shimmering with lights and decorations, and the trees in the park had been strung with lights, turning the place into a strangely warm and sunny Christmas fairyland.

The main street, which the parade would be heading down in a few hours, was lined with lights, garlands and giant baubles. Puddles of coloured fabric was spaced out along the pavements, waiting for the fans to be turned on when they would pop up into brightly coloured Christmas characters that would wave and lead people towards the village school, where the playground was being turned into a snowy scene, straight from the front of a Christmas card, complete with an outdoor, all weather synthetic ice-rink, donated by a company who had a weekend with no bookings – as most of their work was in winter.

They'd also brought with them a firm who specialised in creating fake snow, and he couldn't wait to see what the school would look like when they were finished. And, the pièce de résistance, a giant snow globe in which people would be able to walk, take photos, and meet the village's very own talking badger – once their volunteer was in costume. It was going to be amazing.

'It looks good,' he murmured.

'It does. We've done a bloody good job, mate.' Nick clapped him across the shoulder.

'We couldn't have done it alone. The response from the community has been incredible.' He gave Nick a big hug, thumping him on the back a few times. 'And we couldn't have pulled off anything like this without your help. Thank you.'

'Not a problem. It's going to be awesome.' He hesitated when a coach pulled up and started to offload people. He waved to the driver. 'You're early, Dave.'

'I know. But the car park is already filling up with people. Jim's not far behind me. We thought hanging around the village was better than people hanging around a field.'

'But we're not kicking off for over an hour.'

'I'm just doing what I'm told.' Dave shrugged. 'I'll be heading back for another load of people. And we've called in another coach to help.'

'How many people are there already?'

'Didn't stop to count.' Dave grinned. 'But I reckon we're going to be spilling over into the next field before the end of the morning.'

Summer was struggling to hold still from excitement as the hairdresser wove sparkly clips and pins through her hair to complement the tiara waiting on the bench in front of them.

'Did I tell you what Santa got me?'

230

Mia, the hairdresser working patiently around Summer's excitement, smiled indulgently. 'No, I don't think you did. So, Santa made a special delivery to you?'

'Yeah! Can you believe he came in summer? But Nanny said it's OK, because I didn't get a proper Christmas in winter.'

'So what did he bring you?'

'A hoodie with a big heart and Boston on it, coz that's where the doctors with the special medicine are. And a snow globe which you shake, and then snow and glitter falls in it. And in the middle is Boston. And a puzzle book, and a big bag of sweets for when we're on the plane. Did you know that your ears pop when the plane goes up and down? Nanny said it feels weird, but it doesn't hurt. And if you suck sweets, it isn't so bad.'

'She's right.' Mia nodded.

'Have you been on a plane? I never have.'

'A few times,' Mia replied. 'But not for as long as it will take for you to get to Boston. It's really good fun – you get your own little TV in the back of the seat in front of you, and special food.'

'Wow.' Summer's eyes widened, and Evelyn grinned at her in the mirror.

'So, are you nervous about today?'

'I was a little bit. Nanny and Mum and Nick said there's going to be lots of people, but Jake made it OK.'

Evelyn glanced up at Summer's words, curious to hear that not only had Summer been nervous, but also that she'd spoken to Jake about it rather than her.

'He said everyone would only be there coz they want me to get better,' she continued, not aware of how Evelyn was hanging on her words. 'And that Santa will be next to me to hold my hand if I do get nervous. And that no one can be nervous when they're sitting next to Santa.'

'Jake sounds like a very clever person.' Mia smiled. 'Is he your boyfriend?'

Summer giggled so much that Mia had to pull the curling tongs away from her head to avoid catching her with them. 'That's silly. Jake is Mummy's boyfriend. Not mine!'

'Oops.' Mia winced apologetically. 'He still sounds like he's very clever.'

'He is,' Summer agreed. 'I like him.'

Me too, Evelyn thought. She more than liked him. A lot more.


Jake could feel Evelyn trembling as she stood next to him, her hand squeezing his so much that it made his knuckles creak, but there was no way he was asking her to let go. The music from the silver band – because Broclington didn't just have a *brass* band – swelled and Evelyn's hand tightened even more.

She had smiled and helped Summer into the carriage that would be pulled just behind the silver band, heading up the rest of the carnival. He'd watched, and waved, as Evelyn fussed with Summer's dress and opened up the lacey parasol to protect her from the sun, and given strict instructions to "Santa" to not let her get too hot, or too excited, in spite of who he was beneath the beard and hat. Though, in deference to the heat, he'd forgone the fur lined coat in favour of a red shirt, shorts, and tie covered in elves. Next to him, Summer looked like a snow princess, all sparkling and shining with excitement.

Evelyn had blown her a kiss – careful not to smudge the glittery make-up that Summer was so excited about –

before grabbing Jake's hand and they'd raced from the meeting point to the first corner the carnival would come around, wanting to experience every single moment of the whole event. He looked around the usually quiet pavements and was amazed to see people squashed up four and five abreast, crammed into every spare inch on the pavement. Around them, people balanced on walls, and small children sat proudly on the shoulders of their parents. Jake had never seen the village so busy.

'Are you regretting your decision not to ride with her?' he asked, leaning down to be heard above the crowd.

'Yes, a little,' Evelyn answered. 'But this is her event, and what was I going to do? Don some pointy ears and jingle bells, and play an elf who just happens to be twice her height?'

'I think you'd make an adorable elf.' He gave her a swift kiss, then flicked one of the bells that hung from her tinsel-laden headband.

After a few moments, Evelyn strained, stretching up on tiptoe to ensure she saw the procession as soon as possible, and didn't miss a single moment of Summer's ride. Jake found himself craning his neck to do the same, his phone already out and in video mode to ensure he captured every precious second, even though he knew there were far better cameras already poised to capture everything and play it back on Natalie's show.

A cheer went up as the band rounded the corner, marching in time with the version of jingle bells that they played. The sun bounced off their highly polished instruments, creating dazzling patterns in their eyes. Evelyn's hand tightened around his even more and then pulled away as she spotted the carriage and started waving, even though Summer probably couldn't see her yet.

The local dance school, all bedecked in white leotards and floaty skirts and with tinsel woven into their hair, danced alongside the slow-moving carriage, careful not to distract the white horses pulling it.

The crowds teeming the street appeared to be mostly made up of families, and for a few moments Jake felt jealous of those dads who held their children's hands so tightly. He wasn't under any illusion – he knew that a lot of the people were there for the fun and spectacle of Santa in the sunshine – but at that moment, they were cheering along with him for the little girl sat beside Santa, and pouring out good wishes towards her. For Summer, whose dress sparkled in the sunlight, and who shimmered like a fairy as she waved and blew kisses to everyone waiting to see her.

'Doesn't she look beautiful?' Evelyn's voice was awed.

'Incredibly.' Jake felt his chest tighten with an overwhelming sense of pride and adoration. He was as crazily in love with this little girl as he was the woman standing next to him. And in order to keep them both happy and safe, he was going to have to send them away. The thought soured his mood as he considered life without them. There was no question in his heart about how he felt, but he also knew that the relationship was so new and fragile that the chance of it surviving countless months when they'd be apart – with Evelyn dealing with the most stressful situation that any parent ever could – was incredibly low.

Bile rose in his throat as he struggled not to let his fears for the future destroy the day. So, instead, he tried to focus on the magic of the moment, and lose himself in the goodwill of the people all around. Any trace of misery and self-pity disappeared when Summer's eyes locked with his and she gave him a special wave and blew him a kiss. He waved back furiously, almost forgetting the recording phone in his other hand.

He kept waving and cheering until Summer passed them, and then looked down at Evelyn. Tears ran down her face smearing her make-up, but she looked up at him with so much joy. He quickly wiped her tears away with the tips of his thumbs and gave her a quick hug before offering a tissue.

She took it gratefully, and leaned against him. He slipped his free hand around her shoulder, tucking her against him where she fit so perfectly. She slid her arm around his waist and rested her head against his shoulder, and they stood like that, taking comfort from each other while they watched the rest of the carnival, march, dance and float by in a blaze of colour, hope and fundraising.

Every local children's and young people's group was represented in the carnival: the scouts marched past proudly, dressed in their best uniforms and followed by the cadets from the neighbouring areas. The village school had a float filled with storybook characters, and the senior school from the next town over had scenes from *Grease the Musical*.

The local dramatic group dressed their lorry as a stage, and were in full costume as they performed scenes from their latest show. The Broclington Bell-ringers had their handbells, and supported the choir as they sang Christmas songs.

Some of the local businesses had sponsored floats – and the retirement home Linda worked at part-time were dressed in Hawaiian style shirts and dresses, wearing flower garlands as they waved from the bed of their lorry, which had been dressed to look like a tropical island. Evelyn didn't know how they'd got the residents onto the lorry, or how they planned to get them down, but they did look fantastic, and she appreciated the effort. She laughed as one of the residents shoved a brightly coloured fishing net filled with change under her nose and shook it. Unlike the children on the other floats who had clearly been instructed to be on their best behaviour, the residents had fewer reservations about catcalling the crowd for extra donations.

Even the toddler and baby day-care group were out in force, dressed as sparkly snowflakes and snowmen, with their prams and pushchairs turned into sleighs and sparkling with tinsel and glitter.

As the last float meandered by, Evelyn grabbed Jake's hand and tugged him into the road to follow.

'What are we doing?'

'Becoming part of the parade.' She laughed as more people fell into step around them. 'Can you believe how many people are here? It's amazing.'

'It really is.' Jake felt slightly amazed himself.

As they walked further down the street, more and more people joined them, jumping off the pavements to become part of the parade. As they turned the corner, Evelyn's fingers tightened around his once again, and Jake grinned so much it almost hurt when he realised why: as far as they could see down the main street, people were lining the pavements, squished shoulder to shoulder as they dug into pockets and purses to drop money into the waiting buckets and nets. There were thousands and thousands of people there, a lot of them in festive colours, clothes and hats, and they were all there to support Summer's Christmas.

It was overwhelming, and he was filled with a deep sense of pride – both in what he'd helped to achieve for Summer, and for the brilliant Broclington community. What they'd created here was truly fantastic and he realised, for the first time, that it could be something far bigger than just this one year, and this one event and cause.

He spotted the local news team and Natalie Rosh, front and centre on the podium overlooking the parade route – just as she'd promised.

By the time they reached the car park at the cricket ground, there were more people than there was room, and the crowd spilled out onto the already closed road. After a few moments, everyone quietened as Santa and Summer appeared on the cricket pavilion balcony, and Jake held his breath, worried that the huge crowd would be intimidating, but his concerns were groundless as she stepped forward and waved confidently before blowing kisses to the audience.

A few moments later, Natalie stepped out of the pavilion, looking as though she hadn't just hotfooted it from the parade, and gave the crowd a warm smile. As planned, she took Summer's hand in her left, and raised the microphone in her right. When she'd offered to open the event, Nick had jumped at the opportunity, telling them all that a regional celebrity would attract even more attention – and donations.

And he'd been right. Natalie had been running an advent-style countdown on her show, featuring a different activity every day that would be at the event – advertising for both the event and the vendors who'd donated so much – and it had clearly worked judging from the amount of people already there. She worked the crowd like a pro, as at home in the live setting as she appeared on screen every day, building up the excitement in waves until Jake doubted there was a single person within hearing of the loudspeakers who wasn't engaged and excited.

'All right, all right, thank you so much for your incredibly kind welcome. But we all know that it's not really me you're here to see.' She waited until the noise lulled, and spoke again, this time in a quieter voice that everyone fell almost silent to hear. 'You, me, your friends and family, we're all here because there is something that is more important than anything else we could have planned for today. Because we've heard of a cause that's so vital, and so intrinsically human, that *not* being here was unthinkable. It's a cause for kindness, love, sharing, and light that is found in the darkest, coldest part of the year. It's the cause of Christmas, in summer …' She paused and looked at Summer. 'It's giving hope to a little girl and her family, when no one else could.'

Jake felt goosepimples race over his arms in chills despite the heat of the sun. 'She's brilliant, isn't she?'

Evelyn nodded fervently, not taking her eyes from the balcony that had become a stage.

'So,' Natalie continued, 'I'd like to thank you all for being here, and remind you to dig deep, spend lots of money for this vital cause, and have a wonderful time.'

Summer tugged on her hand, and Natalie held the microphone out to her. 'I was too sick for Christmas last year. I was in a hospital and too sick for visitors. Even Santa. Only my mum was allowed.' She paused as murmurs of sympathy rippled around the crowd, and Jake felt like his heart would burst from pride. 'So I wanted to say thank you. Everyone. For coming to my Christmas.' She hesitated again, before adding, 'I'm Summer, by the way.'

Next to him, almost unheard amongst the laughter and cheers of thousands, Evelyn made a choking noise somewhere between a laugh and a sob. When he saw the sparkle on her cheeks, he pulled her against him, her back against his chest, and his arms tightly around her waist to offer the support and comfort she needed.

When he looked up again, the microphone was in the hand of Santa. 'Ho, ho, ho! Merry Summer's Christmas!' He waited for the applause to wane. 'You've all heard what these two lovely ladies have had to say, and you all know how important this weekend is. So, as the expert on all things Christmas, I now declare Summer's Christmas officially open! Ho, ho, ho!' He waved his hand, and the park gates were swung ceremoniously open.

Another, huge cheer went through the crowd, and people started to file through the gates, through the avenue of decorated trees, and into the waiting fete grounds.

Evelyn laughed as she caught Summer and spun her around in the air.

'Did you see me? Wasn't that awesome!' Summer squealed in delight. 'Jake, did you see when I waved to you? I blew you a special kiss.'

'I know, munchkin.' He wrapped her in a hug when she launched herself at him which ended up in him carrying her. 'And I loved that you blew me my own special kiss.'

'It was the bestest thing ever!' Summer declared, bouncing in his arms. 'Can we go and get reindeer ice creams? And I want to try the ring toss and snowman coconut shy. And I did want to go and see Santa, but,' and she leaned closer to Jake, 'I don't think it's really Santa.'

'What do you mean?' Evelyn felt her heart drop. She didn't want today to be the day when Summer's belief in magic ended.

But, as usual, Jake saved the day.

'Well, obviously he isn't the really real Santa. He'll be busy in his workshop designing new toys, and helping the elves make them all. This is one of his super special, affiliated, and magically approved alternatives. Like how your mum is sometimes a locum nurse, when the normal nurse is busy.' He shot Evelyn a wink. 'Isn't that right?'

Her throat constricted tightly, and not for the first time that day, she wondered if she'd done the wrong thing trying to put limits on their time together. She'd wanted to protect everyone from being hurt when she and Summer left for Boston – but watching how Jake and Summer interacted, she worried they were all in too deep already. She could handle the heartbreak – she'd do anything for her daughter. But the thought that she might be hurting Jake and Summer too tore her up inside.

He nudged her and grinned. 'I said, isn't that right?'

She forced herself to answer. 'I have sometimes been a locum, yes. And people have done the same for me too.'

'So is it OK that I think your dad might be a Santa locum?'

Evelyn grimaced, not quite knowing how to answer.

Jake shrugged. 'Who better to tell Santa who belongs on the naughty list and the nice list than a GP? They always know what's going on.'

'I guess.' Summer seemed mollified, and Evelyn breathed a sigh of relief. She watched as Jake placed Summer carefully on the ground and smiled when he tweaked her nose and made her giggle, and her chest ached. It was so unfair that right when she'd finally met an amazing man who made her feel so happy and safe and loved, and who showed Summer the attention and affection that her own father had withheld, she'd have to leave him. The timing was so bad that she sometimes wondered if she'd been cursed to never be happy in love.

Needing to distract herself from such morose thoughts, she gave Summer a bright smile. 'So what do you want to do next?'

Summer thought for a second, before jumping up and down with excitement. 'Everything. I want to go to the fete, and pet the reindeer, and ride the donkeys, and get a Rudolph ice cream, and go in the snow globe and dance in the snow, and play every game in the whole village.' She slipped one hand into her mum's, and grabbed Jake's hand with her other – the simple act tugging at Evelyn's heart. Summer hadn't even hesitated before reaching out to Jake, and Evelyn envied her the ease and confidence of the gesture. She wished she could pull him as close and hold him tight with as much ease as her daughter did.

'*Annnnd*,' Summer continued, unaware of her mum's inner turmoil, 'I want to go and see Santa in his grotto. Even though I know it's not really the real Father Christmas, if he's approved by the real Santa, he can get a message to him. Do you think?'

'I think that makes a lot of sense.' Evelyn nodded in agreement. 'Did you want to ask for something else?'

'Maybe.' Summer pursed her lips as she thought. 'But I mostly wanted to say thank you. For my presents, and for lending us his magic so we could make Christmas now. Do you think that would be OK?'

'I think that would be very, very OK.' Yet again, Evelyn was amazed by the kindness and thoughtfulness that Summer showed. She'd been through so much pain and suffering – more in the last few years than most people did in a lifetime – and still she was such a beautiful, kind soul who put others first.

'I think that's a great list.' Jake lifted his arm in time with Evelyn's so that Summer could swing between them every few steps. 'But if I get any say in this, food will definitely be involved soon.' As if in agreement, his stomach growled and made Evelyn and Summer both laugh.


The village was absolutely packed, and as they made their way across it, Summer held tightly onto Jake's hand and admitted that she'd never seen so many people in one place. She was asked for photos again and again and smiled and posed patiently each time, even though he sensed her starting to get tired. As he watched, her smile started to droop a little, and on occasion she seemed to stumble and he was reminded of what this whole event was for; though she was a bright, stubborn, sometimes precocious and always adorable little girl, she was still sick, and there was a tumour in her spine.

After a moment of thought, he hustled her into the doorway of one of the beauticians – now closed so staff could enjoy the day and paint faces, and offer hair braids at their stall in the fete. He whipped off the lightweight overshirt he'd not bothered to button over his T-shirt, and wrapped it around Summer, before gently removing her tiara and replacing it with his baseball cap. As disguises went, it was pretty weak, but he figured it might give her enough anonymity to at least get something to eat. His shirt hung almost to her ankles, which made him smile, but it did cover most of her dress.

'Thank you.' Evelyn gave him a smile of such heartfelt gratitude and love that he almost gave in to the urge to drag her against him, and cover her in kisses. If they'd been anywhere else, he was sure he would have. But instead, he contented himself with holding her hand, and taking Summer's hand in his other, and leading her to The Brockle's Paws where Margaret and her team had set up stall to sell Christmas themed ice creams and ice slush drinks – in raspberry and lime flavours.

Within a few minutes, they'd got their refreshments and found a spot on the wall where they could all perch in the shade, and Summer happily bit the cherry nose off an ice cream masquerading as Rudolph. She grinned up at Jake, and offered him one of the chocolate pretzel antlers. When he leaned forward to taste the treat, Summer giggled and pushed it up, daubing his nose with spiced chocolate ice cream.

But instead of grinning at him as he'd expected her to, Jake felt Evelyn stiffen beside him. He looked at her with concern; she'd gone from being happy and laughing to shaking, with horror painted across her features, in just a few seconds.

'Oh please no, no, *no!*' Her voice was a pained whisper. 'What is *he* doing here?' The vehemence and anger she managed to imbue into a single word made him rock back in shock. He'd never heard pure hate from her before.

# Chapter Seventeen

Anger and fear flooded Evelyn's veins. Charlie, that low-down, sorry excuse for an ex and a father had the audacity to show up on Summer's special day and potentially ruin it. He hadn't had the backbone to tell them he was unhappy, had instead cheated and lied, and nearly killed their daughter with his despicable behaviour.

He'd been so invested in impressing his new girlfriend that he'd cut off funds and refused the visits he and Summer were entitled to, and ignored them both for months. She didn't know if it was his way of trying to protect himself from the pain of losing Summer, but she didn't honestly care; when he'd first left, Summer had cried for weeks, asking where her dad was, and why he didn't love her any more. With every one of Summer's sobs, the remnants of Evelyn's love for Charlie had disappeared – washed away by their daughter's tears and replaced with anger.

And Evelyn had never been able to give her daughter any answer that could take away her hurt, ease her tears, or soothe the fact her dad wasn't there for her.

She looked down at Summer, happily engrossed in her ice cream and laughing with Jake. In that moment, Evelyn knew she couldn't bear to let Charlie take away anything else from Summer.

She could feel Jake's eyes on her, and forced herself to stay calm as she met his worried gaze. 'Can you please take Summer to find her nan?'

'But you said I could go see Santa …'

'And you will. But right now, I need you to go with Jake. Please.'

'What's wrong?' Jake mouthed the words over Summer's head.

Evelyn couldn't keep her eyes from flicking to Charlie as he shouldered his way through the crowd, still looking around. He hadn't spotted them yet, but it was only a matter of time. Despite the huge crowds, it wasn't that big of a village.

Jake shook his head, not understanding.

'My ex.' Evelyn murmured the words, not wanting Summer to realise what was happening. 'Now, Summer. Go with Jake to find Nanny, please. No arguments.'

'I'm not sure I'm happy about this …' Jake began.

'Please, Jake …' She took a deep breath, knowing time was running out. 'I'm fine. Please, take Summer to find my mum.'

He nodded reluctantly, before holding a hand out to Summer. 'Come on, let's go find your nan.'

She pouted for a moment, before putting her hand in his and glaring at Evelyn. 'I know something's wrong. I'm not happy about this too.'

'I know.' Evelyn placed a kiss on her daughter's cheek, once again amazed at how insightful she was becoming. 'Thank you. I'll come find you in a bit.'

She waved cheerfully as they headed away, and then turned back to where she'd last seen Charlie and squared her shoulders. She strode towards him.

'What the hell are you doing here?'

'Evie, sweetie.' He smarmed his way towards her, the slick smile and hair that she used to love so much now looking slimy to her. 'What type of greeting is that for your husband?'

'Ex-husband. Or did you miss the decree absolute hitting your doormat?'

He waved dismissively. 'You know what I'm like with paperwork. You look good, Evie.'

'If I do, it's no thanks to you.' She kept her distance from him, but kept her voice down. She was only too aware that she was more in the public eye today than she'd ever been before. But even knowing that, she wasn't willing to put up with any of his nonsense.

'Aww, c'mon Evie. Don't be like that.' He reached out his hand towards her, and she pulled back sharply.

'Why are you here, Charlie?' She'd already spent more time in his company than she wanted to. Ever again. 'You're not welcome.'

Uncertainty clouded his face momentarily before the charming smile was back as he changed tack. 'Where's Summer?'

'Why?'

'Because I'd like to see her. She is my daughter.'

'Oh really?' The anger that had been bubbling in her veins geysered to the surface. 'Where the hell were you when she needed you then? When *we* needed you? When Summer was in a hospital bed, fighting for her life against the infection *you* gave her, where the hell were you? When she was crying in pain and begging for her daddy, where were you?'

'I didn't know.'

'You didn't want to know. You were too busy with your new *girlfriend*.' She spat the word out, trying to rid herself of the bad taste it coated her mouth with.

'I'm only human, Livvy.'

'You know your parents stopped taking my calls too. They cut off all contact with Summer. Any idea why that might be?'

'Not a clue. You know how my parents can be.' He shrugged off the responsibility, just like she knew he would. He was so unlike the man she'd married, that it felt like she was staring at a stranger.

'I'll ask you one more time, not because I'm really all that interested, but because I want you to leave, and not ruin this weekend for Summer. Or any other day. What do you want?'

Charlie tugged at his shirt collar. 'I saw the stories about Summer online. They said if she gets to America, she'll get better. Like properly better. I thought, when she is, I thought maybe we could give it another go. What do you think?'

'What do I think?' Evelyn forced herself to take a few deep breaths, before stepping closer to him, not wanting anyone around them to hear what she was about to say. 'Are you freaking kidding me? You nearly killed Summer!' Evelyn hissed through clenched teeth.

'It was just a stupid mistake. Is it an apology you want? I'm sorry. There we go. Can we move on now?' He stepped even closer to her. 'We were good once, Evie. We could be again. We could be a family.'

'You have a family. What about your new baby?'

'He never stops crying. And I'm not even sure it's really mine. It doesn't look like me.'

'*It*?'

'C'mon, Evie. Don't be mean about this. I'm offering to try again.'

'I'm being *mean*?' Her hold on her anger dissolved. 'Are you for fucking real?!' She jabbed him in the chest, forcing him to step backwards. 'You nearly killed our daughter, then threw us away like something you scraped off the bottom of your shoe. You lied, you cheated, and you broke Summer's heart. And now, as if by magic, when there's a bit of media attention and a spotlight you can crawl into, suddenly you reappear. When did you become such a selfish, arrogant, immature bastard!'

'That's a little harsh …' He started to argue, but Evelyn wasn't about to let him interrupt.

'I'm not even close to finished,' she snapped at him. 'Your selfishness was our biggest problem. It wasn't that we had an unhappy marriage – or a loveless one – it was that Summer needed me more than you did, and you couldn't handle that my world stopped revolving around you. So you slunk off to get your ego stroked somewhere else, and now that she doesn't have time to cater to your every whim and constantly chase away your insecurities, you're back. Trying to steal attention from your daughter. Your sick daughter. What type of person does that?'

'I've made mistakes, I admit that. But it's not like you were perfect either. If I changed, it was because of you.'

'How dare you!' Her fury blinded her. Somewhere behind her, Evelyn was aware of familiar footsteps approaching, but in her anger she ignored them. 'I was trying to keep our daughter from dying, and you're blaming me for that?'

He slunk forward. 'You were so busy with Summer, you never really gave me a chance.'

'Well you weren't stepping up to look after her! One of us had to!'

'You could have made more time for me. More time for us. You changed when Summer got sick.'

'Of course I bloody did! She's our *daughter!*'

'And then you raced back down here, to move in with your mum. You cut me out of your life.'

'*You* were the one who left, remember? You emptied our bank account and left me basically broke.' Evelyn forced her arms to remain at her side – it was that or slap the smarm off his face. 'You ignored my calls. I even had the hospital try and call you.'

'I'm here now.' He rested his hands on her elbows, trying to pull her close.

'Get your hands off me.'

'Evie, please.' He gripped her arms more tightly.

'You're hurting me.'

'I think you'll find she asked you to let go.' Jake's voice was harsh and clipped.

'Just bugger off, mate.' Charlie barely bothered to glance at him.

The casual dismissal didn't bother Jake, but the look on Evelyn's face, and the jerk's hands on her like she was some possession, really did bother him. He wanted to grab the bastard by the scruff of his neck and shake him hard. He couldn't care less about the crowd gathering around them, their attention dragged from the festivities to the progressively louder argument. He glared at "Charlie". He figured he had a couple of inches and at least fifteen pounds in his favour – that and years of experience wrestling with less than co-operative patients. The slimeball in front of him, in his expensive looking clothes, looked like he'd struggle to tell one end of a cow from another.

'She asked you to leave.'

'It's not any of your business.' The slimeball flicked his head at Jake.

'Actually, I think you'll find it is,' Jake all but growled. 'Get your hands off her.'

249

'Oh ...' Realisation dawned over the idiot's face. 'This is why you're not interested. You've already got a new lay.' He shook Evelyn.

The world around Jake ran in slow motion as Evelyn's hair bounced back and forth as her head was jerked by the moron shaking her. He saw red, and almost all thoughts vanished as his focus narrowed on the hands hurting the woman he loved.

He grabbed the moron and jerked him away from Evelyn. 'You *do not* get to speak to her like that. And you *do not* get to touch her.'

The idiot shoved him hard, and grinned like the loser he was as Jake was forced to take a couple of steps back to keep his balance. Charlie took full advantage of the moment to grab Evelyn and drag her away, nearly yanking her arm from its socket. Jake's heart leaped as he watched Evelyn react faster than he could reach her, drawing her arm back and landing a punch square on the dimwit's jaw that sent him staggering backwards, his eyes wide in shock as he crashed into a bin.

Jake put himself firmly between Evelyn and Charlie, just in case the idiot was angry and stupid enough to try and hurt her. 'I suggest you walk away.' He ground the words out, fighting to control his anger and remember everything about how he'd been brought up to use words instead of fists.

'You can keep the dirty whore and her cancer-ridden brat.' He spat the words at Jake.

Before he'd even had a chance to process the disgusting words, Evelyn had already launched herself at the jerk, but Jake caught her around the waist and pulled her into his arms. 'He's not worth it, Evelyn. He's just a boil spewing pus – a disgusting growth no one wants. Don't lower yourself to his level.'

She was shaking with fury in his arms, but he held her tightly until she nodded against his shoulder.

'Just fuck off then. Stupid bitch.'

Jake whirled on the idiot, fighting his own urge to finish what Evelyn had started and really beat some manners into the arsehole. 'Don't you ever, *ever* speak about Evelyn or Summer in those terms. They're far too good for you. You didn't deserve them when they were in your life, and you were stupid enough to let them go. Believe me when I say I won't make the same mistake.'

He wrapped his arm back around Evelyn, wanting to protect her from being hurt. Ever again. 'Shall we go find Summer?'

She nodded, and buried her face against his shoulder, trusting him to guide her.

'I'm going to bloody well sue you. I'll take everything you've got.' Charlie struggled to his feet behind them. 'I'll fucking destroy you, and take Summer.'

Evelyn span back so quickly that she jarred Jake's arm. 'No you won't, Charlie. Because if you do, I'll make sure everyone knows who you are, and everything you've done. I've kept quiet for this long because I didn't want to hurt Summer by letting her find out how pathetic you are. But I don't think she'd be that bothered any more. If you'd stayed in contact at all, you'd know this, but she's stopped calling you "Dad". She doesn't even think of you as her dad any more. And you know what? She's better off without you. We both are. So you just go ahead and try it. I dare you. And when I'm done making sure everyone, everyone whose opinion you care about, knows exactly what type of sleaze you are, then I'll sue you for every penny of child support you owe us. Have I made myself clear?'

Charlie nodded silently.

'Good. Now go sort yourself out, Charlie. Crawl back into your hole and see if you can evolve into someone resembling the man I once thought you were. Maybe then, we can talk. But right now, you can stuff off.' She led Jake away.

'Are your all right, love?' An older man he didn't recognise approached them, speaking to Evelyn.

She nodded. 'I'm fine, thank you, Mr. Mason. I just want to go and sit somewhere quiet for a while.'

'Of course.' The man nodded. 'But if he does try anything, you've got us all as witnesses.'

'Thank you.' Evelyn nodded. 'But he won't.'

'Were you telling the truth, are you really all right?' Jake asked quietly.

'Not here. Please.' Evelyn shot him a glance that was full of tension.

'OK.' He guided her gently away from the crowds. 'We can go to mine?'

She nodded.

Neither of them spoke on the way back, and he kept Evelyn tucked tightly against his side, hoping that he'd help her to stop shaking.

She winced when he took her hand to lead her inside. 'Ouch, your fingers look sore.'

'They're fine.'

'Does that hurt?' He gently took her fingers in his.

'No.' She looked up at him with such honesty and passion that his breath caught in his throat. 'Nothing hurts when you touch me.'

Heck, he could understand that; she managed to drive almost all rational thoughts from his mind. He stared down at her, suddenly incredibly aware of the blood pulsing through him, still fuelled by adrenaline. She met his eyes, and he couldn't stop himself from dragging her into his arms and plundering her lips with a deep and hungry kiss. She responded eagerly, moulding herself against him as she twisted her hands through his hair.

'You know, Summer will be happy hanging out with my mum. We probably won't be missed for some time.'

That was more than fine by him. After seeing that jerk with his hands all over Evelyn, he was left with the primal urge to claim her as his, and leave his mark on her. The urge surprised him. He'd always considered himself to be an evolved and modern man, but then again he'd never been so passionate about anyone that he was – quite literally – willing to fight for them. If Evelyn hadn't handled things herself, he was pretty sure he'd have flattened the idiot to keep her and Summer safe from harm.


Hours later, Summer had exhausted herself playing every stall in the fete, ice skating, and jumping around in the snow globe and on every bouncy castle she could find. With everything she'd eaten, it was amazing that she hadn't been sick. She sat on the picnic rug, with a blanket draped around her shoulders, watching as the sun went down and the lights around the park flickered on.

'Look …' Evelyn stroked Summer's hair. 'Isn't it pretty?'

'Like where fairies live.' Summer sighed happily and leaned up against Jake. 'Can I have a hug?'

'Always, princess.' Jake shifted so she could lean up against him, and wrapped an arm around her shoulders.

Evelyn watched as Summer got comfortable against Jake, and felt that pang of sadness that they'd be separated so soon. Jake couldn't abandon his business for the many months that they'd be gone, and knowing how hard he'd worked to build it – Evelyn wasn't willing to ask him to put it all at risk. The knowledge was a dark cloud over her, but she tried to remember her promise to herself and tried to focus on the moment instead of worrying about what the future would bring, or the unfairness of the situation. She was in a far better position than a lot of people, and was incredibly fortunate that so many people had done so much to help her and her daughter.

'Mum, are you going to cuddle with us?'

There was no way she could refuse Summer's plea, so she moved to sit beside them, stretching her legs out until they rested against Jake's, with Summer wedged comfortably between them as they watched Santa and his elves climb onto the stage and read Christmas stories, tell silly jokes, and sing carols and festive favourites.

By the time the show was over, Summer had fallen asleep against Jake's shoulder.

'I hate to wake her.' Evelyn sighed sadly. 'She needs all the rest she can get.'

'So don't wake her.' Jake shrugged the shoulder Summer wasn't asleep on. 'I'll carry her.'

'I can't ask you to do that.'

'I offered,' he murmured. 'And I can't ask you to wake her when she's such a little thing.' Without waiting for an answer, he moved carefully to twist slightly and slip his arms around Summer. She muttered and stirred when he lifted her, but settled again once he was standing, seemingly happy in his arms. It was a sentiment Evelyn could agree with.

They walked home slowly, Jake being careful not to jostle his precious armful, while they talked softly. After she opened the door, Evelyn reached out to take Summer, but Jake just smiled at her. 'I think she's pretty comfortable, and it's been a long day for you too. I don't mind taking her up, if you're OK with it.'

Evelyn smiled at his thoughtfulness. 'Of course I'm OK with it.' She led him up the stairs, held open the door to Summer's room, and pulled down the covers. She watched as Jake slowly, carefully put Summer on the bed. She stirred and complained slightly, but settled almost immediately when Jake rested his hand on her shoulder and hushed her softly. 'Goodnight, princess,' he whispered as he left the room.

Evelyn worked quickly, peeling off Summer's dress and sliding off her shoes with well-practised ease before pulling on her nightdress and tucking the covers loosely around her. When she was done she tiptoed downstairs to join Jake.

'Thank you.' She fought to stifle a yawn. 'For today, for helping me bring Summer home. For everything.'

He leaned towards her, and she felt her pulse quicken, as it so often did around him. 'You're welcome.' He placed a gentle kiss on her lips. 'For today, for carrying Summer, and for everything.' He laughed as she fought to stifle another yawn. 'I would wrangle an invitation to stay …'

'You don't need to wrangle anything. You're always welcome.' Evelyn yawned again.

'And you're practically asleep on your feet. So I'm going to bid you goodnight, and see you tomorrow.'

'Tomorrow,' Evelyn agreed.

Jake stuffed his hands into his pockets as he walked up the street. His mind was a confused jumble of contradicting thoughts. He had thought he'd made his peace with the idea of Summer and Evelyn leaving in the not-so-distant future, and being away for goodness only knew how long. But when he'd held Summer against him and she'd snuggled against his neck, trusting him to keep her safe, his heart had twinged painfully.

He'd done his best to keep his feelings buried deeply, so that Evelyn wouldn't run scared again. He was in trouble; when he'd seen Charlie grab Evelyn, he'd wanted to beat the jerk into a bloody pulp for what Evelyn and Summer had suffered at his hands. When he'd carried Summer home, and she'd cuddled tiredly against him, his heart had all but melted. They filled his every waking thought, and half of his sleeping ones, and the thought of them leaving made him feel physically ill – even though he was well aware it was the only way Summer could get better. But he didn't think he wanted to be with Evelyn for a couple of weeks – or even months. He wanted forever. With both of them. And that *terrified* him. He'd never wanted anything or anyone *forever.* Even his vet surgery was something he planned to retire from one day.

He didn't know what to think, or do, but he did know there was only one person he could turn to. He pulled out his phone, and hit the speed dial.

Nick answered on the third ring. '*Wasssssssup*?'

Jake snorted in amusement. 'You know that wasn't even cool when we were kids?'

'Then it's a classic. Can't ever go out of fashion. So I repeat, *wassssssssssup*?'

'Mate, you're not making this any easier.'

'Sorry. Seriously, what's up?'

'Maybe everything. I don't know what to do,' Jake admitted quietly, knowing that if there was anyone in the world he could talk to right now, it would be him.

'Can I make a suggestion?'

'Please do. I'm out of any of my own,' Jake answered honestly.

'Come meet me at the pub. I'll get the drinks in, and we can sort out whatever it is.'

'All right. I'll see you in a bit.' He swiped the call off, and stuffed his phone and hands back into his pockets.

True to his word, Nick already had two beers waiting on a table in the corner of the bar when Jake arrived. He waited until Jake had sat down and taken a few sips before starting the interrogation. 'So what's going on, mate?'

'Does there have to be something up?'

'No, but there is. Don't forget, I've known you since we were trading football cards and still thought girls had cooties!'

'Simpler times.' Jake laughed. 'When the most important thing was finding that rare sticker to complete the book.'

'Yeah. Simpler times,' Nick agreed. 'But I wouldn't trade them for now. But you didn't come here to reminisce, so spit it out.' Nick gave him a knowing look.

'How did you know, I mean for sure, that Claudia was the one for you?' The words tumbled out, and he tried to wash the taste of their fear away with a couple of gulps of beer.

'Because she made me want to be a better person, someone who I felt was more worthy of being with her. And I liked who I was when I was around her.' He fiddled with his drink. 'And because the thought of not being with her was physically painful.'

'I think I get that,' Jake admitted quietly.

'You think?' Nick guffawed.

'It's not funny.'

'It kind of is, mate,' he argued. 'You've turned your life upside down, dragged me and almost the whole village along with you, found an experimental treatment for a kid you didn't even know this time last year, and pretty much exhausted yourself making sure she can get it. I heard you had a run in with her ex, and Evelyn knocked him on his arse? And that you read him the riot act.'

'There might be some truth to that. What's your point?'

'My point is, that maybe you've found someone you care about enough to take a risk for. Two someones. So what's the problem?'

Jake took a huge breath. 'I tried to tell her before we found out how ill Summer was. After that, it didn't seem fair. Or that important.'

'Love isn't "that important" to you?'

'It's not like I haven't had girlfriends before.'

'But not like Evelyn,' Nick challenged.

'No, not like Evelyn. I knew I loved her and Summer, but I wasn't sure it was love, love. Like you and Claudia forever type of love.'

'Well what the hell did you think it was?' Nick laughed again.

'I don't know.' Jake gulped down the last of his drink, and waved to the barman for another one. He felt like he'd more than earned it. 'If we pull this off ...'

'We will. I've seen the initial numbers,' Nick interrupted to reassure him.

'Really?' Jake felt his eyebrows raise and a silly grin spread across his face.

'Really.' Nick nodded.

'That's great.' His face fell. 'Now I'm going to sound like a selfish arse.'

'Go on.'

'They're going to leave me. To go to Boston and get Summer's treatment, they're going to leave me. And I can't ask them to stay, and I can't go either. What the hell am I supposed to do?'

Nick sighed, and watched his best friend. 'Do you remember what you told me when I was dithering about asking Claudia to marry me?'

'That you were being an idiot. That she was an amazing woman, and if you could somehow convince her to say yes, you should whisk her down the nearest aisle as fast as you could, before she had a chance to change her mind.'

'Yeah, something like that. But you also told me that you'd never seen me happier than when I was with her, and if I screwed it up, it would be the single worst, most stupid thing I'd ever done. And that you'd drop me in the duck pond if I was that stupid.'

'That does sound like me,' Jake admitted. 'But I was right, wasn't I?'

'Yeah, well stranger things have happened.' He grinned. 'Can't think of any right now, but I'm sure they have somewhere.'

'Christmas in summer in Broclington is pretty strange.'

'Yeah, I guess it is.' He looked up and thanked the waitress for their two fresh pints. After she'd left, Nick fixed him with a serious gaze. 'Pay attention, Jakey-boy. In the last few months, you've been more driven and more focussed than I've seen you in years. Probably since you set up your surgery. You've taken on an incredibly stressful situation – one that already sent another man running for the hills, and you know what? I've never seen you happier.'

Jake said nothing, instead flipping a beer mat over and over in his hand.

'You know I'm not usually one for unsolicited advice, but you started this conversation, so you're stuck listening to me now. If Evelyn is it for you – if she's your Claudia – and I think she is, then you owe it to them, and to yourself, to say something. Before it's too late. And before I have to give you a bath with the local ducks.'

# Chapter Eighteen

Evelyn laughed as Jake spun her around the dance floor again and again. Summer had already said goodnight and headed home with Linda, who was yawning almost as much as her granddaughter after the long – and truly magical – weekend.

Evelyn had enjoyed the champagne and cocktails, and the lights strung throughout the marquee seemed to twinkle and reflect off her silvery, floaty dress as she twirled around the bandstand. Jake's arms were warm around her, and his face was alight with happiness as he dipped her and laughed at the way she clung to him. If she closed her eyes, she could have imagined herself Cinderella in the arms of her prince.

Her feet certainly hurt enough to imagine she was wearing glass slippers. When the song ended, she tugged at Jake's hand, and tried not to limp too obviously as she headed back to their seats. It was definitely time to switch to the flats she'd stashed under their table.

'Do you want anything?' Jake's smile mixed with the champagne fizzing through her veins, filling her with warmth and happiness. On a night like this, dancing under countless thousands of stars that draped from the tent poles, hung by the hands of a community that she'd grown to love, and who clearly loved her and her daughter back … On a night like this, almost anything seemed possible.

'No, I'm fine thank you. Just not as young as I used to be when it comes to dancing all night long. What time is it?'

Jake checked his watch. 'Late enough that it's almost tomorrow.'

'It's been a wonderful night.' Evelyn sighed happily as she slid her feet into blissfully flat, cool shoes. 'It's been a wonderful weekend.'

'It's not over yet.' Jake held out his hand. 'Do you fancy some fresh air and a walk in the park?'

'That would be nice.' Evelyn let him help her to her feet and tucked her arm through his. He led her to the end of the marquee, and through the double layer of curtains that separated them from the cool night air. The lights that had been strung throughout the park glistened and sparkled in the slight breeze, and seemed to reflect in Jake's eyes as he smiled at her. The chills that raced over her skin were far less to do with the cool air on her skin, and far more caused by the heat of his lips as they brushed against hers.

The park seemed to glow and swirl as his hands skimmed down her sides to rest on her waist and draw her against him. She pressed herself against his warmth, moulding her body against his and revelling in their heat as he kissed her thoroughly. The world around her came into pinpoint focus, while at the same time, conscious thought evaporated until all she could think about was the feel, taste, and scent of him as he plundered her senses. She was going to miss him so much.

After what seemed like an age, and not nearly long enough at the same time, Jake drew away. 'Have I told you how absolutely stunning you look tonight?' His voice was gruff in his throat and incredibly sexy.

'You might have mentioned it once or twice.' Her voice caught in her throat and came out breathless.

'Once or twice? That's not nearly enough.' He teased her lips again, and ran kisses along her chin. She shivered against him, and he pulled away reluctantly. 'You're cold.' He ran his hands over her bare arms.

'Not really.'

'You've got goosepimples.' He laughed and shrugged off his jacket, and placed a kiss on her forehead as he wrapped it around her shoulders.

She sniffed the jacket, inhaling his clean, slightly spicy scent. It was warm from his body, and the silk lining swished against her skin and dress. 'You always do this.'

'Do what?' He sat on a park bench, and patted the spot next to him.

She sat down. 'Take care of me. Make sure I have the things I need, before I even know I want them. Thank you.'

'You don't ever have to thank me for anything.' She felt him stiffen slightly beside her, and then take a deep breath. 'I'd like to keep taking care of you, and making sure you have everything you ever need and want.'

'It's a nice thought.' Evelyn rested her head on his shoulder, wanting to pretend for a while that it really could be true. But the reality was, it wasn't a choice that was within her gift to make. She had to do what was best for Summer, and it didn't matter what sacrifices she had to make personally – she'd gladly give her world to keep her daughter safe.

'We could make it more than just a nice thought.' Jake tucked a loose strand of hair behind her ear, and let his hand linger on her cheek.

Evelyn forced herself not to nuzzle against him. 'No, we can't. I wish we could, Jake, but we can't have a future together.'

'Why not?'

263

'You know why.'

'Because you're going to Boston?'

'Which is more than three thousand miles away.'

'And?'

'And it's three thousand miles, Jake. And your business is right here.'

'And I'll be busy working, and you're going to be busy looking after Summer, and in and out of the hospital, and in a different time zone. And you've no idea how long you're likely to be out there, because you don't know how Summer's going to react to the treatment, so you can't possibly ask me to wait. And it's not like we're even a proper couple. We're just having fun, right?'

Just fun. Exactly what they'd agreed, and what she wanted. Which was why she didn't understand the hollow, sick feeling in her stomach, or why her palms now felt clammy at the thought of the farewell she'd soon have to say. She already knew Boston was going to be hard, and the fact that she'd be alone was only going to make it more difficult. But she'd managed before, and she'd manage again. There's nothing she wouldn't do for Summer. But she wished so, so much that things could be different.

'Hey.' Jake nudged her shoulder with his. 'Is that about it? Busy with Summer and hospital, three thousand miles and different time zones for an unknown length of time. Are those all your objections?'

'I think they're reason enough, don't you?' Evelyn looked out at the lights, watching as they started to blur behind the veil of her tears.

'No. I don't.' He tucked his fingers under her chin and lifted her face to his. 'Evelyn, it's taken me my whole life to find you and Summer.' He used the pads of his thumbs to wipe away her tears, and took a deep breath. 'I know you've said you're not ready to hear this, but if I don't tell you, I'll always wonder. I love you. And Summer. I think I've known since the Spring Fling. I wanted to tell you the day you met with her specialists, and you came to the surgery afterwards. When you said goodbye to me, the bottom fell out of my world. And the day when the council voted to make Summer's Christmas a reality …'

'… You mean when I kissed you?'

'Yes. It felt like almost everything was right in my world again. And that when we'd gotten Summer her treatment, it would all be right.' He took both of her hands in his. 'I love you both, and I think you should give us a chance. I think you should give us all a chance.'

'But what about the distance? Do you know how many couples don't survive long distance relationships?'

'No, do you?'

'Well, no. Not exactly. But I know it's a lot.' She sighed. 'Long-distance is hard, Jake. And it's not like this is even normal, easy long-distance.'

'No, this is going to be really stressful for you. I appreciate that.' He squeezed her hand. 'That's part of the reason I want to be here for you.'

'Only part?'

'The other part is selfish. I love you and don't want to lose you. Boston isn't *that* far, Evelyn. I can visit. You're making excuses and putting obstacles in the way. And you don't need to. There's only one thing I need to know – do you love me?'

Evelyn nodded, her throat too tight with emotion to get the words out.

'I already know Summer does. So what do you say, will you give us a chance? At love, and happiness, and maybe even a future? We can figure out the logistics later, you just have to say yes.'

'Evelyn'—he squeezed her fingers in his—'I know what you're thinking, and if you say yes I promise I won't let you down. I can't promise I might not make mistakes – I probably will – but I promise I will never, *ever* let you or Summer down. Just please, please say you'll give us a chance. I don't want to lose you. Either of you. My life has been so much better since you've become a part of it. I don't want this – us – to end before we've really started.'

His words filled her with hope, offering the promise of the future that she had barely dreamed possible: one with a real family, a partner who loved her as much as she loved him, and a loving father who would fight for Summer's happiness and wellbeing every day. Evelyn nodded slowly. 'OK.' Her voice was barely more than a whisper, but it was more than enough for Jake. He scooped her up from the bench, and span her around while laughing, and then kissed her thoroughly until she was breathless.

When they finally broke apart, he rested his forehead against hers, with laughter dancing in his eyes. 'I promise you Evelyn, I won't give you cause to regret it. Ever. I love you.' He delighted in saying the words aloud.

'I love you, too.' Her words came far more easily than she expected, and felt so right that she laughed and yelled them into the night air. 'I love Jake Macpearson!'

By the time Jake walked into The Brockle's Paws café the next afternoon, Evelyn, Summer and Linda were already there waiting. Summer was happily eating a Brockle cake and had a milkshake moustache, and Linda was chatting with her granddaughter. But he could feel Evelyn's worry from the door, and see her tense movements as she crumbled her cake into tiny pieces. Almost as if she felt his presence, she looked up and shot him a tight smile.

He could understand her stress. Although Nick had already told them he thought they were going to clear their fundraising target easily, Jake wouldn't be happy until he'd seen the final figures – and he knew Evelyn wouldn't be able to relax either. But Evelyn had enough of her own worries, so he pasted a casual smile across his face and raised his hand in greeting.

'Hi, does anyone want anything else to eat or drink?' He kissed Evelyn's cheek, and gave Summer a hug. 'Well you seem well set, but do you think I should buy your mum something else that she might actually eat?'

'Maybe.' Summer pursed her lips. 'She likes the fruit buns.'

'Noted.' Jake nodded. 'How about you, Linda? Anything for you?'

'No thank you.' Linda shook her head.

'I'll be right back.' He looked to Evelyn. 'Do you want to come see if there's anything you fancy?'

She slipped her hand into his, and he helped her to her feet. As soon as they were out of hearing range, Jake stepped closer to her and lowered his voice. 'Are you OK?'

'Yeah.' Evelyn nodded. Now she was out of the corner where their table was, he could see how tired she was.

'Do you want to try that again?'

'Not really.' She rubbed her eyes, then cursed and checked her fingers. 'Have I just rubbed mascara all over my face?'

'No.' He peered at her closely. 'Just a tiny bit, right here.' He swept the smudge away with the edge of his thumb. 'I have to ask, is it just the stress of today or'—he took a deep breath—'is it that you've changed your mind about what you said last night? Because, in case you're wondering, I haven't.'

Evelyn's face softened as he watched her, and her hand found his. 'No, I've not changed my mind. I meant what I said. I think you're crazy for hoping it will work, because I'm still not so sure, but I'd like to be wrong. Just this once.' She sighed hugely. 'Assuming we even get there at all.'

'You will,' Jake reassured her as he guided her towards the café's counter. 'I'm sure of it. Now, can I get you anything to eat? Another drink.' He ordered quickly – including a coffee and a doughnut for Nick and fruit buns for himself and Evelyn, and carried the tray back to their table.

After what seemed like an age of uncomfortable small talk in which they all tried to politely skirt around the elephant-sized issue worrying them all, Nick finally arrived, laptop in hand and looking hot and sweaty.

'Sorry to have kept you all waiting.' He sat on the bench next to Summer. 'I was just waiting to make sure we had all the figures from last night in and confirmed.' He took the mug Jake offered and took a few long sips. 'Delicious. I must remember to see if they'll sell me some of their bean mix. I think I'm getting slightly addicted. What is it, Brazilian? Columbian?'

'Mate.' Jake struggled to keep the frustration out of his voice. As much as he'd spent weeks reassuring Evelyn that they were going to pull this off, and as much as Nick reassured him they were in good shape, he needed to know for certain and to see the final figures himself.

'Yes.' Nick gave him a bright grin through the mouthful of doughnut.

'We're all waiting.' He glanced over to Summer, wary that she was listening. 'As much as I love you like a brother, if you don't put us out of our misery, I'm going to drop you in the duck pond like when we were kids.'

'All right, all right. Sorry, I'm starving.' He shoved the rest of the doughnut in his mouth and dusted off his fingers before opening his laptop. He pressed a few buttons, and a spreadsheet lit up the screen. He scrolled rapidly, the figures racing by in a frustrating blur. When he reached the bottom of the sheet, he typed in a formula so quickly that Jake couldn't read all of it.

'Can I get a drum roll please?' He grinned at Summer who beat out something resembling a rhythm on the table, before hitting enter and sitting back, looking pleased with himself.

They all leaned forward eagerly to read the bold, black figure at the bottom of the page. Evelyn exchanged a glance with Jake, then looked over to her mum, confusion and worry filling her eyes.

'Fifty-three thousand? That's it? But …'

Jake danced his fingers across the keyboard, scrolling backwards rapidly, before grinning.

'Nick, are you sure about these numbers?'

'Checked them twice. And then a third time because I still couldn't believe it. It's why I was late. I'm sure.'

Jake couldn't help it. The relief burst from his lips in a bubble of laughter.

'I don't understand what's so funny?' Evelyn demanded. 'Surely we raised more than that. We have to have.'

'Look.' Jake ran his finger along the bottom line.

'I don't understand what these numbers are telling me.' Evelyn looked close to tears.

'This is the target figure.' Jake pointed to the astronomical amount in one of the left-hand columns. 'These are the amounts raised by different events and revenue sources – like the online pages. And this'—he let his finger hover over the bold figure again—'this is the surplus.'

'What's surplus?' Summer asked. 'Are we going to Boston or not?'

'Yes, sweetheart.' Evelyn's voice was choked by tears. 'We're going.' She threw her arms around her daughter, who was immediately squished by Linda hugging her as well.

Jake watched them, awed by the feelings of love that were so strong they made his chest ache and his stomach clench. They'd done it. They'd really bloody gone and done it! He punched the air and let out a whoop.

'Uhhh, need to breathe.' Summer's voice was muffled from the hug.

'Sorry, sorry.' Evelyn smoothed her hair back into place. 'I'm just so happy.'

Jake pushed a napkin into Evelyn's hands, and waited patiently while she dried her tears.

'I'm glad we're going to Boston.' Summer grinned up at him, making his heart squeeze again. 'But what's surplus?'

'It's all the extra money we raised.'

'We raised more?'

'Yes.' Nick nodded. 'Quite a lot more than we needed.'

'That's so cool!' Summer grinned. 'We'll have to do something good with it.'

'Definitely.' Evelyn nodded. 'We'll have to think about it.'

'I've got an idea now,' Summer said. 'Do you think the hospital could use it? I know they couldn't make me better, so I've got to go to Boston, but they make lots of other kids better, don't they?'

Jake stared at her in amazement. Even with everything she'd been through, and all the pain and disappointment she'd experienced, and facing a journey that would literally be life or death for her – Summer still showed compassion that a lot of adults lacked. He snuck an arm around her shoulder.

'I think that's a lovely idea.' He gave her a squeeze and had to cough some of the pride and love from his throat to speak clearly. 'You're right, the hospital charity could do a lot with that money.'

'You know what,' Linda mused, 'you've given me an idea, Summer. You're right, there's a lot of children who will benefit from help from the hospital charity. The WI have already started talking about running the event again.'

'It's a good idea,' Nick agreed. 'You'll probably raise less without the figurehead that Summer's been, and you'll miss the novelty value – but equally we're going to get tonnes of social media attention and word of mouth advertising. This could be a thing. Just, next year, we'll try not to plan it all in a matter of weeks.'

'You've been wonderful, Nick.' Evelyn kissed his cheek. 'We'd never have done this without you.'

A few moments later, Margaret appeared from behind the café counter, a laden tray in her hands. 'From the way you're all acting, I think you might be needing this.' She put the tray down on the table. 'The one with the pink roses is for Summer.' She shot Evelyn a wink. 'Fizzy apple.'

They all reached for the delicate, mismatched, bone china cups and Jake laughed when he saw what it was: champagne. He raised his tea/champagne cup in toast. 'To the best community in England. To Broclington!'

'To Broclington!' The others joined in the toast.

'And, if I may,' Margaret added, 'to Summer. Wishing her every health and happiness.'

'To Summer! Health and happiness!'

Summer held up her sparkling apple juice. 'Look out Boston, here we come!'

# *Epilogue*

Jake stood nervously in the arrivals lounge. He knew it was ridiculous to be nervous, but somehow he couldn't stop the butterflies waging an all-out war in his stomach. He hadn't seen Evelyn or Summer without a set of screens and three thousand miles between them since he'd flown home after Christmas. That had been nearly five months ago. They'd missed their first Valentine's Day together, birthdays, and months of the normal, everyday things that were the foundation for any new relationship. He'd desperately wanted to be in Boston with them, but his parents had headed off on their adventure soon after Evelyn and Summer had left for Boston – and he'd been caught out trying to balance running his vet surgery while also trying to help Callum manage his duties as the sole practice manager. He'd stepped in with Sarah – being the best uncle he could – as often as possible, but it hadn't made missing Summer and Evelyn any easier.

He'd made it to the States for Christmas – seeing his parents for long enough to exchange gifts and hugs before they jetted off again to save another part of the world. He wasn't surprised they'd been bitten by the travelling bug: apparently the heat helped with his mum's arthritis, while they both relished the challenge of helping some of the most vulnerable, deprived people on the planet.

He was thrilled for them, but every email from a far off place had made him wish *he* could have dropped everything and leaped on a plane to Boston. But he needed to work and build a life.

There was a lot he, Evelyn and Summer had missed out on – and he was planning to make up for all of those missed moments, and then some. But none of it mattered.

273

Because Summer had responded well to the treatment, and her medical team were happy for her to continue at home. She was back in chemical remission – with no measurable trace of the cancer – and she was tolerating the immunotherapy well. It was showing every sign that it was working and successfully teaching Summer's own immune system to fight the cancer. It truly was remarkable. Evelyn had requested every report, and sent them all to him. He and Cal – and his dad via email from his sabbatical – had devoured them – not only because they cared about Summer, but for the ongoing possibilities for so many other people in the future.

The last five months had dragged miserably for him – even worse than the weeks before Christmas – and now the minutes while he was waiting for their arrival time to tick by and for their flight information to flick over to "disembarking" was starting to feel almost as long as all those lonely weeks. He'd spoken to them both almost every day, and was still sure of his feelings – and Evelyn reassured him regularly of hers – but it was different having a relationship squeezed into calls, promises and pixels than it was being physically together every day. For one thing, he'd have to get better at cleaning up the kitchen and not "leaving things to soak" for quite so long.

The glowing figures on the arrival screen tormented him. There were definitely moving far more slowly than the normal rules of physics allowed.

He flicked his phone screen on again, hoping for a message from Evelyn to let him know they had landed. Still nothing. He was at risk of driving himself insane before they arrived. Trying not to be too irritable, he stomped over to a seat and flopped down, and thumbed open his picture gallery. He smiled to himself, instantly cheered, as he flicked through the photos of his last visit.

Summer grinned at him proudly from behind the glass screen, with Tilly close to heel on a purple leash that matched her new vest as they walked down a brightly lit hospital corridor.

Every time Jake saw that image, he knew all the effort, emails, calls and paperwork to get the little dog out there had been worth it. She'd had to be vaccinated, and quarantined from other dogs for a month before he'd been allowed to take her in to the country. None of that was particularly difficult, though Tilly had developed a wonderful array of stares and whimpers to make him feel guilty every time he had needed to shut her away from other dogs, or lock her in his flat when he went to work. She'd even taken to her travel crate with the minimal amount of fuss or bribery.

The training hadn't been a problem either – he'd known she had the perfect temperament for supporting people and making them feel a little less bad. He'd emailed back and forth and video chatted with the Boston charity responsible for taking therapy dogs into hospitals, and managed to convince them to arrange an "interview" for Tilly at a time when Summer would be in treatment. He hadn't liked lying to the little girl, but Evelyn was right – and it had all been worth it when he'd seen her face as she'd spotted her best four-legged friend trotting towards her, dressed in her purple Therapy Dog vest.

Just as he'd told the charity, it worked out perfectly. Because of the trial nature of her treatment, Summer had to spend a lot more time on site than most patients, and most of that time was spent waiting for tests between appointments and infusions. She'd rapidly grown bored of the hospital gardens and playrooms, and was now thrilled to introduce the younger members of the trial to Tilly. Tilly, of course had lapped up all the fuss and thoroughly enjoyed all the extra hugs and pats as she helped the children to not be so scared or upset by the procedures they were all having to go through.

He flicked to the next picture, and grinned at the image of himself with Summer, both of them covered in flour and chocolate as they tried to make breakfast for Evelyn together. The pancakes had been horrible, but the laughter and time shared with Summer made it all worthwhile. Especially when Evelyn stumbled into the kitchen looking for her morning caffeine fix, and saw the disaster zone they'd created.

He flicked through a few more images, smiling to himself as he let his hand slip into his pocket to check the small gift bag was still there. Even through the coloured fabric, he could feel the cold metal against his fingers. He just hoped he wasn't moving too fast.

Evelyn rubbed her temples tiredly. It had been a really, really long flight, made even longer by Tilly's whining and Summer's constant begging. Tilly had had to be bribed and shoved into her travel crate, and Summer had almost been in tears to see her best friend locked up, despite the fact that it was the only way the little dog was allowed to travel, and Jake's reassurances that she'd been fine when he'd originally flown her over. Though she half-wondered if it was Summer's presence that made Tilly less settled, and more vocal in her complaints as she tried to get to her girl.

Eventually, when they'd learned she was a registered therapy dog, the on-flight steward team had given in to

Summer's begging, and Tilly was released, much to everyone's relief because the whimpering from the crate ceased. Once out, Tilly was the very definition of well behaved – even climbing back into her crate to potty on the special pads that the airline had sold Evelyn.

But while unlocking Tilly had helped her and Summer to relax, it had put Evelyn immediately on edge as she knew she had to watch the dog for every second. She was well behaved, but in a confined space where she and Summer were both bored? It was only too easy for total chaos to break out. So she'd spent the entire flight either comforting the little dog and little girl, or watching them for the smallest sign of mischief.

And she was worried. Of course she trusted the English hospitals, and Callum Macpearson to keep up Summer's treatments and the near-miraculous therapy that was already keeping the cancer at bay far better than anything else before had. But she was nervous. She knew it was silly, but until they'd had their first appointment with the new team in a few weeks, and until she'd seen the medication there in the UK, she knew she'd struggle to be completely happy.

By the time they'd reloaded the little dog for landing, and the tires hit the tarmac, she felt utterly frazzled and wanted nothing more than to climb into her mum's car and finally relax. She couldn't wait to get home, shower the travel grime off her skin, and crawl into bed.

'We're home. We've landed! Come on, Mum!' She had to bite her tongue to not snap at Summer.

'Calm down. We're still going to be here for a while. Other people have to get off first.'

'But that's not fair,' Summer whined in a tone that set Evelyn's teeth on edge. 'We've been on here forever!'

'Everyone has, Summer, and we've got Tilly with us. It'll take time to get her offloaded, so we should let everyone else go first.'

'Fine.' Summer flopped back down in her seat and glared mutinously out of the window for the next few minutes as the plane emptied. Evelyn pulled and tugged at Tilly's carrier, grumbling under her breath as it caught somewhere. After a few more tugs, and a yelp of complaint, the carrier and Tilly shot forward and caught Evelyn's fingers between the hard plastic and the base of the chair. She closed her eyes and exhaled slowly, forcing her temper back under control. 'Come on.' She lifted her cabin bag onto her shoulder, checked Summer had her backpack, and lifted Tilly.

'Finally!' Summer rolled her eyes and all but dashed off the plane, ignoring Evelyn's pleas that she was careful on the stairs.

She struggled with Tilly's carrier, banging her knees every other step and trying not to lose her footing on the stairs from the plane. The corridor to the baggage claim seem endless, and of course she had to scrabble around for the pound coin she needed to release the trolley from its stand. Eventually she had Tilly secured next to their bags, and she could drag them all to the baggage claim. Naturally, because sod's law was real and liked to strike at the worst possible moment, she'd managed to pick the trolley with the wonky wheel, so had to fight all the way there.

By the time she, her bruised shins, and overtired daughter had made it to the carousels, Evelyn was having to fight back the tears. She was exhausted, her legs and back hurt, and she could hear Tilly scratching at the inside of the carrier as it wobbled back and forth. Trying to ignore all the irritations, and her grumbling stomach, she glanced around to try and find the right luggage carousel for their flight. When she finally spotted it, she turned to Summer.

'Stay here with Tilly,' she ordered Summer. 'I'm going to grab our bags. You can look around and see if you can spot Nanny, but *do not move from this spot or open Tilly's crate.*' The last thing she needed now was to lose Summer or Tilly. 'I mean it. If you move so much as an inch from Tilly's side, there'll be no Brockle cakes for tea!'

'OK.' Summer sulked and sat on the end of the trolley, clearly not willing to risk missing out on her favourite treat for a second longer than she already had.

After a couple of revolutions, she finally spotted the ribbons she'd tied around their cases. Of course, all three had come out at once, so she'd probably have to wait another full revolution to claim them all. There was no way she'd be quick enough to grab them all at once. With a sigh, she leaned forward and grabbed the first.

She turned around to put it behind her, and winced when her back complained. By the time she turned back, the bags had vanished, and she cursed under her breath. Hands on hips, she stared at the opening where they would reappear and took a couple more, deep, calming breaths. She waited for the cases to reappear and pounced, wrangling them from the carousel. 'You're going to have to walk please.'

'Ugh, do I have to?'

'Unless you want me to put these cases on top of you, yes. But keep your hand on the trolley. If you let go …'

'I know. No Brockle cakes for tea.' Summer rolled her eyes as she hopped off the trolley and obediently grabbed hold of the handle.

Tiredness made Evelyn short, and she wedged the cases onto the trolley. She pushed the trolley, and it refused to move, so she shoved all her weight against it and cursed as it shot off in the wrong direction.

She had just barrelled, bullied and cajoled the thing through customs and into the busy arrivals lounge when her phone started bleeping. She juggled it out of her pocket and then swore.

'Ummm, that's a bad word.'

Evelyn gritted her teeth. 'Yes darling, I know. I'm sorry. Nanny has just texted to say she can't drive us home. We'll have to get the train.' Which was the last thing she wanted to do; with three big cases, Tilly and Summer the thought of the multiple-change journey made her want to cry.

When she turned around, Summer was trying to smother her giggles behind her hands.

'What's going on? Summer, can you please just try to behave. We need to find the train station, and work out how to get all these cases on board.'

'No we don't.' The little girl was wriggling and still trying to avoid making eye contact.

'What is wrong with you?' Evelyn's last nerve was dangerously close to breaking. 'Can you and Tilly please just behave while I try and figure out how to get us all home?'

'You could just get a lift with me.' The voice behind her froze her to the spot and sent goosepimples racing over her skin, and she instantly forgot how tired she was and how much her body ached.

'Jake …' The name slipped out with the type of reverence she usually reserved for prayer.

'I'm right here. Just turn around.'

Sure enough, when she did, he was stood there smiling. He grinned and held his arms out to her. Within seconds, she was in them, pressed tightly against his chest and burying her face against his shoulder.

'I've missed you so, so much,' she murmured the words against his neck.

'I've missed you too.' He squeezed her so tightly that she struggled to breathe.

'I've missed you three!' Summer complained. '*Muuumm*?'

'Sorry. Of course you can move. I just didn't want you getting lost. Sorry.' Before she'd even finished, Summer had launched herself at Jake, who caught her in an awkward one-armed hug.

Reluctantly, Evelyn stepped aside and let Jake pick Summer up and spin her around. She placed a kiss on his nose before he put her down.

'You know, I think you're getting heavier,' he jokingly complained. 'And are you taller?'

'Yup.' Summer grinned proudly. 'Nearly a whole inch.'

'And so much hair!' Jake tousled her curls, making her laugh. 'You're going to have to get it cut soon, or we'll lose you under it.'

'*Nah uh*. I'm going to grow it so long I can sit on it. But not as long as Rapunzel's. That would need lots of brushing, and I've got better things to do than brush my hair all day.'

'Really?' Jake asked. 'Like what?'

'Like eating Brockle cakes with Nanny, and going on badger hunts with you.'

'That sounds great.' Jake grinned at her again. 'But right now, I want to say hello to your mum properly.'

'Ugh, do you mean kissy faces?' Summer rolled her eyes in disgust.

'Yes I do.' His reply sent shivers of anticipation down Evelyn's spine.

'I …' She couldn't get the words out as he stepped towards her and cupped her face in his hands.

'Yes?' The intensity in his eyes filled her stomach with butterflies and sent heat racing through her.

'This should probably wait. I'm grubby and need to clean my teeth, and my hair's a mess …'

'You look perfect to me.' His lips grazed hers, electrifying her. 'And I've missed you.' He kissed her again, more firmly, and for a few moments all the stresses of the last few months, all the noise of the airport, and even the pukey noises Summer was making faded away until it was just the two of them, warm, welcoming, and back together.

In that moment, she realised why she'd felt so out of sorts for so long: because she'd left a part of herself behind, with him. And she didn't want to be apart from him again. 'I've missed you too. So much.' She wanted to say more – so much more – but the middle of the busy airport was hardly the place.

'*Muuuuum.*' And there was Summer to think of. 'Tilly's getting bored. And so am I. Can we go home now?'

A thought occurred to Evelyn and she whirled suspiciously on her daughter. 'Did you know about this?'

'Maybe.' Summer fiddled with her sleeve.

'Of course she did. I needed a partner in crime to make sure you didn't actually get on the train.' His eyes sparkled. 'But I'm sure you'll forgive me, right?'

'Maybe,' Evelyn teased, her bad mood forgotten. 'If you really do give us a lift home.'

'About that.' He took a deep breath and reached into his pocket to pull out a small, blue gift bag, sparkling with silver snowflakes. A Christmas gift bag. 'I know you might think I'm moving too fast, and there's a lot to consider and talk about, but I really, really do mean this …' He lifted her hand in his, and dropped the bag into her palm.

'What is it?' Summer peered at it eagerly.

'I don't know.' Evelyn gave Jake a confused look.

'Why don't you open it and find out?'

She fumbled with the ribbons for a moment, before emptying the contents into her palm. 'I don't understand.' She looked at the two keys attached to a heart-shaped key ring.

'They're the keys to my front door. My new front door.' He took her hands in his. 'I've rented a house. Just a little one. But it's got two bedrooms, and a garden. And my flat really wasn't big enough for all of us.' He swallowed hard. 'I thought … I was hoping … that I could take you home with me. To our new home. Where we can be a family.'

Evelyn stared at him, speechless. She felt like she was in a dream – this couldn't possibly be happening to her.

'I've been glad for every moment that Summer has got the help that she needed. And I'm thrilled that Boston has given you everything we all prayed for, but I have missed you – both of you – more than I knew it was possible to ever miss another person. And I don't want to

283

miss you any more. Ever again.' His eyes searched hers for long moments before he reached out a hand to Summer. 'So, what do you say? Will you move in with me?'

Evelyn had to fight to break his gaze before she could look down at Summer, who was grinning like the cat who had gotten the whole Brockle cake smothered in cream. She looked at her daughter's tiny hand, dwarfed in Jake's, and failed to come up with a single, solitary argument. She threw her arms around his neck and kissed him thoroughly, no longer caring where they were, or who could see.

When they finally broke apart, both breathless, Jake gave her a smile filled with such hope and warmth that her knees went weak.

'Is that a yes?'

'Yes.' Evelyn nodded. 'It's a yes. I love you.'

'I love you, too.' He rested his forehead against hers.

'Jake.' Summer tugged at his hand.

'Yes, sweetheart?'

'Do you think Tilly can come to our new home?'

'Who do you think the garden is for?' He laughed. 'Of course she's coming too.'

'Thanks, Jake!' She wrapped her arms around his waist, and once again Evelyn was overcome with gratitude that she'd met someone who loved her daughter as much as he loved her, and that Summer was finally getting the father figure she deserved.

'Jake?' Summer wheedled.

'Yes, Summer?' He was wary now, and Evelyn realised that he knew Summer was after something.

'Can we stop for cakes on the way home?'

'You mean Brockle cakes?'

'Yes please.'

'Like the ones I picked up on the way here?'

'Did you really?' Summer's eyes were wide.

'Of course I did. I know they're your favourite, and that you've missed them.'

'Jake?'

'Yes, sweetheart?'

'I missed you more than Brockle cakes.' Summer took a deep breath before blurting out her next words. 'I love you, Jake.'

He knelt to her level, and Evelyn had to fight to hold back tears. 'I love you too, Summer.' He gave her a huge hug before standing again, and holding his hand out to Evelyn. 'Let's go home. To our new home.'

She placed her hand back in his. 'That sounds perfect.'

# *Thank You*

Dear Reader,

Thank you for choosing *Summer's Christmas*. I hope you've enjoyed visiting Broclington and meeting some of the characters who live there – they will be back ☺

And if you have enjoyed this book, please let others know by leaving a review on the website where you bought the book, Goodreads, or any other book review sites – it really, really does help us independent authors and publishers hugely.

You can also follow me on Twitter (@ellacookwrites) for news on my next book, and maybe share some of your own favourite festive moments – or just pop by and say hi!

Love and light,

Ella x

## *About the Author*

Ella is one of those people who is addicted to the written word. She's been obsessed with books since before she could walk. She decided to become a writer as soon as she realised that stringing letters together in the right order could actually be a career.

She grew up in the outskirts of London, where fairies lived at the bottom of her Grandma's garden, so it isn't surprising that she still looks for magic in every day life – and often finds it.

When she's not living in a fantasy world of her own creation, she writes bids and develops programmes for children's services, and lives in rural Warwickshire (where there are probably more fairies). She shares her house with two small parrots, one of whom likes to critique her writing from his favourite spot on her shoulder, and her husband who is ever loving and understanding and makes her gallons of tea in magical cups that can keep drinks warm for whole chapters.

Please spend a couple of minutes to leave a review and tell your friends about *Summer's Christmas* – it's one of the best ways for new authors to meet readers.

Ella also writes for Ruby Fiction and details of her book can be found on the next page.

To find out more about Ella, follow her on social media:
Twitter: @EllaCookWrites

# *Ruby Fiction from Ella Cook*

*Beyond Grey*

**What if you became an outsider in your own life?**

Jennifer Hughes doesn't have an extraordinary life, but that doesn't matter – she loves her family and enjoys her job as a teacher. In her eyes, her unextraordinary life is utterly perfect.

But then, in the blink of an eye, Jennifer finds herself cut off from everything she knew and loved, confined to a strange new world and forced to watch from a distance as her family and friends pick up the pieces.

Can Jennifer hold her perfect life together, even though she's not living it herself?

**Visit www.ruby-fiction.com for more details.**

# *Introducing Choc Lit*

We're an independent publisher creating
a delicious selection of fiction.
*Where heroes are like chocolate – irresistible!*
Quality stories with a romance at the heart.

*See our selection here:*
**www.choc-lit.com**

We'd love to hear how you enjoyed *Summer's Christmas*.
Please leave a review where you purchased the novel or
visit: **www.choc-lit.com** and give your feedback.

Choc Lit novels are selected by genuine readers like
yourself. We only publish stories our Choc Lit Tasting
Panel want to see in print. Our reviews and awards speak
for themselves.

**Could you be a Star Selector and join our Tasting
Panel?**
Would you like to play a role in choosing which novels
we decide to publish? Do you enjoy reading romance
novels? Then you could be perfect for our Choc Lit
Tasting Panel.

Visit here for more details …
www.choc-lit.com/join-the-choc-lit-tasting-panel

***Keep in touch:***
Sign up for our newsletter for all the latest news and
offers: www.spread.choc-lit.com.
Follow us on Twitter: @ChocLituk and
Facebook: Choc Lit.

Printed in Great Britain
by Amazon